From the Chicken House

I went to a boys' boarding school – we had straw hats
and silly rules, but I loved living with a bunch of friends
all day, every day. It was like being on a desert island
with prefects! Of course, we imagined all the visitors
were criminals and there was a dire secret in the clock
tower. But actually, maybe Esme Kerr's right; it was
the teachers who had the *real* secrets all the time . . .

Barry Cunningham
Publisher

The Glass Bird Girl

ESME KERR

Chicken House

2 Palmer Street, Frome, Somerset BA11 1DS
www.doublecluck.com

Text © Esme Kerr 2014
First published in Great Britain in 2014
The Chicken House
2 Palmer Street
Frome, Somerset, BA11 1DS
United Kingdom
www.doublecluck.com

Cover and interior design by Helen Crawford-White
Cover photograph (house) © Michael Trevillion/Trevillion Images
Cover photograph (girl) © BestPhotoStudio/Shutterstock.com
Typeset by Dorchester Typesetting Group Ltd
Printed and bound in Great Britain by CPI Group (UK) Ltd, Croydon, CR0 4YY

The paper used in this Chicken House book is made from wood grown in
sustainable forests.

1 3 5 7 9 10 8 6 4 2

British Library Cataloguing in Publication data available.

ISBN 978-1-908435-99-6
eISBN 978-1-909489-55-4

For Freya who will read it and Wolsey who won't

Fish for Breakfast

Edie crouched on her bedroom windowsill, training her field glasses on the three boys by the stone pond. Their names were Lyle, Jason and Tom, and she hated them. They were like foxes, thin and cunning, with eyes that flashed through mops of filthy hair.

It was nearly a month since Edie had come to live with her cousins at Folly Farm, and she had learnt to keep out of their way. If she wanted to know what they were doing, she spied. She peered down at them now, making a quick adjustment to her lens. Lyle, the eldest at thirteen, was holding a fishing net. His twin brothers watched as he thrust it into the middle of the pond, and stabbed it into the water. The stick started to bend and writhe and the others grabbed it too, three pairs of hands pulling the jerking net from the lilies.

Edie saw the fish tossed, gasping, onto the grass, and dropped her field glasses in horror.

They had caught Tilly.

'Pigs!' she choked, stumbling to her bedroom door. 'Pigs! Pigs! Pigs!'

Tilly was Edie's goldfish. She had grown huge, as long as a ruler, since Edie had brought her from her London tank and put her to live in the dirty stone pond. Edie fed her every morning, and loved to watch the metallic flash of her skin as she moved through the murky water. She was proud of the way Tilly had grown into her new country life, even if she herself had not. *At least one of us is flourishing*, she had thought grimly, when considering her own failure to settle at Folly Farm.

'Let her go!' she shouted, as she crashed down the stairs three at a time, but she was too late. When she reached the pond the boys and Tilly had gone.

The camp! she thought desperately, veering off at breakneck speed towards the woods.

The boys' camp was dank, made out of rusting corrugated-iron sheets camouflaged with peat and bracken. Edie had only discovered it last week, when she had been exploring on her own and had seen Lyle's quad bike parked outside. Lyle said if she ever came back he'd tie her up.

As she got nearer she saw feathers of smoke rising from the bracken and a nauseous smell flooded towards her. She felt faint, but staggered on.

'How could you! How could you!'

Lyle looked up, smirking, and tossed a cigarette into

the camp fire. 'You're just in time for breakfast,' he said, turning the fish in the pan.

The twins, sitting on either side of him, giggled nervously. It was Lyle who'd had the idea of cooking Tilly, but something told them they would be in trouble if their mother found out. When there was trouble the twins usually took Lyle's share of it – they were nine, and that was the deal if they wanted to play with him. Now they looked at Edie with frightened eyes.

Lyle smiled, showing pointed teeth. 'Go on, eat it!' he said, pointing to the pan. 'You like fish.'

'Beast!' Edie shouted, hurling herself on him with flaying fists.

Lyle was thin, but bigger than Edie and strong as wire. He stepped back, caught her arms and twisted them behind her back.

'Give her some!'

The twins looked at him, uncertain. Edie was struggling and kicking but Lyle had her tight.

'Let me go, you pig!'

'*Give her some!*' Lyle snarled.

Tom poked his stick in the fire. He looked as though he wanted the game to stop. But Jason stood up, and lifted the pan from the flames.

'Go on. See if she likes it.'

Jason pulled off some of the fish with his fingers. It was still rubbery, half raw. Lyle's hands were twisting Edie's wrists behind her back, burning her flesh. She kept her mouth tight shut, willing herself not to scream as the lump of pink fish was thrust under her nose.

When she was sick it went everywhere, into the pan, over Jason's hand, over Lyle's trainers.

Afterwards, she was aware of Tom's bowed head, and of a strange, fearful look in Jason's eyes. But Lyle stood gazing at her calmly, wiping his shoes on the leaves as he lit another cigarette.

As she ran away his expressionless voice swam after her: 'Go on, run away. Run back to Granny. Run back to your blind old Babka.'

Edie stumbled on, out of the woods and across the field, then collapsed, exhausted, by the pond. The damp grass soaked through her jeans but she did not move. She sat frozen, staring at the motionless grey water, thinking of Tilly writhing in the net, Tilly smoking in the pan.

She hated Lyle as she had never hated anyone before. And he was always there. Wherever she went, she could feel his pale eyes following her. And next week it would be even worse. Next week, after half-term, she would be starting at his school, going with him every day on a bus into the local town. 'Don't expect me to look after you,' he'd said to her, 'though people will expect things of you, as my cousin.'

What will they expect of me? Edie wondered with a shudder. Lyle had been expelled from two schools already.

'Savages.' That's what her grandmother had said, after she and Edie had stayed at Folly Farm one Easter. After three nights they had both been glad to escape. 'A filthy, cold house and three filthy, cold children,' Babka had muttered on the train home, pursing her lips over her sweetened coffee.

When Edie had been sent to live at Folly Farm, Babka had refused to look her in the eye as she directed her what to pack.

'You'll be going to school again. That's what you wanted,' was all she had said.

'I wanted to stay at my old school,' Edie had replied. 'I don't want to go to school with *them*.'

But Babka, defeated by blindness, had just shrugged.

Folly Farm was good enough for Edie, though not for Kitty – Babka had arranged for her fat old cat to go to an animal shelter. 'Why can't I take her with me?' Edie had pleaded.

'Your cousins would not be kind to her,' Babka replied.

'You don't care if they're not kind to me,' Edie said quietly.

Edie had lived as long as she could remember with Babka in a little flat perched at the top of a grey building near Hyde Park. There was a Chinese restaurant in the street below them, with gold lights in the window, and next to it a Polish grocer where Babka would buy jars of beetroot and red cabbage and, on good days, little cakes with bright yellow custard.

Edie had gone to a school a few streets away, but when she was nine her grandmother had started teaching her at home. Babka didn't want anyone coming to the flat; she didn't want anyone to know that she was going blind. 'If they find out,' she had warned, 'they'll take you away.'

But Edie had hated the long, friendless afternoons, with Babka drilling her impatiently in whatever subject took her mood. She was never allowed to invite her old school friends to tea – Babka said that sometimes you needed to be secret to be safe. But the social services had found out about Babka's blindness in the end, so Babka had been sent to a home. She'd refused to go to the one they'd found for her in London – 'I want to die in a room with a view,' Babka had said – and she had dug into her meagre savings to make her wish come true. Babka had ended up in a home near Oxford, but Edie had been given no choice about where she was to live – and Folly Farm was just as bad as she had feared.

'Things will be easier when you start school and make some friends of your own,' Aunt Sophia had said, in her vague, careless way. 'You can bring girls back to play.' Somehow, though, even Aunt Sophia seemed to understand that her going to school with Lyle would not be easy.

Edie stared at the pond. She had betrayed Tilly by not keeping her feelings secret – Babka was right, you had to be secret to be safe. Lyle had killed Tilly because he had seen Edie feeding her. If he could do that to a fish friend, what would he do to a human one? Edie shook her head. She would never bring anyone back to Folly Farm, never.

She thought with sudden longing of the flat in London, and the street full of people. Here there was nothing. The village was more than a mile away, hidden beyond the wood. Wherever Edie looked, all she could see was green – an endless mass of green, rising around her like a prison. Was this what Babka meant by a view?

She gazed out at it, the stale taste of sick on her tongue. Her body was aching, but some force rose inside her and she knew she could not stay here any longer. She took her mobile out of her pocket, and looked again at the number of Babka's nursing home.

But it was useless – there was no signal in the valley. And it was no good calling Babka. Babka would tell her she had to stay and make the best of it. If Edie turned up at the nursing home, Babka would send her back.

Her stomach felt hollow. She thought of Babka's kitchen with the rusty gold tins and the glass cake stand, and the smell of cooking that rose to meet you as the lift doors opened onto the thin concrete corridor on the sixth floor. Then she sat up with a start, thinking of the cracked stone pig beside the front door. Babka had always kept the key hidden under the pig. It would still be there, Babka wouldn't have moved it . . . She could let herself in, then in the block she was sure to find someone to help her. Maybe the Polish grocer would come to her rescue. So long as she could get back to the flat she would be all right; London was full of friendly people.

She heard Lyle's words floating back to her: '*If you hate us, go. Go on, run away . . . Run back to your blind Babka.*'

I will, she thought defiantly. *I will run away. But not where you think.*

Blood Families

Several hundred miles away from Folly Farm the golden October sun was slanting into the drawing room of a tall Mayfair town house, dappling an interior of gilt, marble and chintz. Here stood Charles Rodriguez, one of the city's richest and most secretive art dealers, welcoming one of the richest and most secretive of his clients.

'Thirsty?'

'Parched,' Prince Stolonov sighed, sinking into an armchair. He watched silently, his foot drumming restlessly on the floor, as his friend mixed the drinks.

Charles threw him a questioning glance: 'Something tells me you haven't come to buy a picture.'

'Quite right,' replied the prince. 'I've come to you as a friend, Charles, in need of help.'

Charles inclined his head. 'I have long thought of my friends as my family, on account of my blood family being so thoroughly unsatisfactory.'

'I didn't know you had any blood family.'

'Everyone has blood family. I just choose not to play with mine.'

'Of course, you have no children,' the prince murmured.

'None that I know about.' Charles smiled.

'I wish, sometimes, that I was in your position.'

Charles raised an eyebrow. 'I hope that your enchanting little Anastasia has not been giving you trouble?'

'Not trouble, exactly. But . . . well, you know what it's like, Charles, it's her first time away from home without a bodyguard and one can't help worrying.'

'*You* can't help worrying, Stolly. The British tradition is to send your children to boarding school then forget all about them.'

The prince shook his head. 'This country is barbaric. I wish I'd never agreed to let Ansti go away to school.'

'I thought she wanted to go.'

'She didn't want to live at home with her stepfather. And her mother didn't want her roaming the world with me. Boarding was the compromise and Venetia insisted it should be her old school, even though she never liked it there herself. Why are English people so attached to places where they have been unhappy?'

'I had a letter from Anastasia a couple of weeks ago and she sounded quite cheerful,' Charles said. Anastasia was his god-daughter.

'That must have been before the problems started.'

'Problems?'

'I spoke to her on the telephone yesterday and she was in quite a rattled state. I'm afraid she's being teased, Charles. *Horribly teased.*' The prince gave the words the weight of torture.

Charles looked at him thoughtfully. 'Go on.'

'Well, it might not amount to anything of course, but Anastasia's reported things going missing – nothing valuable, just pens, homework, a diary, but it seems to go and on. It's . . . Oh, syrup and pancakes, Charles. I know it sounds nonsense, and it probably is. But she's usually so meticulous about her things – at home she even keeps her books in alphabetical order. You know what she's like, dreamy in some ways, but well ordered in others. So it does seem odd she should suddenly start losing everything. And if it is a question of her being teased, then—'

'You want to cap the knees of whoever's doing it,' Charles concluded, smiling.

'It might strike you I'm being over-protective. But she is my only child and I reserve the right to protect her. For God's sake, what else are parents for?'

Charles opened his mouth as though to answer this question, then seemed to think better of it. The prince was mid-flow.

'It's not easy to judge the situation. I tell you, Charles, this English school is quite absurdly old-fashioned, even by your standards. It's run on some modish principle of keeping children cosseted from the outside world. No computers or mobile telephones . . . letters home every Sunday . . . no television . . . even the school uniform looks as if it belongs to the nineteen-fifties – you should see the brown tunics they wear.'

'You probably didn't choose it for the uniform,' Charles said.

'I didn't choose it full stop,' the prince replied. 'It's like a prison. This business about not being allowed mobile telephones is grotesque. They have to ring from a call box in a freezing corridor at a prescribed time, and most nights the bell rings for bed before Ansti can get to the front of the queue. The older years get to barge in front of the younger ones. Always, my little Ansti is shunted to the back of the queue!

'But yesterday we managed to talk, and I could hear the unhappiness in her voice. She was trying not to cry – and she wouldn't tell me exactly what was wrong. You see, Charles, she wants to prove to her fusspot papa that she can manage on her own. She made such a song and dance about not having a personal protection officer and wanting to live as a "normal" schoolgirl, and now she's determined to prove she can cope, even when—'

'When the evidence suggests otherwise,' Charles concluded.

'*Exactement!*' the prince replied.

'Have you spoken to the school?' Charles asked.

'Yes, I talked to the dragon headmistress, a Miss Fotheringay, and she promised she'd look into it. But when I called again a week later she gave me some spiel about school matters being best left to the school. My fear is that they will do nothing at all.' The prince turned his drink in his hands. 'I think, Charles, that I am going to have to follow this up myself.'

'What do you plan to do – turn up and search everyone's drawers?' Charles asked, looking amused.

'Don't be an idiot,' the prince replied impatiently. 'This is a job for a professional. My first thought was to approach a member of staff and pay them to keep a special eye on Ansti. But I have become rather nervous of the dragon finding me out. Or Venetia. So now I have a much better idea. We import a child to be her special friend and protector.'

'*We?*' said Charles. '*We* import a *child*?'

'Correct. I want to plant a child in the school to watch the other girls day and night and find out what the devil's going on. It shouldn't take a clever urchin more than a few weeks to get to the bottom of it. It could be Ansti's just being careless, but if I can get proof that someone's persecuting her, then—'

'You don't think an urchin would stick out rather, among the rich girls of Knight's Haddon?'

'Not a clever one. Anyone with brains can fit in anywhere. You surely don't need me to tell you that.'

'Mmm,' Charles replied.

'And I take it you don't want Anastasia's mother to find out?'

'For heaven's sake, Charles, what kind of fool do you take me for? You know Venetia's mental health is fragile at the best of times. Any anxiety over Anastasia could tip her over the edge.'

'I'm sorry,' Charles said quietly. 'I thought she was better.'

'So did I. But her brute of a husband has sent her back into the arms of her doctors. Ansti knows better than to trouble her with this, and so do I. Besides, she's convinced Ansti's safe there. After all, it was *her* old school, and she loves the fact it's hidden away in the middle of a huge park, miles from anywhere.'

'Aren't you reassured by that too?'

'Yes and no. I would prefer to have my own people on the premises. And to set my own rules around my daughter's freedom. So, my friend, are you going to help me in this matter? Find a suitable waif to be playmate and protector for your favourite god-daughter?'

'My dear Stolly,' Charles protested, 'you're surely not serious? You seem to forget I am an art dealer, not a child recruitment officer. What you propose is quite outlandish, and perhaps even outside the law.'

'Nonsense,' said Stolly. 'You find the child, I offer to educate her – at least for a term or two. Lemon squeezy. Ansti told me there was a spare bed in her dormitory. I want it filled before I return to Russia.'

'But, Stolly—'

'No, Charles. I have to know if my daughter is being persecuted at school. You've helped me out of more awkward spots before now,' the prince reminded him gently, 'and I don't believe I've ever given you cause to regret it.'

Charles Rodriguez inclined his head. Friendship didn't come into it. He was one of nature's fixers, and the prince was his paymaster.

'All you have to do is find me a smart eleven-year-old girl capable of keeping a secret. Surely, Charles, one of those can't be so hard to find?'

A Chance Encounter

It was dark by the time Edie passed the church and started along the road that led to the small country station. The warm lights of the village soon paled behind her; ahead there was only the weak beam of her torch dancing on the tarmac.

Edie wished she had brought a stronger torch. She had never known darkness like this – in London the streetlights beneath her bedroom window had glowed all night, and she had always fallen asleep to the hum of voices and music drifting from the pavement below.

But here there was nothing, no sound, no light. Even the moon had retreated behind a cloud.

The station had seemed near when they had made the journey in Aunt Sophia's car, but now the road stretched on for ever, in a tunnel of black. She kept her eyes fixed

on the flickering torchlight, and tried to think ahead –
to the flat in Queensway . . . to the key hidden under the
cracked stone pig by the door.

Her back was aching under the weight of her rucksack, and she could feel the straps cutting like wire into
her shoulders. She decided to stop and put on some
extra layers, thinking it would make her load lighter.
She slid the rucksack from her back, then knelt down on
the thin grass verge beside the hedgerow and started
tugging out a jumble of hastily packed clothes.

But then she heard a low humming noise, which rose
swiftly to a roar, and suddenly found herself blinded by
the headlights of a car. Edie screamed, stumbling back
into the hedge in terror. She heard the engine stop, and
when she removed her hands from her face the lights
had dimmed to a soft yellow. She looked up and saw a
man standing over her, reaching out a hand. His face
was hidden by shadow, but she felt the softness of his
overcoat as he bent down to help her to her feet.

'I'm relieved to see I didn't hit you,' he observed
calmly.

Edie just stared.

'I take it that belongs to you?' the man enquired,
pointing to her rucksack.

Edie nodded, and watched as he picked it up and
retrieved the bits of clothing from the grass.

'Aren't you rather young to be out at this time?' he
said, handing them back to her.

Edie shrugged. She wondered if he was going to start
probing, but his next question took her unawares:

'I'm trying to find Folly Farm. I've been there before, but I think I must have taken a wrong turn out of the village. Do you know it?'

'I'm sorry, I've never heard of it, I'm not from round here,' Edie said, the lies tripping from her tongue. 'I'm camping with some friends up the lane. I'd better get back or they'll wonder what's happened to me.'

As she spoke she stuffed her clothes into her rucksack and swung it onto her back. Then she picked up her torch and marched on in the direction of the station. Only when she heard the engine start into life behind her, and the car drive off towards the village, did she clench her fist in a little mime of triumph.

Edie felt bolder having survived this challenge. A careless word would have given her away, but the stranger had clearly fallen for her story. Even so, the fact that he was on his way to Folly Farm made her even more anxious to reach the station. She looked at her watch and saw she had less than twelve minutes until the London train. The next one was an hour later and by then Aunt Sophia would have noticed she had gone. If a visitor told her that he'd seen a child hurrying through the night with a rucksack she would be straight on her trail.

She pointed her torch into the darkness and hurried on. Finally she came to a small cluster of cottages, then the lane turned and she saw the lights of the station up ahead. A surge of excitement shot through her – then alarm when she saw the train already at the platform. She bent her back under the weight of the rucksack and started to run.

She heard the slamming of train doors – but not the footsteps gaining quietly on the road behind her. It was only at the sound of a familiar menacing laugh that she turned to see three thin, feral faces leering at her in the torchlight.

'Gotcha!' said Lyle.

Before Edie could scream his hand closed over her mouth, and she heard the shrill of a whistle as the train slid away into the night.

The front door at Folly Farm was never locked. It opened into the long, low kitchen, where Sophia Fairlight, Edie's aunt, was huddled by the wood-burning stove, clutching a telephone and a glass of gin. 'Oh, Lyle darling, is that you – and have you found her?' she called out as she heard a door slam. 'Please say yes.'

'No,' came the reply. 'And no.'

Sophia, recognising the voice, stood up with an expression of languid delight. 'Cousin Charles! What a treat, do you know I had completely forgotten you were coming.'

'How flattering,' replied the tall, velvet-collared man.

'But I remember now,' Sophia went on, draping her arms around his neck. 'You had a funeral nearby?'

'Something like that.'

'Oh, darling, you're always so mysterious,' she sighed.

'Good,' Charles said. 'I would hate to think I had lost my touch. Where are all your ghastly menfolk?'

'Tony's away, leaving me to cope all on my own,'

Sophia replied in a tone of theatrical self-pity.

'What a treat.'

'Don't be unpleasant, you've never seen the point of him.'

'I'm sorry, my dear, but you can't expect me to like the man who took away the one cousin whose company I could bear and buried her in the middle of the dank countryside. Why couldn't you have found yourself a banker and stayed in London?'

Sophia did not rise to this familiar bait. 'Are you spending the night?'

'Certainly not. I've booked a hotel in Chagford. But I'll stay for dinner.'

'Oh God, darling, I wonder if there is any—'

'Where are your horrible sons? Can't we eat them?'

Sophia grimaced. 'Eugh! You'd have to chew them for ever they'd be so tough. They really are horrible. They've been so vile to Edie that she's run away and now they're out looking for her.'

'Who's Edie?'

'Charles, darling, don't be dim, it doesn't suit you. Edith Wilson, my little orphaned niece – and your cousin, though I know you've never held our family in much store.'

'What's she doing here? I thought you hardly saw her.'

'She's come to live with us. It's a complete nightmare – she hates it here and is furious all the time and the boys hate her, but . . .' Sophia shrugged. 'Oh, darling, what can I do? The long and short of it is that I'm her guardian and this is her new home.'

'How old is she?'

'Eleven,' Sophia replied.

'And aren't you worried about her?'

'Not really. She's bound to have made for the station.'

'I'd better go after her,' Charles said, putting down his glass. 'I think I saw her on the road.'

'Oh, don't bother, darling. The boys will hunt her down—'

'Why didn't you go?'

'*Me?*' Sophia sounded amazed by the suggestion. 'I don't really feel this drama is anything to do with me. You wouldn't understand, Charles, you're not a parent, but children have to sort these things out by themselves. There's no point in *us* getting involved. I told the boys they had to promise to be nice to Edie from now on. But the trouble is, they're wild.'

'That, my dear, is because no one has tamed them,' Charles replied. 'Is this them now?' he added, hearing scuffling in the hall.

A moment later the door blew open and through it appeared the child he had met earlier that night, with Lyle and the twins dragging her by the arms like gaolers.

Charles looked at her, intrigued. He saw what had prompted his flash of recognition by the roadside: she had her mother's eyes, the same intense yet furtive stare. But it was the change in her appearance that struck him most. In the car headlights her thin, ivory face had been lit with adventure, but now it was sallow and streaked with tears.

Charles did not move. 'Let her go,' he said.

The boys released her and Edie pulled away, rubbing her arms where their hands had gripped her and thanking Charles with a sullen stare.

'We caught her by the station,' Jason said proudly. 'We got there just in time. She was going to get the train to London.'

'Bet she wishes she had,' Lyle sneered.

'Oh, boys, do try and be a bit nicer,' Aunt Sophia said feebly, as Edie stormed upstairs.

Charles looked at the slammed door, and something in him stirred. It was not so much pity that he felt as an agreeable inkling that he might be in luck. This was a child, he calculated silently, in need of a new master.

4

KNIGHT'S HADDON

Beware the Sideways Move

Edie sat in the car dressed in her stiff new clothes, with her trunk stowed on the back seat. The school uniform – brown tunic, yellow shirts, brown overpants (*Overpants!* Edie had thought, wrinkling her nose in disgust) and grey tights – had arrived in a series of brown paper parcels, each one to Edie's mind containing something even more frumpy than the last. Everything had been unpacked and sorted by Cousin Charles's silent Spanish maid. Her handkerchiefs had been counted and ironed; name tapes had been sewn into her socks; even her tuck box had been neatly engraved with her initials. And yet Edie felt ill-prepared.

'Remember, Edith, you're not going to Knight's Haddon as an ordinary schoolgirl,' said Cousin Charles, hooting at a cyclist on Hyde Park Corner.

'I know that. I'm not a schoolgirl, I'm a spy,' Edie said, rehearsing her brief.

'That is one way of seeing it,' Charles replied, smiling.

'But you said—'

'You are a spy, but you are also Anastasia's servant. It is the prince, you would do well to remember, who is paying your fees.'

Edie scowled. She did not want to be anyone's servant, least of all to a girl her own age. And she did not like Charles's warning tone.

'More secret servant than secret service,' he continued. 'The roles are distinct, but not dissimilar. The important thing is not to get too close to anyone. If you start forming sentimental attachments to the other girls it will cloud your judgement. And that applies to Anastasia too. You must act like her friend, but never forget that you are, in fact, her servant – and a servant, as you will shortly learn, can never be a friend.'

Edie looked out forlornly at the whirl of traffic. It felt like just her strain of luck to be going to school with the specific instruction not to make any real friends at all.

She had been secretly elated when Cousin Charles had offered to take charge of her education. Such was her excitement at escaping from her cousins she hadn't thought to ask what sort of school he was going to send her to. It was only when putting her on the train to London that Aunt Sophia had said, 'He wants to send you to boarding school, God knows why. But you might as well give it a go, darling. It's not as though you've been very happy with us.'

Of course I haven't, Edie had thought sullenly. *Your sons are savages.* But boarding school! The only person she knew who had gone to a boarding school was Lyle, who had lasted less than three weeks before being expelled for reasons even he wouldn't talk about.

'The school is famously strict and I don't want you stepping out of line,' Charles went on, his eyes fixed on the road. 'Your job is to blend in.'

'But I thought you said I might have to break the rules—'

'I said you can break any rules you like so long as you break them quietly. And that includes your mobile phone. Strictly against regulations, but you'll need it to keep me informed of your findings. I don't want to hear it's been confiscated, Edith. Keep it well hidden. It's your first test.'

'I don't see why we're not allowed them anyway.'

'The school prides itself on keeping the world at bay. Parents like to think of their daughters being protected—'

'From what?'

'Oh, I don't know,' said Charles with sudden impatience. 'And don't whine. I've only told you to hold on to your phone.'

Edie snorted. She thought one mobile was pretty poor payment for the job in hand. And the new phone he had given her with such ceremony was little improvement on her last. She had hoped at the very least Cousin Charles might equip her with some useful gadgets – devices for secretly recording people, or listening through walls – but he had met this suggestion with contempt: *Romantic nonsense, Edith. You've been watching too many films. I've told you, all you'll need are your eyes and ears.* Her mobile didn't even have a camera.

Cousin Charles had put Edie's eyes to the test during the few days they had just spent together in Mayfair. One afternoon he made her face the drawing-room wall and tell him what was in the room. He looked surprised when she listed every piece of furniture.

'When Babka started going blind I became her second pair of eyes,' Edie had explained with a hint of pride. 'She'd ask me what I could see and she always seemed to know if I'd left anything out.'

'She has trained you well,' Cousin Charles had said, impressed. By way of contrast he had given Edie no training at all – until this last-minute pep talk.

'It's possible that Anastasia is simply imagining that she is being teased. In which case your job is simply to get in there and act like her friend and stop her feeling strange and lonely. Remember, this is a child who's used to travelling around the world in a private jet and being waited on hand and foot. She's made a fuss about wanting to manage on her own and she's not managing.'

'You don't think she's being teased at all?' asked Edie in a puzzled voice. 'I thought—'

'I don't know if she is being teased,' said Charles. 'Nor does her father. We can't know, as we're not there. It's your job to find out.'

'And if I think she *is* being teased,' said Edie, 'then what do I do about it?'

'First you have to discover who is doing the teasing. If, for instance, someone really is messing with her possessions, you probably have to catch them in the act.'

'Without telling anyone what I'm up to?'

'Exactly. In the end it's about covering your tracks. To that end you can lie all you like, although it's best to stick to the same one. Sometimes the only thing you have to go on is the fact of a deception; you have to work backwards from there. Remember everything, Edith, never let anything go: most mysteries are solved by attention to the most trivial-seeming details.'

Privately Edie thought the whole affair was trivial. Cousin Charles talked as though it were quite natural for a father to send another child into a school to investigate whether or not someone was stealing his daughter's pencils, but Edie thought it was plain weird. Cousin Charles needn't worry about her and Anastasia becoming friends: Edie could not imagine liking someone so spoilt.

'You say she's always travelling, but where's Anastasia's home?' she asked.

'Moscow, Paris, the South of France – her father's got houses everywhere,' Charles said, sounding bored. 'And her mother lives in Yorkshire.'

Edie was intrigued. She wondered if Anastasia ever felt homeless having so many homes to choose from. 'And does she have a Russian accent?' she asked.

'Certainly not,' Charles replied. 'I told you, her mother's English and the prince was at school with me. He sounds more English than the Queen.'

'You say she's dreamy, but that she keeps all her things in perfect order and arranges her books alphabetically, and that she never loses anything,' Edie said, thinking over the information she had been given, 'but isn't it the case that dreamy people *always* lose things?'

'You have a lot to learn, Edith. People's characters are not so easy to define.'

'Babka thinks they are,' Edie replied. 'She says there are good people and bad people – she doesn't believe in shades of grey.'

Cousin Charles gave a derisive laugh; but then his face suddenly darkened. 'Babka, blow it,' he said, checking his watch. 'We're running late. I might have to take you to see her another time.'

Edie looked stricken. 'But – it – it's on the way . . . and . . . *and you promised—*'

'All right, we'll go,' Cousin Charles gave in grumpily. 'But remember in future, Edith, never pay any attention to a promise unless it's been made by someone you know you can trust.'

It was raining when they arrived at the St Benedict Nursing Home, a bare, red-brick villa on the outskirts of Oxford. The reception area smelt of cabbage, and there was a trolley piled with bedpans parked beside the desk.

'I'll take a walk round the garden and come back for you in half an hour,' Cousin Charles said, turning away with distaste.

Edie felt relieved. She had an instinct he and Babka would not get on. A moment later a nurse appeared, and led her to Babka's room. Edie gave a start when she saw it. She had expected something drab, in keeping with the rest of the home; but instead it was filled with a bright confusion of clutter and colours – pictures and ornaments, books, china and gold-threaded tapestries and quilts from the flat in London.

Babka was sitting at a small table in the corner, in the glow of a heavily shaded lamp. When Edie came in she looked up, unsmiling, from the chess game she had been playing against herself.

'They tried to take them all away,' she said, gesturing blindly at her possessions, 'but I say I go on the hunger strike.'

Edie sat on the end of the bed, and Babka reached out a hand and felt her face. 'You have been unhappy,' she said. 'Are your cousins being bad to you?'

'I'm not staying there any more – I'm . . . I'm going to boarding school,' Edie said.

Babka's face hardened. 'Boarding school? Who's paying for that?'

'I don't know,' Edie lied. She did not want to tell her grandmother about her secret mission. Edie knew she would be contemptuous – but what could Babka do? She could offer Edie no alternative.

'What a lot of things you don't know. Which makes two of us.'

'No!' protested Edie. 'Not you, Babka. You know everything.'

'Not any more,' Babka said bitterly. 'It's falling away. There is no necessity, here, to hold on to what you know.' She turned away, nodding towards the chess-board. 'But I still have the game,' she said, deftly feeling the pieces as she moved them back into their starting positions. 'You be white this time.'

Edie did not want to play chess; she wanted to talk. 'I . . . I haven't got long—' she began, but Babka silenced her with a curt wave of her hand.

Edie pulled up a chair to the table, and moved a pawn. Babka had never taught Edie how to play chess: '*You cannot teach chess; you can only learn. Study the moves, Editha, and work out the rules.*' Edie had done this, watching Babka play with the Polish grocer down the street, in the room behind his shop. When Edie had learnt enough she and Babka had started playing together, always in silence, always with a clock.

Edie did not enjoy chess. But Babka wouldn't play anything else.

'Give us twenty,' Babka said, handing Edie a stop-watch; but in the end it took Edie only ten minutes to lose.

'You were afraid of losing a piece, and so you lost the game,' Babka said. 'It often happens that way.' Then she raised a hand, and her fingers reached out, trembling, as if feeling something in the air. 'There is a dark knight in the room,' she announced, looking up with unseeing eyes.

Edie turned to see Cousin Charles standing in the doorway. She made a motion to say something, but he put his finger to his lips, then tapped his watch and left the room.

'That was Cousin Charles,' Edie said when he had gone. 'He's taking me to the school. Oh, Babka, there's so much to tell you and now there's no time.'

Babka nodded. 'Don't fret. You are ready for school, I think. But I would take your Cousin Charles with a pinch of salt. Be prepared for the sideways move.' Then she reached back to the board, and moved her knight.

A Cosy Tone

A mile or so beyond the village they came to a pair of tall stone gateposts with a sign saying KNIGHT'S HADDON.

Edie sat in silence as Cousin Charles drove over a cattle-grid and into a thick tunnel of trees with branches that hung low over the windscreen.

'Why do they let the road get so overgrown?' Edie wondered.

'It is not a road,' Cousin Charles said impatiently. 'It is a drive.'

'Like saying *prep* for *homework*?' Edie asked.

'Not unlike,' Charles replied.

As he spoke the drive opened out into wide fields – 'a park' Cousin Charles explained – but Edie thought how different it looked from any of the parks she had been to in London. It was huge and empty, sloping down on one side of them towards a swollen river, surrounded by sodden grey marsh, and on the other side rising up into a low ridge of hills. There were no buildings, not even a barn, and beyond the river the view ended in thick black woods. Edie leant her face into the coldness of the car window. The drive went on so long that even though it was a single road, leading only one way, she had a strange sense of being lost.

Eventually they turned the corner, and in front of them, towering above a sloping lawn, appeared a huge, pale stone building, with four spearing turrets.

'Your new home,' Charles said in a bored voice as Edie gave a sharp intake of breath.

Everything about the house seemed to spike and soar. There were row upon row of sharp, pointed windows frowning down at her through curtains of flowerless creepers, and the turrets, which stood at each corner of the building, rose high up above the long, jagged roof. Edie thought how unlike a school it looked, with a frosty beauty that seemed strangely out of keeping with the surrounding patchwork of tennis courts and playing fields.

Charles drove on in silence into a paved courtyard and pulled up in front of a flight of stone steps. As the car stopped, a short, round woman came hurrying down to greet them. She seemed to be bursting out of her green wool suit, her face beaming beneath a cap of black hair.

'Now you must be Mr Rodriguez,' she said warmly, as she clutched Cousin Charles's hand. Edie recognised the faint Irish lilt in her accent, for the woman living in the next-door flat in London had been Irish too, and the memory gave her a sudden pang of homesickness. 'And you must be our new girl!' the woman went on. 'I'm Matron, that's what I'm known as here.' She said it with a slightly harsh laugh, as if she thought it a foolish name, and assumed others would too.

'It is very kind of you to take Edith at such short notice,' Cousin Charles said smoothly. Edie noticed the change in his manner since the nursing home, where he had seemed less keen to make a good impression. 'I hope she won't be too much trouble for you. Boarding school might come as a bit of a shock to her – she's been taught at home for the last two years.'

'Would that be with a governess?' Matron asked, looking at Edie with interest.

'A grandmother.'

'Well, well, you are unusual,' Matron murmured, gazing at Edie over folded arms. 'I don't think we've ever had a child who's been taught at home before.'

Her expression was kind, but Edie felt self-conscious. If Cousin Charles wanted her to blend in she wondered why he had revealed so much.

Matron turned and summoned a man to unload the luggage from the car, and Edie watched nervously as her trunk and tuck box were wheeled away. She knew from the schoolgirl books she had read that tuck boxes were intended for keeping food in, but Cousin Charles hadn't given her any to put in hers. Instead, she had filled it with all her most personal treasures – letters, photographs, some old schoolbooks of her mother's –

and as it disappeared she surreptitiously reached into her pocket to reassure herself that the key to the padlock was still there.

'Don't worry, dear, they'll be taken to your dormitory,' Matron said, noting Edie's anxiety. 'You can unpack yourself – there'll be plenty of time before supper. And I hope your tuck box hasn't got anything contraband in it,' she added, turning to Cousin Charles with a smile. 'We do reserve the right to search them once in a while!'

'Quite right,' Cousin Charles replied jovially; but he shot Edie a meaningful glance.

'I'm very sorry Miss Fotheringay isn't here to greet you in person, but she's on her way back from a head-mistress's conference in Oxford,' Matron said, assuming a more businesslike tone. 'But I can assure you, Mr Rodriguez, Edith will be very well looked after. And the girls write a proper letter home every Sunday – no email nonsense here.'

What's nonsense about a letter that doesn't need an envelope or a stamp? thought Edie crossly in the awkward pause which followed. She realised that Matron was waiting for her and Cousin Charles to say goodbye, and she detected a shadow of uncertainty on her cousin's face, as though this was an act he had forgotten to rehearse. He had never kissed her before, but he did it now, stooping to touch his lips against her cheek, while his arms remained stiffly by his side.

When he had gone Edie followed Matron inside, and found herself in a large hall filled with trophies and shiny silver shields. Everything looked clean and polished, and very old. The walls were covered in panels of dark wood, and there were carvings on the ceiling, and gloomy-looking portraits hanging up the stairs. It reminded Edie of a country house she had once visited with her class at primary school, and it felt strange to think she was going to live in such a place.

She looked about her carefully, trying to make a mental inventory of the doors and corridors that led off in every direction. Charles had said that she should waste no time in learning her way around – but she felt overwhelmed by how much there was to take in. As she was peering about her a bell rang, and Edie felt the floor shake, then all at once a flood of girls appeared from the landing above and came crashing down the stairs like a wave about to swallow her.

'Girls! Girls!' Matron cried, clapping her hands for attention. 'Lower IV are still in music practice – *QUIET, PLEASE!*'

The noise subsided a little, and Edie felt a swarm of eyes settling on her face. She was wearing exactly the same brown uniform as everyone else, but felt as conspicuous as if she were dressed as a clown. It was a relief when a voice hollered '*TEA!*', at which the girls streamed away through a door on the right.

Matron smoothed down her skirt as though she had been set upon. 'I'll take you to your dormitory,' she said, 'then when Miss Fotheringay's back I'll fetch you for tea.'

Edie was surprised. She had not been expecting a

private audience with the headmistress.

Matron smiled. 'Don't look so worried. She always has tea with the new girls – you're not in trouble yet. And when you are, just come to Matron and she'll sort things out for you. They don't call me Matron Mend for nothing.'

'Thank you,' Edie said, but something in the cosy tone made her uneasy. Cousin Charles had warned her that she was to avoid getting into trouble at all costs. Why did Matron 'Mend' seem so certain that she would?

Matron led her down a maze of corridors, with so many twists and turns that Edie was sure she would never find her way back to the hall. It was only when they started climbing a steep spiral staircase that she realised they must have entered one of the turrets. When they had climbed two floors they came to a curved landing, leading onto a long corridor with doors on either side.

'This is you,' Matron said, stopping halfway down.

There was a list of names on the door written in beautiful italic letters. Edie saw *Stolonov, A* and her own name *Wilson, E* at the bottom. The sight of her name underneath the others gave Edie a jolt. *As if I belonged here,* she thought, almost guiltily.

The door opened into a large, bright dormitory overlooking the park. The five tall wooden beds were all set wide apart, each with a green candlewick cover and a pine bedside table. There were also five identical chests of drawers, and a large enamel sink. Despite its orderliness the room had a lived-in feel, with each girl marking her territory with photographs and ornaments, toys and teddy bears. Edie's trunk and tuck box had been placed at the end of the bed nearest to the door; it looked very bare in comparison to the others.

'There you are,' Matron said, fluffing up the pillow, then briskly marching off to pick up a stray sock.

Edie, uncertain what to do with herself, took off her coat and laid it on her bed.

Matron shook her head. 'Coats, gloves, scarves and outdoor shoes are all hung in the cloakroom downstairs – one of the others will show you where,' she explained. 'And you'll unpack later, but when you do, remember that it's strictly two ornaments only on your bedside table – most girls choose two photographs, but you can have one photograph and a clock if you prefer, so long as it's not a radio clock – radios aren't allowed. And as for i-anything!' Matron rolled her eyes. 'None of that fancy technology here, young lady! And you can have six things on your chest of drawers, one of which should be your hairbrush . . . and a hairband or a hair-clip would count as another item, but if you put all your hairbands and hairclips together in a box, then you could have as many hairbands and hairclips as you could fit in the box and it would only count as one thing. Is that all clear, dear? Good,' she went on, taking Edie's blank stare for an answer. 'Now you tidy yourself up, and I'll be back in ten ticks.'

Edie had never shared a bedroom with anyone before, and when Matron had gone she suddenly felt self-conscious. She stood frozen a moment by her bed, then ventured around the room, peeking furtively at the toys and photographs.

The corner bed had a rather haughty-looking china doll on the pillow, with glassy emerald eyes. Edie walked over, and recognised a photograph of Anastasia's father on the chest of drawers – but looking very different from the solemn portrait Cousin Charles had shown her of the prince. Here he was leaning against the side of a sailing boat, his green eyes smiling from beneath windswept, pepper-grey hair.

Then something next to the photograph caught Edie's eye. At first she thought it was a jewel, but when she moved closer she saw that it was a glass bird, with sculpted feathers and a fanned tail, and shining violet beads for its eyes. Edie thought it was the prettiest thing she had ever seen, tiny and flawless, and though the glass was shining it had an ancient, centuries-old air, like an ornament peered at in a museum. It looked much too fragile to touch, and yet before she quite knew what she was doing she had reached to pick it up. As she did, she heard the door burst open behind her.

'Oh!' Edie gasped, jumping round to see four girls appear. One was Anastasia – Edie recognised her at once from the photographs she had seen, taking in the dark eyes and pale skin, and the hair that tumbled over her shoulders in thick brown ringlets. It struck Edie there was something fragile and exotic about her, like the glass bird.

The other girls looked at Edie curiously, but Anastasia did not seem to notice that Edie had been rifling through her things. She sat down on her bed with a dreamy expression, as if her thoughts were somewhere quite different.

'Hello, I'm Sally,' said a plump, pleasant-looking girl with a pink face and a bouncing bob of straw-coloured hair. 'Hey! What's that you're holding? Isn't that Anastasia's bird?'

Edie's checks burned. 'I . . . I'm sorry . . . I . . . I just . . . I just wanted to look at it!' she stammered, fighting back a sudden sting of tears.

Anastasia watched carefully as she replaced the bird on the chest of drawers, but did not say a word.

'You won't get off to a very good start here if you poke about in other people's things,' said a tall, pinched-faced girl. 'How would you like it if we—'

'Oh, leave her alone, Phoebe, she's new,' piped another girl. 'You can see she's sorry and I'm sure she didn't mean to snoop. I'm Alice, by the way,' she said, turning to Edie with a warm smile.

Edie looked at her gratefully, feeling she had been pulled from a ditch. Something about Alice was very reassuring. She had brown hair scraped briskly into a ponytail and wore a badge that said 'Form Monitor'.

'I've told you, Anastasia,' Alice said teasingly, 'if you insist on bringing back all these beautiful things and turning the dormitory into a museum then you must expect people to want to look at them.'

Anastasia shrugged. 'I don't mind if people give Birdy a stroke,' she said, gazing at Edie from beneath thick black lashes. Her voice was gentle, and despite what

Cousin Charles had said about her having no trace of a Russian accent, Edie detected something foreign.

As Edie walked back to her own bed she caught Phoebe's hissed warning: *'We'd better look out for* her.' Edie wished the floor could swallow her, but the others chattered on as if quite used to Phoebe's spite.

'Lucky you, having a full tuck box,' said Sally. 'It's only a week since half-term but we've finished ours already.'

'It's a pity you've arrived so late,' Alice said sympathetically. 'You've missed the choir auditions, *and* the trials for the first-year lacrosse team – but they might still let you try out.'

Edie tried to look interested, though she suspected her mission would leave no time for such things.

Sally meanwhile was staring hungrily at her tuck box. 'Oh, do show us what you've got! I'd love to see!'

Edie felt herself reddening again – she was too embarrassed to admit she had nothing to offer them. And she didn't want anyone to see her phone.

'It *is* the custom for new girls to share their tuck,' Phoebe said. 'But I suppose we can't force you.'

'Oh, don't start up again, Phoebe,' Alice said. 'It's all right, you know – you don't have to share with us if you don't want to. And you can lock it if you like,' she said, pointing to the padlock on Edie's tuck box. 'But you'll have to hand over the key when they do an inspection.'

Edie looked horrified.

'They search them,' Sally said darkly. 'And if you've got any sweets they'll be confiscated and you won't get them back until the end of term!'

'If Matron greedy pig Mend doesn't eat them first,' Alice giggled.

'I don't have any sweets,' Edie mumbled. 'I don't have any cake either . . . I . . .'

Anastasia turned and looked at Edie thoughtfully. 'Don't worry about Phoebe,' she said, speaking with quiet authority. 'It's up to you to decide what you want to show us.'

Phoebe looked furious and Edie was relieved when Matron reappeared. It was time to meet the headmistress.

Miss Fotheringay's study was on the other side of the school, down another series of corridors, and Edie tried to compose herself on the way. She had been nervous about meeting her head teacher, but now she was more concerned about the scene she had just fled.

'*Whatever you do, don't draw attention to yourself,*' Cousin Charles had warned her. But she had been caught snooping before she had even unpacked. And after the business over her tuck box they'd all think she was mean.

What's it matter whether or not they like me? she thought, as Matron knocked on the headmistress's door. *As soon as my job's done I'll be gone from this stupid place for ever!*

6

KNIGHT'S HADDON

In Loco Parentis

'In you go,' Matron said, nudging her through the door.

It took Edie's eyes a moment to adjust to the dim lighting. When they did she found herself in a large fire-lit study filled with books. The walls followed the gentle curve of the tower, and a tall arched window showed the sun sinking in a brilliant blaze across the park.

In the corner of the room a figure was seated behind a wide leather desk, her head bowed over a pile of papers. A black cat crouched beside the brass desk lamp, tracking the progress of the woman's fountain pen as she turned over a document and signed her name with a flourish.

'Done,' she said, returning the pen to its lid and looking up with the flicker of a smile.

Edie looked back, unnerved. Cousin Charles had been dismissive of Miss Fotheringay – *she hasn't been there long . . . a bit at sea, I'm told . . . Stolly said she was a dragon, keep your head down, though, and she shouldn't take much notice of you . . .* – but the woman sitting behind the desk was not what she had been expecting. Her face was beautiful, long and narrow with features that looked as though they had been carved out of stone; but more than anything Edie was struck by the eyes, blue and unblinking beneath hooded lids. She felt herself being scrutinised in a way that was quite unfamiliar to her, as if everything inside her were being turned out and searched.

'Close the door, Edith, and come and sit down,' Miss Fotheringay said at last. Edie followed her towards the fire, noting the whispers of grey in the headmistress's pale brown hair, and the gold thread in her dress.

'Here,' Miss Fotheringay said, patting the sofa.

Edie perched uneasily. A delicate tea was laid out on a low table in front of her, flowered china and cakes on a glass stand.

Miss Fotheringay sat beside her and reached for the teapot. 'No, Black Puss, you keep off the food,' she said, batting away the cat that had approached the table with its tail erect. 'Although I agree that Miss Wilson here has the air of a bird ready for flight,' she added in an amused voice. 'I hope we can hold on to you long enough, Edith, to stop you wanting to leave.'

Edie didn't know how to respond. Had she been found out already? But Miss Fotheringay was calmly busying herself with the tea things, and gave no sign of having meant more than she said.

'Eat,' she ordered, choosing her two little cakes.

Edie balanced her plate on her lap, crumbling her food with her fingers.

Miss Fotheringay sipped her tea. 'Tell me, Edith,' she said, 'what brings you to Knight's Haddon in the middle of term?'

Edie felt a tightening in her throat. The question was unexpected, and she needed time to think. She looked up into the headmistress's face but as quickly looked away again. There was something in her eyes that made Edie flinch.

'I did not press your guardian for too much information,' Miss Fotheringay went on. 'Sometimes parents are afraid to tell me things because they think I'll refuse to accept children who have been in trouble. It is, for the most part, an unnecessary caution – I'm reluctant to turn away any child I have room for. But if something went wrong at your last school then I should like to hear about it.'

Edie remained silent. Her orders were to blend in. Should she make up a story to fit Miss Fotheringay's assumption that she was some sort of delinquent?

'Tell me, child. Were you unhappy there?'

'No – no,' Edie said, surprised into telling the truth. 'I liked it.'

'You just happen not to have attended for the last two years,' Miss Fotheringay observed.

Edie, failing to think of a story, decided to stick to the

facts. To some of them, anyway: 'Babka – that's my grandmother – took me out of school. She . . . she needed me at home, so she taught me herself.'

'I see . . .'

'But then Babka had to go into a home, and my guardian wanted . . . decided to send me here.' Edie finished clumsily.

Miss Fotheringay nodded. 'Mr Rodriguez mentioned how keen you were to come here. He was afraid you might have a romantic idea of boarding school from all the old-fashioned storybooks you've read.'

Edie felt ambushed. Cousin Charles had warned her that she would have to lie – *you can lie all you like, Edith, so long as you stick to the same one* – yet she found herself shocked to discover that he had lied about her.

'Perhaps he was the one who was keen, Edith, not you,' Miss Fotheringay continued. 'You don't strike me as the sort of girl who comes to a school like this with fixed ideas about how much fun it is going to be.'

Edie said nothing. There was something about this dramatic-looking woman with searchlight eyes and a quiet, probing voice that made Edie want her approval, but an instinct told her to hold back. *'There are some people,'* Babka had warned her, *'who always want to know more than it is safe to tell.'*

'When did you stop living with your grandmother?' was Miss Fotheringay's next question. 'I had understood that you lived with your uncle and aunt.'

'I left Babka a month ago,' Edie replied, 'when she went into a home.'

'Ah,' Miss Fotheringay said. 'So your grandmother has been the important one.'

Edie had a vision of Babka sitting alone with her chessmen, and fought a sudden sting of tears. 'Yes . . . yes, I suppose . . .' she began, wishing Miss Fotheringay would take charge of the conversation again. But her headmistress was watching her in silence. *She is waiting for me to cry*, Edie thought; and she did, her tears dripping onto her crumbled cakes. Miss Fotheringay gave her a handkerchief, and through glazed eyes Edie saw the initials C.F. embroidered in crimson thread, and wondered what the C stood for. But Edie was not crying because of Babka. She was crying because someone was being kind to her.

Miss Fotheringay did not seem at all awkward or embarrassed. Black Puss jumped up into the space between them on the sofa, and began to purr. 'I hope you're not afraid of cats,' Miss Fotheringay said, stroking him lovingly. 'This one was a stray. He used to be afraid of me, but I think I've won him round.'

'We had a cat, when I lived with Babka,' Edie said, trying to keep her voice even. 'Then when Babka went blind I was sent to live with my aunt and uncle and their three sons but they . . . they lived in the country and they didn't really want . . . then . . . then Cousin Charles asked me to live with him in London and then . . .' Edie faltered, suffocated by secrets. 'I miss my grandmother,' she said finally, for this at least was true. Then it occurred to her that it was better than true – that missing Babka could be her alibi for all the other feelings she could not confess.

Edie talked a little more, about Babka and her failing sight. Miss Fotheringay asked the occasional question such as 'Who did the cooking?' and 'What happened to the cat?' and Edie explained about the eating out of tins and the cat being sent to an animal shelter. But mostly Miss Fotheringay just listened, and when Edie had stopped talking she had the look of someone who was still listening, or at least thinking very hard about what she had heard.

At length she said, 'I have a hunch about you, Edith. I think you will have something extra to offer. It is often the way with children who have suffered more than is quite fair. I hope that Knight's Haddon will be the beginning of a more settled period in your life. The first few weeks at a new school are always difficult, and you may find you are behind in certain subjects. But you'll catch up soon enough, and in the meantime you must try not to get anxious about your work. The teachers are here to help you. Of course, this is true of staff in other schools, but at boarding school all the teachers are *in loco parentis*. Do you know what that means?'

Edie shook her head.

'It's Latin. Can you try to work it out?'

'I don't know any Latin.'

Miss Fotheringay smiled. 'You will. *Locus* is Latin for place – it's where the word "location" comes from. *In loco parentis* means in the place of parents. You are used to being the only child without parents, but here at Knight's Haddon all the pupils are, in a sense, parentless.

My staff and I try to make that up to you.'

Edie bit her lip, trying to take this in.

'But a boarding school can only thrive so long as its members are truthful and trusting. There is no place, at Knight's Haddon, for secrets or lies. Your success – now and in the future – will depend on your ability to be open and honest – it is the open, honest girls, Edith, of whom I am truly proud.'

Edie's heart gave a confused lurch. This was very different from the talk Cousin Charles had given her in the car. She stared at the cat, not daring to meet her headmistress's eye. She would not be here long, she reminded herself – it hardly mattered if she failed to please Miss Fotheringay. And yet this short speech made her very uncomfortable.

'Have you met the girls in your dormitory?'

Edie nodded.

'Now let me see, you're with Sally Lanyon, aren't you, and Alice and . . . Phoebe, is it?'

'Yes,' said Edie nervously.

'There must be one more,' said Miss Fotheringay, frowning as she replaced her teacup on the tray. 'Who's your fifth?'

Edie had a sudden fear that Miss Fotheringay suspected something of her connection to Anastasia. Why else was she watching her so intently, waiting for her to say her name?

'I c-can't remember,' she faltered, and felt the red rising.

Miss Fotheringay looked thoughtful. 'Isn't it

Anastasia Stolonov?' she said. 'Perhaps you haven't met her yet?'

'Yes . . . no . . . I think I have . . . I – I'm not sure.'

Miss Fotheringay looked at her carefully, before seeming to shake an idea from her head.

'Of course, you'll take time to settle in,' she went on. 'But not too long, I hope. You've missed half a term of Latin so I shall tutor you myself in that. Meanwhile it's probably a good idea to involve yourself in as many things as possible. Have you ever played lacrosse?'

Edie shook her head.

'What about music? Perhaps you could audition for the orchestra.'

'I don't play anything.'

'Or the choir?'

'I can't sing.'

'Mmm. There is a school of thought which says that everyone can sing, but not being able to myself I don't belong to it. Drama!' she said suddenly. 'There are auditions tomorrow for the first-year play. It's to be *The Merchant of Venice*, directed by one of the prefects. Perhaps you would like to try for that.'

'Yes, I – I'd like to – but . . . but I can't act,' Edie said uncertainly.

'I don't believe you, Edith?' Miss Fotheringay said, smiling. 'I suspect you might be rather good at it.'

The Strictest School in England

When Edie returned to the dormitory, Sally was there. 'Matron said I could stay behind during prep to help you unpack,' she said, looking very pleased. 'I'm your shadow, by the way. All new girls have a shadow, someone who shows them round and looks out for them and tells them what to d— well, helps them if they don't know what to do,' she corrected herself.

Edie was glad it was Sally, not Phoebe, who had been appointed to look after her.

'Miss Fotheringay asked me,' Sally went on excitedly. 'I'm the first of the first-years to be made a shadow. The others will have to wait until next year, when we get the next lot of new girls in. I thought she'd ask Alice. She's the good one – she's a form monitor.' Sally sighed. 'I *always* seem to be in trouble.'

They set about unpacking Edie's things. Sally showed her how everything had to be arranged in a particular way – shirts on one side of the wardrobe, dresses on another, toothbrushes on a particular glass shelf in the bathroom – 'and you'd better get it right, because if anything's found in the wrong place you'll be given an order mark. And you'll have to put that back,' Sally said, as Edie unpacked a blue dress Babka had made her. 'We're only allowed one set of home clothes.' Edie put the dress back in the trunk, but took the opportunity of pulling out her torch and sneaking it into her bedside table.

A bell rang. 'Supper,' Sally said, her face brightening. 'Come on. All the meals are at different times on different days,' she explained, leading Edie down the stairs. 'Supper's at quarter to seven today because there's no school council – that's when all the notices are read out – but on other days it's at six-thirty, and breakfast is at half past seven on Monday to Thursday and quarter to eight on Friday because . . . Oh, don't worry, you can always ask me,' she finished hurriedly.

They passed through a stone archway and came to some steps leading up to a heavy oak door, which they arrived at in time to see swing shut. 'We're late,' Sally groaned, hurrying up the stairs and pushing it open. Edie followed her into a dim panelled dining room full of girls sitting silently at trestle tables. The door creaked as it closed behind them, and everyone turned to stare. There were so many faces Edie felt dizzy, but it was the mistress standing at the end of the nearest table whose presence she found most disconcerting. She was solidly built, with a flushed face and dark, bulging eyes, a pair of spectacles hanging round her neck. As she looked at them her head seemed to lower, reminding Edie of a bull about to charge.

'If you are going to take responsibility for a new girl, Sally, you might at least have the courtesy to ensure that she arrives in the dining hall in time for Grace,' she said in a ringing voice.

'Sorry, Miss Mannering,' Sally mumbled.

'So you should be. Lateness is a vice which loses wars.'

'Yes, Miss Mannering,' Sally sighed.

'Now hurry up and sit down,' Miss Mannering said crisply, holding the room in silence as Sally led Edie to a table in the corner. Then: 'You may begin,' Miss Mannering said, and all at once the room exploded with the sound of chattering and clattering.

Edie and Sally were the only first-years on their table, and the older girls hardly acknowledged them, other than the occasional remark such as, 'Butter, please.'

'Miss Mannering's the deputy headmistress,' Sally explained, helping her to water from a huge tin pitcher. 'She goes bright red and shouts a lot but you'll get used to it. Phoebe says she's going through the menopause,' she added in a thrilled whisper.

'Oh,' Edie replied, not sure what this meant.

'Anyway, you've got to watch out for her,' Sally went on. 'She loves gating people at the weekends. And she'll send you to Fothy for the slightest thing – the two of them are thick as thieves. And *that*,' Sally went on in a lowered voice, 'is Helen. She's the head girl.'

At the end of the table, a statuesque young woman was serving the cottage pie. She was beautiful, with wide hazel eyes and a tumbling mass of golden hair. Edie found it hard to believe that she and Helen were members of the same schoolgirl race.

'Helen's ancestors lived at Knight's Haddon years ago before it became a school, and the family still owns part of the park,' Sally explained furtively. 'She's got her own place on the other side of the woods, a little brick tower – the prefects are allowed to have picnics there—'

'Sally,' Helen said, with a gentle half-smile. 'Don't whisper at table. It's rude.'

Sally blushed, and Edie noticed how much more chastened she seemed by Helen's mild telling-off than she had by the rebuke from Miss Mannering.

Edie was curious. She had never before heard of any schoolgirl owning her own tower. But the snippets of conversation she picked up at supper gave her a glimpse of a very different world.

'If I get a good report this term Daddy's going to buy me a new pony. Clopper's got so fat we can't enter any of the gymkhanas . . .'

'We're going heli-skiing this Christmas. I can't wait . . .'

'Our cook gave in her notice the day before my birthday. Mummy was furious. She says that if she can't find another one we'll all have to spend Christmas in a hotel . . .'

Edie felt she had nothing to contribute. She

remembered Babka once working as a cook in a Polish restaurant, but she had never met children with cooks of their own. At her old school they had talked about the TV, and Edie had always watched plenty of that. But here, she remembered ruefully, there wasn't one.

'The food's not bad, is it?' Sally said, passing up her plate for a second helping of treacle tart. 'They say it used to be disgusting, boiled fish and cabbage and stuff like that, but Fothy put her foot down. Are you any good at tennis?' she asked suddenly, digging greedily into a bowl of clotted cream.

Edie was about to admit she had never played; but then she remembered Cousin Charles's warning about pretending to be the same as everyone else. 'I'm a bit out of practice,' she said.

It was a relief when a bell clanged, and supper was over.

'Why did your parents choose this school for you, Edie?' Sally asked as they were walking back to the dormitory.

'I think . . . I don't really know.'

'My mother chose it because she came here. Anastasia's mother was here too – they were in the same year and they were so naughty. They used to sneak into the kitchens at night to steal food, and once they ran away together and spent a night in the tower!'

'Lucky them,' Edie said, thinking of her miserable attempt to run away from her cousins.

'I know, it must have been fun,' Sally said wistfully. 'But we can't do things like that any more. It's much,

much stricter than it used to be. It's probably the strictest school in England now. Didn't they warn you?' she laughed, seeing Edie's startled expression. *Old-fashioned manners by old-fashioned methods*, that's what it says in the prospectus. That's why we're not allowed mobiles or computers, and why we have to write lines, and walk up corridors one side, and down them another, and jump to attention every time a mistress enters the room. Our parents think it's good for us. My mother's an actress and my father works in the City,' she finished breathlessly. 'What do your parents do?'

Edie bit her lip. She hated telling people that her parents were dead, and then having to deal with their embarrassed reaction. Sally was sure to find out the truth soon enough, but Edie wasn't going to help her.

'They're journalists,' she replied.

Sally looked uncertain. 'I don't know anyone else here whose parents are journalists. You might be the only one!'

Edie deflected. 'Are we *ever* allowed out?' she asked, thinking of London, where she had run messages for Babka up and down their busy street.

'We're allowed to walk to the village on Saturday afternoons in pairs. But there's not much there, just a couple of tea rooms – and when you're new you end up being gated half the time as you're still learning the rules. Oh, don't look so worried, it's not as bad as that,' Sally said. 'Most of the teachers are OK. Even the Man is more bark than bite.'

'The Man?'

Sally giggled. 'Miss Mannering. That's what everyone calls her.'

Edie thought of the thickset woman glaring at her across the dining room with a lowered head, and thought the nickname very fitting. 'What's Matron like?' she asked.

'We call her Matron Mend because she's so good at fixing stuff. She can put anything back together. She even fixed a string on my tennis racquet once.'

'Is she nice?'

'Oh, she's all right – but I'm not one of her favourites like Anastasia. She's her complete pet.' Edie detected a note of envy in Sally's voice. 'I'm too naughty to be anyone's pet,' she went on, taking Edie's arm. 'Oh, Edie, I'm glad you've come. I didn't like having an empty bed in the dormitory. And some of the others are a bit . . . well, you need to look out for Phoebe – she's always in a bad mood.'

'Why?'

'I don't know why.' Sally shrugged. 'She's just like that. And Alice is nice, but she's a bit of a goody-goody. I think it's because she's on a scholarship and is always afraid of losing it. Her father lost his job.'

'How do you know so much?' asked Edie, who was making a mental note of everything Sally told her.

Sally shrugged. 'I just do.'

'And what about Anastasia?' Edie asked, in as casual a voice as she could muster.

'Her father's a Russian prince!' Sally said, clearly thrilled to be so well informed. 'He's got a palace in

Moscow and a place in the South of France. Phoebe says he's richer than the Queen.'

'She seems cool, though,' Edie said, hoping Sally might expand.

'She's a bit—' Sally paused. 'She's a bit strange. Actually, she's more than a bit strange. She's seriously weird. You probably didn't see it just now in the dormitory but you will soon.'

'What sort of seriously weird?' Edie wondered.

'Well, she doesn't say much and you think she's just very dreamy, then suddenly something will upset her and she'll get in a real strop. And then she tears through books, like someone seriously clever, but her spelling's atrocious. But weirdest of all is the way she gets upset about losing stuff – she's always accusing other people of taking her things even though whatever she's lost always turns up somewhere she's obviously hidden it herself.'

'Like what?'

'Before half-term she accused me of stealing her diary – but then it turned up under her pillow. I pretended not to mind. But Alice could see that I did mind and she said she understood why and that she would have minded too, if Anastasia had accused her. She's basically a real drama queen, anyone can see that.'

When they got back to the dormitory Edie saw to her alarm that her tuck box had gone. 'Don't worry, Matron will have taken it to the lower-school common room, that's where all the tuck boxes are kept,' Sally said.

'Come on, I'll show you.'

Edie followed her down the corridor to a long, brightly lit room with dozens of identical black tuck boxes arranged in a neat row along the wall, each with its owner's initials marked on top. Edie sensed this was not the time to rescue her phone from its hiding place – the common room was full of girls, some shouting raucously, others talking in secret huddles.

'Belinda! . . . Rose! . . . Becky! . . .' Sally trilled, as girls came over to be introduced, but Edie was too over-whelmed to take in all the new names and faces. She was starting to feel very tired, and it seemed for ever until a bell rang, signalling that it was time for bed.

As they returned to the dormitory a woman came down the corridor towards them. Something in her appearance made Edie want to stare. She was tall, with a sculpted bob of jet-black hair, and a body as thin and bendy as a blade of grass. Edie noticed the awed glances she attracted from the other girls as they hurried to bed.

'That's Miss Winifred, head of Lower School,' Sally whispered. 'She's pretty, isn't she? She only arrived this term, like us. Apparently she used to live in Monaco!'

'Will we have any lessons with her?'

'You bet! She's our form teacher and she takes us for maths. She can be quite strict – before half-term she gave me an order mark for being late with my homework – but she's so much cooler than any of the other teachers. You'll see for yourself tomorrow.'

As Edie changed into her pyjamas she watched the other girls from the corner of her eye. Alice was hanging her uniform in the wardrobe, while Phoebe was sitting on her bed, angrily brushing the tangles from her hair.

'You shouldn't brush so hard or you'll have no hair left,' Sally said teasingly. Phoebe scowled. Anastasia, meanwhile, seemed altogether elsewhere. When the others had all got into bed she was still standing by her chest of drawers, quietly rearranging her little ornaments and hairclips into a painted wooden box. Edie thought about what Sally had said. She could see exactly why Anastasia might be described as dreamy, but as for wanting to whip up the action – she had seen no sign of that. She was still standing there when Miss Winifred appeared.

'What are we up to, Anastasia?' she asked, smiling. 'Rearranging the family jewels?' The other girls laughed but Anastasia looked embarrassed. Miss Winifred waited until they were all in bed. Then, 'Goodnight girls,' she said in her sweet, fluting voice, and left them in darkness.

The dormitory soon fell quiet but Edie couldn't sleep. The school seemed so big and confusing – if there really was an intrigue going on around Anastasia, she wondered how she would ever get to the bottom of it. And she was worried about her mobile. She knew it had been foolish to leave it in her tuck box when there was a threat it might be searched. If it was confiscated she would have failed Cousin Charles's first test. She heard the school clock strike nine and wondered if she should risk creeping along to the common room to fetch it. Would the feather-like Miss Winifred still be breezing about in the corridor?

There was only one way to find out . . .

The dormitory door squealed as Edie opened it. She flashed her torch along the corridor, and saw a glint of glass from the common-room door at the other end. She tiptoed towards it, and crept inside. She shone her torch over the tuck boxes and soon found her own. She had hidden the phone in a tattered blue shoe box along with some photographs and other little treasures. Edie decided to take them all, and as she returned to the dormitory with the box tucked under her arm she felt a new confidence in her ability to carry out her secret role.

But then the corridor lights came on.

Edie stood like a startled rabbit as a hawk-like figure loomed towards her. She looked up, expecting to see Miss Winifred. But it was the Man. 'Edith Wilson! What *on earth* are you doing?' she demanded.

Edie clutched the shoe box to her stomach. She remembered what Sally had said – '*she's more bark than bite*' – but at that moment the Man looked as if she might swallow her whole.

'Well?'

'I . . . I went to get something from my tuck box,' Edie stammered.

'*You went to get something from your tuck box?*' Miss Mannering sounded incredulous, as if Edith had admitted to breaking into the school safe. '*At nine o'clock at night?*'

'Y-yes.'

Miss Mannering let out a loud breath. 'You have a lot

to learn, Edith Wilson, if you wish to stay on the right side of me.'

Edie thought with longing of her bed, wishing she could dive inside it and hide under the covers. She realised suddenly that she was shining her torch onto Miss Mannering's boots, and made to hide it in her pocket.

'Give that to me please, Edith,' Miss Mannering said, stretching out a hand.

Edie gave it to her.

'And that, whatever it is.'

Edie shook her head, holding the shoe box tight. She felt a rising panic. She didn't care what else happened – she couldn't let the Man have it.

'Give it to me, Edith. *At once!*'

'No!' Edie choked, making no effort to fight her tears.

A door banged down the corridor, and Edie turned and saw Miss Fotheringay appear.

'Ah, it's you, Miss Mannering,' the headmistress said in a calm voice. 'I saw a light and wondered what was going on. Is everything all right?'

'No,' Miss Mannering replied shortly. 'I have found this child emerging from the common room. She tells me she *went to get something from her tuck box.*'

'Is this right, Edith?' Miss Fotheringay asked, looking at her kindly.

'Yes,' Edie whispered.

'What was it you needed so badly?'

Edie could not say.

'She has refused to hand it over,' Miss Mannering said. 'If this weren't her first night at school, I'd—'

Miss Fotheringay cleared her throat meaningfully, and Miss Mannering stopped. 'Give it to me, Edith,' Miss Fotheringay said.

Edith looked at her hesitantly; but something in her expression made her relinquish the box without further protest.

'Thank you,' Miss Fotheringay said quietly. 'I can assure you I shall take good care of it.' She gently steered Edie back into the dormitory and stood over her while she got into bed.

When she had gone Edie lay on her back, watching the shadows from the window slip across the grey ceiling. As she drifted off to sleep it was not Babka but Miss Fotheringay whom she saw, gazing down at her with searching eyes.

8

KNIGHT'S HADDON

First Impressions

Alone in her study Miss Fotheringay's face took on a look of frowning concentration very different from the kindly vision which Edie had seen on her way to sleep.

She made first to close the curtains then, seeing the moon, changed her mind and went instead to her bookcase, running her hand over a small, perfectly disguised section of fake leather spines. The shelf sprang open to reveal a secret chamber containing a leather notebook, a square brown bottle of fiery orange liquor and two delicate crystal glasses.

She poured herself a drink, then picked up the notebook and slid back the chamber door. At her desk she opened the book at the section titled *Register of Staff and Pupils; D&P (Diagnosis & Prescription)* and made an entry about her newest pupil:

The years of keeping watch for her grandmother have left her with a habit of defiant reserve . . . a slow introduction to school life would in this case be a mistake . . . let the child be stripped free of time to think and she will have a chance of flourishing.

Miss Fotheringay put down her pen and gazed out of the window at the disc of white in the black October sky, mocking her attempts at clarity. The headmistress of her first school had taught her to record her first impressions of new pupils. '*It will be a record, for the most part, of your own mistakes,*' Mother Bridget had said.

Miss Fotheringay put her impressions of Edith straight to the test with a glimpse inside the shoe box which lay on the desk in front of her. The headmistress of Knight's Haddon did not believe that the girls in her charge had any right to privacy.

The mobile phone did not surprise her. It always amused her how many parents said they supported the school's ban but failed to prevent their daughters trying to smuggle one in. It was as though even that bit of discipline was too much for them.

Miss Fotheringay switched the phone on and checked the contacts. There were only two – Babka and Charles. She noted with relief that it was not the instrument of a regular user – there were no text messages, no stored voicemails.

She looked to see what else the box contained. There were two photographs in frames and a curious-looking rag doll about ten centimetres tall in black velvet fancy dress. Miss Fotheringay had a horror of dolls and was careful not to touch this one, but she put the framed photographs on the desk in front of her and studied them closely.

One was of an elderly woman dressed in a fashion-less pale wool coat sitting on a balcony with mountains behind her. Her eyes were closed against the sun, but there was something shrewd in the knot of hands that lay in her lap and something determined in the tilt of her head. The other photograph was of a baby in a christening gown, sitting on a woman's knee. The woman's face was bent towards the baby, and the focus was blurred. Miss Fotheringay stared at this picture for some time.

She was about to replace the contents in the box when she saw the small brown envelope she had missed. She paused briefly, before dipping her long fingers inside. She drew out first a list of what looked like commandments, hand-written in a language she recognised as Slavic, and then another photograph – in colour, of two schoolgirls standing next to one another, holding tennis racquets.

Miss Fotheringay gave a start. It was the uniform which held her attention – distinctive pale blue blazers with a red cross on the breast pocket. The colours were faded, but present. She held the photograph up to her eyes and nodded slowly as her memory released the faces to match. Then she turned it round and read 'Anna & Sophia Carter' in the same lettering as the list of commandments. Underneath this was written *my mother and my arnt* in a looping, childish hand.

Miss Fotheringay continued to stare at the photograph for a long time. 'Oh, Anna! Why did I ever think you would *not* come back to haunt me?' she said at last, in a low, trembling voice.

Acting Up

Edie rose to a day of great confusion. Every event was announced by a loud bell, which would be followed by a rush of girls marching up and down the stairs and corridors. Edie was quite bewildered by so much clanging, and soon she was hearing bells echoing in her head even when there were none ringing.

'You're in my form, York,' Sally explained as everyone made their way to the classrooms after breakfast. 'It used to be known as One-B, until Fothy read us *Richard III* and discovered none of us knew about the Wars of the Roses. Anastasia's with us too, and Phoebe, but Alice is in Lancaster, so we won't have any lessons with her except games. It suits me. Alice has become a bit of a prig since she was made a form prefect. And, of course, we're lucky having Miss Winifred. And we're even luckier that we haven't got Fothy for Latin like the other class do.'

'Don't you like her?' Edie wondered, not mentioning that she was to have her own private tutorials.

'Oh, I don't know, she's just – just *weird*,' Sally said. 'All those funny clothes, and not brushing her hair and everything. And you should see her when she goes for walks – she's got a filthy old tweed jacket she always wears, just like a tramp. And sometimes she turns up to assembly wearing walking boots! Anyway, you've met her. Didn't you think she was a bit weird?'

Edie wondered if Sally ever got fed up of using that word.

'She makes me really nervous,' Sally went on emphatically. 'She always appears out of nowhere, just when you're doing something you shouldn't.' Sally tossed back her head and gave a poor imitation of Miss Fotheringay's low, lilting voice: '*What's that you have there, Sally? Ah, a letter! How interesting, Sally. Who's it from?* She's always poking her nose into things. She wants us to tell her *everything*.'

Edie frowned, thinking of her shoe box. '*Do* you tell her things?'

'No way!' Sally replied. 'But she finds out all the same. Did she give you the *in loco parentis* speech? It's her excuse for giving us no privacy at all. Fothy sends the Man snooping around the dormitories when we're not there. She even does it herself sometimes. I went back to our dorm a couple of weeks ago at break time because I'd forgotten something and Fothy was coming out!'

'What had she been doing?'

Sally shrugged. 'A drawer search, I suppose.'

Edie tried to imagine Miss Fotheringay alone in the dormitory, searching through the bedside tables, but instead she kept seeing Miss Fotheringay's black cat, the tea laid out by the fire in her study, and her calm, inscrutable face.

'And best friends are *strictly* against the rules,' Sally went on, in a mocking voice. 'Fothy *hates* it when anyone gets too close to anyone else.'

'But there can't be a rule against friendship!'

Sally made a face. 'Fothy can have rules against anything – you'll learn. Anyway, she doesn't have a rule against friendship, just a general suspicion of best-friendship. Have you met Belinda and Rose yet?' she asked excitedly. 'They're both in our class, and they're totally inseparable. They knew each other from out of school and neither of them bothers much with anyone else. Fothy's furious about it – she tried to put them in different dormitories after half-term but their mothers complained. They didn't see anything wrong with their daughters being best friends, so Fothy had to climb down for once.'

'This is us,' Sally announced then, and pushed open a door bearing a picture of a white rose. It led into a lofty classroom with a sloping ceiling and a tall, arched window with panes of coloured glass. There were rows of wooden desks with opening lids and a large, old-fashioned blackboard specked with green light from the window. Edie thought how different it looked from the classrooms at her last school, with their shared plastic tables and whiteboards.

The room was full of girls, all talking and clattering their desk lids.

'You're here,' Sally said, pointing Edie to a desk between hers and Anastasia's in the front row. 'It's the worst place, of course, right under the mistress's nose. Anastasia and I used to be in the back row but Miss Winifred wanted to keep a closer eye on us.'

Edie could see why Miss Winifred might want to keep a closer eye on Sally, who never stopped talking. But why had she had moved Anastasia, who seemed so quiet?

'Hello, are you the new girl? I'm Belinda,' came a voice from behind them, and Edie turned round to see a fat, friendly-looking girl with thick blonde bunches sprouting from a smiling face. 'And this is Rose,' she added, turning to a slight, but striking girl at the desk next to her, with curly black hair and wide, slightly startled-looking green eyes. It struck Edie there was something protective in Belinda's manner.

Rose smiled at Edie shyly.

'You should watch out with Sally in charge of you,' Belinda went on teasingly. 'She managed to get herself gated before the rest of us had even unpacked.'

'Oh, shut up!' Sally replied good-naturedly. 'I haven't been in trouble for *at least* two weeks. And you should have seen my half-term report. Miss Winifred said—'

Before she could finish, a bell clanged and everyone fell into their seats like a game of musical bumps. Then the door opened and Miss Winifred made her entrance. She wore a long, swirling red skirt which seemed to float her to the front of the class where she dropped a pile of exercise books on her desk.

'Good morning, girls.'

'Good morning, Miss Winifred,' the class replied, rising to its feet. But Anastasia remained seated, searching for something in her desk.

'Good morning, girls,' Miss Winifred repeated in a playful tone; but Anastasia went on scrabbling among her books. Her head was ducked behind her desk lid, and she seemed unaware the mistress had entered the room. Edie wondered why Phoebe, who was on the other side of Anastasia, didn't prod her, and wondered if she should.

An expectant giggle rippled round the class.

'You must be hiding something very interesting, Anastasia,' Miss Winifred said, smiling down at her over the desk lid. 'Perhaps you might show us.'

Anastasia looked up with a fright. 'No . . . I'm not hiding anything. I've . . . *I've lost something!*'

The girls laughed again, as if sharing a private joke. But Miss Winifred seemed concerned. 'Lost something? Not your watch again, I hope.'

'No. It's Birdy. Someone must have taken— I . . . I mean— I didn't mean . . .' Anastasia faltered, as if suddenly wishing she could take the words back.

'*Your glass bird?*' Miss Winifred repeated, her voice shocked.

'Y-yes,' said Anastasia, with a startled look. 'I put Birdy

in my desk before breakfast this morning – I always bring it in when we've got a test, for good luck, you see, and – and we've got a spelling test this afternoon, so—'

'Of course, I quite see,' Miss Winifred said softly, but the class rocked with laughter, as if it saw something quite different. 'Girls!' Miss Winifred said sternly. 'Please, this is an extremely serious matter. Has anyone seen Birdy?'

There was tittering, but no one spoke.

'But – but someone must have taken it – moved it—' Anastasia protested, turning crimson. 'It was here, I swear it was, and now it's gone!'

'Like the homework you thought had been stolen before half-term, and the watch that disappeared during lacrosse?' Phoebe said gleefully, prompting another burst of laughter from the class. Everyone seemed to be enjoying a familiar joke. Even Miss Winifred's face betrayed the briefest flicker of a smile.

'Please!' she said, raising a hand for quiet. 'Anastasia, dear, the bird was a piece of Stolonov crystal, I believe? I am sure Miss Fotheringay would take something of this nature very seriously indeed. Would you like to go and report it to her now?'

'No,' Anastasia whispered.

'Good. In that case we shall salvage what remains of our maths lesson. Sit down girls, and open your books at page twenty-two.'

Everyone sat down and the maths lesson began, but Edie did not even try to concentrate on the complicated-looking sums being scrawled across the blackboard. She was watching Anastasia out of the corner of her eye, thinking how wretched she looked. Then she glanced again at Phoebe, whose face had worn a look of spiteful scorn throughout Miss Winifred's interrogation.

It was clear that Anastasia's accusations of thieving had become a well-rehearsed joke among the first-years, and the evidence pointed to her being very absent-minded. But Edie recalled her tidiness in the dormitory and felt puzzled. It didn't make sense that she should lose things so often.

'How are you getting on, Edith?'

Edie looked up to see Miss Winifred peering at her. She expected a telling-off, but when the mistress saw she had completed none of her sums she stayed by her desk and patiently explained everything all over again. Edie forced herself to listen and after a few minutes she picked up a dim idea of what she was meant to do.

'I think you have the makings of a perfectly respectable mathematician, Edith,' the teacher said at last, and Edie felt a glow of pleasure.

'See what I mean about Miss Winifred?' Sally whispered as they filed out to their next lesson. 'She's lovely, isn't she? I do like her clothes, don't you? And imagine being that tall and thin. I'd give up cake and sweets right now if I thought I could grow up to be as tall and thin as that, but my mother says I'll never be thin because I'm not that build.'

'It was strange about Anastasia's bird,' Edie said.

'Oh, that! It will just be another false alarm. Whenever she loses something she complains it's been stolen.

Sometimes I think she does it on purpose, to try and get us into trouble. You can see that's what Miss Winifred thinks. She tries to be nice about it but I reckon her patience is running out. Everyone's fed up with Anastasia.'

The rest of the day passed in a blur of lessons and bells and Edie found it took all her concentration just to be in the right place at the right time. At her primary school all the classes had taken place in the same room, but at Knight's Haddon every subject was taught in a different part of the school, miles from the last. Edie was glad to be able to tag along after Sally.

After supper she returned to the dormitory to write to Cousin Charles. She knew she had to tell him about her mobile being confiscated. By the time he got her letter he'd have had no word from her for three days. She wondered if he had tried to ring her, and imagined the phone vibrating impatiently on Miss Fotheringay's desk.

But as she was beginning her letter Alice and Anastasia walked in.

'There you are, Edie, we've been looking for you,' Alice said excitedly. 'It's time for the play auditions. They're starting now, in the lower-school common room.'

'All right,' Edie said, slipping the letter into the drawer of her bedside table.

'Wait for me,' said Anastasia, arranging her hair in the mirror. Edie watched her, intrigued, noticing for the first time the little emerald beads in her hairband, and the initials A.S. beautifully engraved on her silver-backed brush. There was something strangely childlike about the way Anastasia pulled the brush through her hair, as if she were playing with a doll.

'Oh, come on, Anastasia,' Alice teased. 'You don't need to get all spruced up – you're not trying out for Hollywood!'

Anastasia smiled, but Edie could see she had been crying. She supposed it was about the glass bird. But then, 'Oh!' Anastasia said suddenly. 'Look!' She turned, holding it up for them to see. 'It . . . it was here . . . behind the photograph of Papa. But I don't understand – I was sure I left it in my desk before assembly. And now – oh, Alice, what will everyone say?'

'You are an idiot, Anastasia, accusing people of stealing things before you've even looked for them properly,' said Alice, who had heard all about the incident in the classroom from Sally. 'I bet you'd lose your own mother on Speech Day given half a chance!'

'But I was *sure* I left it in my desk . . . I've never been so sure. I—'

'Oh, never mind,' Alice said sensibly. 'You'll have to own up to Miss Winifred in the morning and then it will all be forgotten. Now come on, or we'll miss the auditions.'

'I don't think I'll come,' Anastasia said dejectedly.

'Don't be stupid,' Alice replied. 'You know how much you want a part in the play.'

'Do you like acting?' Edie asked Anastasia.

'Does she just!' Alice answered for her. 'We read a play

of *Alice's Adventures in Wonderland* before half-term and you should have heard her Mad Hatter!'

Anastasia smiled and changed her expression into one of comic anxiety. She tapped Edie on the arm like a fussy old man, before taking her watch from her wrist and shaking it up and down.

'"It's gone horribly wrong,"' she said, in a quavering voice. '"You should never butter a watch with a bread knife. Some crumbs must have got in at the same time. And by the way, if you knew Time as well as I do, you wouldn't talk about wasting *it*. It's *him*."'

'See what I mean?' said Alice to Edie, smiling. Anastasia made a gesture, as if doffing a hat, then switched back into being herself as suddenly as she had changed into being the Mad Hatter.

Edie followed them from the dormitory, feeling she had learnt something interesting. Anastasia clearly loved acting, and just from the few lines she had flung out, Edie could see that she was very good at it. But she didn't suppose that was what Sally had meant when she had called her a drama queen.

Was it possible that Anastasia had been causing all this fuss simply to create a dramatic role for herself? There had certainly been a sense of drama in the classroom this morning. But then Edie thought of Anastasia's face when she had found the bird on her chest of drawers. There had been something fearful in her expression, which Edie could not believe she was putting on.

Striking Down

A notice on the door of the common room announced that this year's play was to be *The Merchant of Venice*, directed by Helen Greyling, the head girl.

'Shakespeare,' Alice groaned.

'It's a wonderful play,' Anastasia said, her eyes shining. 'Papa took me to see it in Stratford last year.'

'What's it about?' Edie asked.

'Choosing husbands,' Anastasia said, knowingly.

'We won't all get speaking parts,' Alice whispered as they went in. 'Some of us will just be attendants and things. But I only want a small part – I've got lacrosse matches every Saturday afternoon so I'd miss half the rehearsals anyway.'

Edie had no desire to be cast as a 'thing'. She experienced a sudden glimmer of determination, which surprised her, then saw Helen sitting at the far end of the common room, and felt a rush of nerves.

Everyone was handed a short passage from the play, and had to step up in turn to read it out loud while Helen took notes, watching with one of her amused smiles. It struck Edie there was something detached in Helen's manner, as if she thought it were all a game that she was too grown up for. It was almost as though she had left school already, and was coming back to visit.

Everyone seemed much more confident than Edie. But it was Anastasia's performance that startled her. As she stepped up to the front, all her dreaminess seemed to disappear:

'If to do were as easy as to know what were good to do, chapels had been churches, and poor men's cottages princes' palaces,' she recited in her strange, resonant voice.

This time there was none of the hostility Edie had noted in class. Everyone watched in admiring silence. 'Very good, Anastasia,' Helen smiled when she had finished, making Anastasia blush. As soon as she stopped reading, Edie noticed, she became shy again.

Then Edie heard her own name being called. 'Just read it slowly and clearly, there's no rush,' Helen said kindly, but as Edie held her page up in front of her she was dismayed to find her hands shaking. As she read out loud her voice sounded strange and uncertain, and she stumbled twice.

'Thank you, Edith, that was good,' Helen said sweetly, but Edie felt sure it hadn't been, and she worried about it all evening, wondering if her reading had sounded as bad as she feared. As she lay awake after lights out she felt a little rueful, reflecting how different her concerns were from the night before.

The following afternoon, when the cast list was pinned up outside the dining room, Edie arrived to find a large crowd of first-years all searching eagerly for their names. Anastasia was standing to the side of the group, looking quietly pleased.

'I'm playing Portia,' she said, turning to Edie. 'And you're playing Nerissa! That means we do most of our scenes together.'

Edie looked at the list in disbelief, astonished to have been given a speaking part. Anastasia's name was at the very top, so Edie supposed Portia must be the lead role.

She was glad to see Anastasia happy again after her miserable morning. When she had told Miss Winifred about finding the glass bird, she had been made to stand in front of the whole class and admit her mistake. She had looked so embarrassed Edie had found herself squirming.

'Who *is* Nerissa?' Edie finally thought to ask.

'She's my maid,' Anastasia said innocently.

Edie recalled Cousin Charles's warning in the car: '*More secret servant than secret service.*' She had not much liked the idea of being Anastasia's servant in real life but in a play it felt like a good omen. 'I think it will be cool to play your maid,' she said, smiling.

But Phoebe, who was standing nearby, gave a derisive snort. 'Trust you to have a maid, Anastasia! I'm surprised your father doesn't send you one from Russia!'

Everyone laughed. But Anastasia looked as if she had been struck and Edie felt a flush of anger on her behalf. 'It's only a play, Phoebe,' she said shortly. 'There's no need to be like that.'

'I think Phoebe's jealous,' Belinda teased. 'She's just a gaoler!'

'Oh, shut up, Belinda,' Phoebe said spitefully. 'We all know why Helen's made you a Venetian magnifico – because you're fat!'

Belinda's face crumpled.

'That's horrid,' Rose said quietly.

'Oh, shut up, clinging Rose!' Phoebe said tauntingly. 'It's a good thing Belinda's so fat – if she was any smaller you'd smother her!'

'Lay off, Phoebe,' Edie said in disgust.

But Phoebe had not finished. 'And we all know why you've been cast as the maid, little Edie,' she sneered. 'It's because you're *like* a maid. Anyone can see you don't belong here.'

Then, 'Ouch!' Phoebe cried, as she was silenced by a resounding slap.

Everyone gasped. But Edie looked more startled than anyone. She stood staring stupidly at her hand, as if it were something quite separate from her.

'*Edith Wilson!*' came a voice that made her heart turn. The Man had appeared. Her face was dark red, and her eyes looked even more protuberant than usual. 'Come here,' she said.

Edie walked up to her, wondering what was going to

happen next. She had an unusual feeling that the whole incident had nothing to do with her, as though she were merely watching a scene in a play.

'What provoked this?'

To tell or not to tell? Edie said nothing. The other girls watched uneasily, for Miss Mannering's expression did not bode well. But then Anastasia spoke up.

'It wasn't Edie's fault, Miss Mannering. It was Phoebe who started it. Edie was only trying to stick up for me.'

'Phoebe? Have you anything to say?' Miss Mannering asked briskly.

Phoebe shook her head, nursing her cheek theatrically. 'I don't know what it was about,' she lied.

Miss Mannering looked doubtful. 'I suspect there was more to this altercation than meets the eye. But in this school we do not settle our differences with physical violence. Edith,' she said, folding her arms, 'you will apologise to Phoebe immediately.'

Edie turned to Phoebe, but when she saw Phoebe's satisfied smirk her throat burned with anger.

'Edith?'

Edie glowered. She wasn't sorry. This time she couldn't lie.

'Very well, I have no option but to report this incident to Miss Fotheringay,' Miss Mannering said coldly. 'And meanwhile, to help you reflect on your behaviour, you will look up in your Bible the twenty-ninth verse of the fourteenth chapter of *Proverbs*, and write it out one hundred times. You will have plenty of time in which to do so – until you have proven to me that you can control your temper you will be gated on Saturdays. And for the rest of this week you will go without cake at tea.'

The other girls looked shocked. Edie supposed that even by Miss Mannering's standards this punishment was harsh. She burned with humiliation. She didn't care about cake or gatings – she'd be out of here soon enough – but the thought of going to see Miss Fotheringay worried her more than she cared to admit.

As they filed into the dining room for tea Edie was aware of the other girls looking at her. She sensed they all felt she had gone too far.

'Poor you,' said Sally, sitting next to her and watching as Edie picked at her slice of buttered bread. 'The Man's not usually as bad as that. It may be the . . . you know, the thing I told you about. But I bet she'll lift the punishments when you apologise.'

But Edie was still simmering. She would not apologize to Phoebe, not after the things she'd said. And if Miss Mannering wasn't usually so bad, then why had she come down on her so hard? Edie was starting to suspect the deputy headmistress had developed a particular dislike for her after the incident over the shoe box.

'Edie, you – you *will* apologise, won't you?' Sally asked anxiously.

'No,' Edie replied.

'But you *must*. If you don't say sorry the Man will gate you until the end of term. You've only got to *say* it, you don't have to mean it.' Sally lowered her voice. 'You can just lie!'

Edie shook her head. Even the thought of an insincere apology was more than she could bear. Sally seemed puzzled by her refusal to give in, and when tea was over Edie found herself walking to prep on her own. But as she was about to enter the classroom, Anastasia came hurrying up.

'Thanks for sticking up for me with the Man,' Edie said gloomily.

'That was nothing,' Anastasia said, looking at her shyly. 'Thank *you* for shutting Phoebe up. She's always going on and sometimes I want to kill her, but – oh, Edie, I'd never have dared hit her like that!'

'That's because you're more sensible than me,' Edie said, reflecting that it was she who had behaved like the drama queen, not Anastasia.

'I don't know,' Anastasia said thoughtfully. 'Sometimes words have to be backed up by actions, that's what Papa says, but I'm just too much of a coward. And anyway, no one would be on my side. The others all think that because— Oh, you know, they just think it's all right to tease me.'

'Well, *I* don't think it's all right,' Edie said.

'But now you're going to be in trouble with Miss Fotheringay, and all because of me. I hope she isn't *too* cross.'

'Oh, I'm not worried about her. And she's certainly not going to make me apologise to Phoebe,' Edie said bullishly.

Anastasia looked at her with interest. 'You are brave,' she said.

Hidden Meanings

Edie might have felt less brave had she seen Miss Fotheringay's expression when Miss Mannering reported her offence. The headmistress stood resting her hand on the mantelpiece, her eyes cold as steel, not a shadow of emotion crossing her face.

'If you take my advice, Caroline, you'd make her give up her part in the school play,' Miss Mannering said. 'Children start as they mean to go on and if you don't bring her to heel, her behaviour will get worse.'

'So,' Miss Fotheringay murmured, 'the child has a temper, like her mother.'

'Her mother? I thought she was an orphan.'

'Even orphans have mothers, Diana. They just happen not to be alive.'

'You are saying that you know something about Edith

Wilson's mother?'

Miss Fotheringay shrugged. 'I know something about her. Her name is – or was – Anna Carter. We were at school together.'

Miss Mannering looked surprised: 'Wasn't she the one—'

'Yes,' said Miss Fotheringay abruptly. 'She was the journalist who got herself killed in Moscow eleven years ago.'

'Really, Caroline, you make it sound as though it was her fault.'

'We were no longer in touch at the time of her death,' Miss Fotheringay replied tersely. 'I know very little about the circumstances.'

'What an extraordinary coincidence.'

'I can assure you, Diana, I knew nothing about the connection until I discovered it by chance from a photograph in the shoe box you confiscated on Edith's first night. I've had nothing to do with the family since . . .'

'Since you were accused of wanting too much that wasn't on offer?'

'I don't know what you mean.'

'I only know what you've told me, Caroline. But I must admit that your having the child at Knight's Haddon bodes ill for—'

'She has been delivered to my care,' Miss Fotheringay returned sharply. 'I did not seek her out.'

'All the more reason for you to resist the temptation to revisit the past. You have always maintained that boarding school should provide every child with a clean slate.'

Miss Fotheringay did not reply. She turned and stoked the fire with a pair of brass tongs.

'I am due to take lower-school prep,' Miss Mannering said with sudden briskness. 'I assume you will send for the child?'

Miss Fotheringay hesitated. Then: 'Of course,' she said quietly. 'Send her to me at six.'

Miss Fotheringay waited until the door had clicked shut before crossing the room and running a hand along the secret compartment in her bookshelf. She took out a black box, which she placed on her desk and proceeded to open carefully, drawing out a faded letter from inside. As she unfolded it her mouth hardened. It was her last communication from Anna Carter – written six weeks before Edith was born. Miss Fotheringay turned by force of habit to the second page, and read again the hate-fuelled words that had haunted her for eleven years.

'Leave me alone . . . this child has nothing to do with you.'

'We'll see about that,' Miss Fotheringay whispered, returning the letter to its box.

Edie was in prep when the summons came.

'Edith Wilson,' Miss Mannering said, barely looking up from her marking. 'You are to report to Miss Fotheringay.'

Edie packed away her things, aware of everyone staring at her. By now there could not be a single girl in the whole school who did not know she had slapped

Phoebe, and as she walked out of the classroom something in their watching faces told her she should fear the worst. When she knocked on Miss Fotheringay's door, her hand was shaking.

'Come in,' said a familiar voice from inside.

Miss Fotheringay was sitting at her desk, with the shoe box placed in front of her. The fire was lit, but there was no tea this time, and no cat.

'I gather that you and Phoebe Phillips have had a difference of opinion, Edith,' Miss Fotheringay said, steering her to the sofa. 'Perhaps you would like to tell me what happened.'

Edie flushed. She had felt hot and angry all afternoon but now she could hardly remember what Phoebe had said. In her mind the whole drama had been reduced to one single scene – that of her arm lashing towards Phoebe's face, and the smack that had silenced the whole corridor.

'I slapped her,' she mumbled.

'Yes, I gather that much from Miss Mannering. But I am interested to know why. I am assuming you don't slap people every time you have an argument, Edith. Or perhaps you do?' Miss Fotheringay seemed interested, as if they were discussing a painting, or a poem they had both read. There was no reproof in her voice. 'I would like to know what Phoebe did to upset you, Edith,' she went on. 'I imagine there must have been some provocation?'

'Phoebe was being nasty to Anastasia,' Edie replied at last, squirming at how babyish the whole affair now sounded. 'She said she was stuck up, and that she should have her own maid, and she said that I'd been cast as her maid in the play because I . . . don't belong here.'

'Background trouble,' Miss Fotheringay surmised, in a tone of sudden impatience. 'What is the matter with you all? Can't you see that Knight's Haddon is a chance to leave your old identities behind? I had put this hour aside to teach you some Latin, not to read you the riot act on losing your temper. I view it as an unwelcome change to my timetable.' Miss Fotheringay paused, and Edie wondered if the riot act was over or if it was about to begin. 'What is the point, Edith, of learning Latin?' the headmistress asked.

'So you can speak it?' Edie ventured.

Miss Fotheringay smiled. 'No one speaks Latin, Edith. But those who know Latin speak their own language better. Words have roots, like trees, and in English the roots are often Latin. Unless you can dig to the roots you will often mislay a word's true meaning.'

Edie frowned, not sure she was quite following, but there was something conspiratorial in Miss Fotheringay's tone which made her listen very closely.

'Let us take the word temper,' Miss Fotheringay went on. 'It comes from the Latin verb *temperare*, meaning to moderate. We also have the verb "to temper", meaning to soften. And yet you probably think of temper as something hard and uncontrollable.'

Edie nodded shyly.

'You need to keep both meanings in mind, Edith. You

will learn to temper your temper, and you will, of course, apologise to Phoebe.'

Edie did not protest.

'Meanwhile Miss Mannering has suggested that I exclude you from the play.'

Edie's face fell.

'But under the circumstances,' Miss Fotheringay smiled, 'I feel that might be a little severe. Tell me,' she added, as though the thought had only just struck her, 'did Miss Mannering take any action herself?'

Edie nodded. 'She's gated me on Saturday afternoons, and I'm not allowed cake at tea time, and I have to write out the twenty-ninth verse of the fourteenth chapter of *Proverbs* one hundred times.'

'I see,' Miss Fotheringay said. 'I'm not sure I remember the twenty-ninth verse of the fourteenth chapter of *Proverbs*. Perhaps you could remind me.'

Edie could, for she had already written it out fifty times during prep. '"He that is slow to wrath is of great understanding: but he that is hasty of spirit exalteth folly,"' she recited in a bold, unhappy voice.

'Very apt,' Miss Fotheringay murmured. Then, 'Are you hungry?' she asked, and without waiting for an answer she stood up and disappeared through a small, internal door at the back of her study. She returned with a tray laid with a teapot and the remains of a marbled cake. 'You might as well eat some now, if Miss Mannering intends to starve you,' she said, cutting Edie a large slice.

Edie was honoured to be part of this plot. She wondered if Miss Fotheringay had cooked the cake herself, and who had eaten the rest of it.

'Now,' Miss Fotheringay said briskly. 'Latin.' She placed a book in Edie's lap, and pointed to a line at the top of the page. 'Read that.'

The strangeness of the words brought a flush of panic to Edie's face. 'F . . . fas . . . e . . . est et ab h . . . hos . . . d . . . do . . . doc,' she stammered.

'Fas est et ab hoste doceri,' Miss Fotheringay corrected her. '"Right it is to be taught, even by the enemy." You will do well to remember those words, Edith, during your time at Knight's Haddon. Although I hope you do not consider yourself to have any enemies among my staff, Edith?'

Edie thought of the Man, and was startled to realise her thoughts were being read.

'If you wish to establish better relations with Miss Mannering, Edith, I would advise you to prove yourself in class,' Miss Fotheringay said.

Edie chewed her cheeks. Despite her reservations about the Man, she had enjoyed her first history lesson. The only history Babka had ever taught her had been to do with Poland. Her grandmother had remembered her country's historic sufferings bitterly, banging her fist on the kitchen table while recounting the wickedness of the Nazis and the Communists. Miss Mannering's lessons were much more fun. She talked about the past as an exciting story which had to be pieced together from clues, and Edie always found herself wanting to know more. But she hadn't yet put her hand up to ask a question, suspecting how much the Man disliked her.

'Knight's Haddon might seem strict in comparison with a day school, Edith, but we all want to help you settle in,' Miss Fotheringay said.

Edie looked guarded, feeling guilty about having so much to hide.

'I am always here if you need to talk,' Miss Fotheringay added, and Edie felt even worse.

It was almost a relief when they returned to Latin. But when Edie opened her pencil case and took out her green fountain pen, she noticed Miss Fotheringay's eyes fix on it. 'It belonged to my mother,' Edie said awkwardly, sensing an explanation was required. 'It's got her initials on it, A.L.C. – or . . . or at least they used to be her initials before she got married and became a W.' She wondered if Miss Fotheringay was going to say that tortoise-shell fountain pens engraved with parents' initials were against the school rules, for she was giving it very close attention. 'I don't have many things belonging to my mother,' she heard herself saying instead. 'My parents lived abroad and after they were— after they died, everything got left behind. There aren't even many photographs left and I haven't got any of my mother's letters or—'

Edie stopped. She tended never to discuss these things, and she wondered if Miss Fotheringay would show impatience, as Babka would have done.

But Miss Fotheringay had put the Latin books to one side. 'How much do you know about your mother?' she asked.

'Not as much as I would like. Babka is my father's mother and she never really talks about my mother. Nor does Aunt Sophia, even though she was her sister. And I don't even know who her friends were.' Edie frowned. 'Maybe she didn't have many – she was a war correspondent, so she was always travelling. But then sometimes I wonder if . . .'

'What?' Miss Fotheringay prompted.

'Sometimes I wonder if there are things Babka doesn't want me know.'

Miss Fotheringay was silent a moment, as she sat examining a gold ring on her right hand. 'What about your Cousin Charles?' she asked eventually. 'Have you talked to him about your mother?'

'He says he hardly remembers her,' Edie said. 'He saw her a bit as a child, I think, but not after she grew up. They're not close cousins. He'd never even met me before he came to supper at Aunt Sophia's.'

'Had he not?' Miss Fotheringay paused, as if to take this in. 'How do you get on with him?' she asked unexpectedly.

Edie hesitated. Cousin Charles had warned her never to trust anyone. But she thought with a sudden longing what a relief it would be to tell Miss Fotheringay the truth – that his pretence at being a loving guardian was all a sham, and that she wasn't really his ward, but the prince's plant.

Miss Fotheringay, as if anticipating a confession, quietly got up and went to stand by the window.

'Cousin Charles, he's not . . . oh, he's all right,' Edie said hurriedly.

A bell clanged, signalling the end of prep. Miss

Fotheringay got up and returned holding the shoe box. Edie knew, as it was handed back to her, that its entire contents had been gone through. *How dare she?* But her silent protest was insincere. Edie didn't care. As she looked up, into her headmistress's eyes, she was aware of some force she had no will to resist.

'I have removed the mobile telephone. As I'm sure you know, they are strictly forbidden.'

'I know, I'm sorry, It was just—'

'Everyone tries it on in the beginning,' Miss Fotheringay said dismissively. 'No one succeeds. You'll find, in the end, that it's a relief not to be in touch with the outside world. Knight's Haddon is your world now, Edith. So long as you are here, in my care, there is no other.'

Thwack!

'Y ou'll be fine,' Sally said, as Edie followed the class reluctantly towards the lacrosse pitch, wearing a vest with the letters 'W.A.' embroidered on it in bright orange. The class had been divided into two teams, the Blues, of which Edie was a member along with Phoebe, and the Reds, which included Alice, Sally and Anastasia. Miss Mannering, dressed in a purple tracksuit, and with a whistle slung round her neck, was leading the players at a brisk march towards the first of the three huge grass playing fields that lay to the side of the West Tower.

'They all take it so seriously, it's pretty babyish if you ask me – so it's much better not to try and catch the ball than to try and catch it and bosh it all up,' Sally went on knowingly, as she and Edie trooped behind their excited classmates. 'Do what I do – just wave your stick about a bit to look like you're trying, and if you see the ball coming anywhere near you, hide behind someone else. It usually works. But it's bad luck being wing attack,' she added, looking at Edie's vest. 'It means you have to run up and down all the time.'

'Which way?' Edie asked nervously, trying to take all these instructions in.

'Whichever way the ball's going,' Sally shrugged. 'Just follow everyone else. You're over there, by the way,' she said – gesturing vaguely down the pitch.

'Where?' Edie asked helplessly – but Sally seemed clueless too. The other girls were all rushing to their starting positions, where they stood half crouched, twirling their sticks in front of them as they waited for the action to begin.

'Edith, over there!' Miss Mannering shouted, pointing across the pitch with a red flag – but Edie still hadn't worked out where she should be standing when the whistle shrilled, and the game began. The ball flew like lightning, now on one side of the pitch, now on the other, swishing from one stick to the next, with girls shouting from all sides:

'Belinda!'

'Clemmie!'

'Here! Here! Over here!'

Edie pretended to follow the ball, though all the time she was working out who she would hide behind if it came too close.

But there seemed to be so many rules that the ball never stayed in play for long without the Man blowing her whistle and telling someone off. Edie watched with relief when the action moved towards the far end of the pitch, where Belinda was standing in goal for the Blues, and noted with admiration how Alice clashed sticks with another player, then gracefully scooped up the ball and flew like a bird towards the goal while the other girls thundered clumsily behind her. Edie was confused about which direction she wanted the ball to go in, and when Belinda saved Alice's attempt at a goal she had to check the colour of her vest to work out whether she should be cheering or groaning. But everyone else seemed to be taking the game very seriously, and the Reds returned to their positions agreeing that with Belinda in goal they'd never be able to score.

'She should have to swap teams each week so we all get a turn with her on our side, otherwise it's not really fair,' Rose said, clearly proud of her best friend, even though they were playing on opposing teams. 'She's probably the best goalkeeper in the whole school.'

'Hardly surprising,' said Phoebe snidely, when Rose was out of earshot. 'With Belinda in goal there's no room for the ball to get through.'

Edie bristled, but pretended not to hear. Anastasia, meanwhile, seemed in a world of her own. She was in the goal for the Reds at Edie's end of the pitch, and stood slouched against a goalpost, twirling her stick in a pretence of readiness while surreptitiously reading a book.

So much for what Sally had said about Anastasia being a drama queen – on this occasion she seemed to be the only person who wanted no part of the action.

Edie felt she had found an ally and she was still watching her, amused, when the whistle blew, and the game started up again with a clattering of wooden sticks:

'Emerald!'

'Hatty!'

'Over here!'

But to Edie's surprise Anastasia just went on reading, oblivious to the game being played out furiously around her.

Then suddenly Edie heard her own name being called, and looked round to see the ball spinning towards her. She flung up her stick, but the ball shot straight past, without even clipping the frame, and she turned to see Phoebe and Rose clashing sticks behind her.

'Play on!' shouted the Man, as Phoebe tackled the ball from Rose and turned, spinning towards the goal. Girls from both teams came crashing up the pitch, screeching encouragement, but Anastasia went on reading.

'Anastasia!' Edie shouted, for Phoebe had dived for the goal, with the ball cradled in her stick –

'*Anastasia!*'

Anastasia finally looked up, and dropped her book in fright as she saw Phoebe whip the ball towards her. There was a thwack, and at first Edie thought Phoebe had hit the goalpost, but then Anastasia let out a shriek and fell to the ground, yelping.

Edie at once ran towards her. A crowd of girls had already gathered around the goal, ignoring Miss Mannering's whistle, but Edie noticed that Phoebe stayed well back. Anastasia was rolling in the mud, clutching her ankle and moaning. To Edie's surprise some of the girls were sniggering, though Anastasia's pain looked very real.

'Where does it hurt?' Edie asked, kneeling down in the mud beside her.

'It was Phoebe, she – she . . . aaaah!' Anastasia winced, sucking in her breath. 'She's broken my leg! Oh, Edie, please – *get someone*!'

Edie was startled – and for once she felt relieved when the Man appeared.

'What have we here, a casualty of war!' Miss Mannering said briskly. The others were all sent back to their positions, and Miss Mannering remained tending to Anastasia in the goal for several minutes. Then she strode purposefully back down the pitch, and sent Alice to fetch Matron before instructing everyone to return inside.

Edie looked back at Anastasia anxiously, but no one else seemed to feel any sympathy for her, and she was glad her friend could not hear the chorus of condemnation as they walked back to the classroom.

'This is the second time she's ruined a game with her hysterics – I can't believe the Man still falls for it . . .'

'I bet it's just a bruise . . .'

'And she says Phoebe hit her on purpose, when the only reason she got hit was because she was reading a book. I mean, how stupid is that?'

'The Man would never have called off the game for one of us. They're all just terrified of the *princess* coming to harm.'

'She'll cry wolf once too often, then she'll learn . . .'

'Learn? Oh, don't be stupid, that's the one thing she'll never do,' Phoebe cut in suddenly. '*She's just mad. Completely mad.*'

Both forms were gathered in the lower-school common room when Miss Winifred arrived, followed by Matron wheeling a cocoa trolley on which sat two steaming tureens. Behind them appeared a sheepish-looking Anastasia, carrying a tray of ginger nut biscuits.

'I bring you Anastasia, bloody but unbowed,' Miss Winifred said in a cheerful voice, placing one hand in the small of Anastasia's back and gently steering her forwards. 'I am sure you will all be relieved to hear that nothing is broken after all, and Anastasia is full of contrition for bringing the match to an end so soon. Aren't you, my dear?' she enquired, flashing her one of her sweet smiles.

Anastasia nodded, but kept her eyes lowered as she placed the biscuits on the table.

'I assured her there would be no hard feelings if we made her lucky escape from Death in Goal an occasion for cocoa and biscuits,' Miss Winifred went on, gesturing at the refreshments 'Am I right, girls?'

'Rather,' said Sally, rushing forward to be first in the queue. 'Thanks for the treat, Anastasia.'

'It's nothing to do with me,' Anastasia said quietly.

'Of course it's to do with you,' Miss Winifred replied. 'You seem to forget, dear, that we discussed in the san how you could make amends. You said that life was so much easier at home because you could always order nice things for people you upset, and I said I thought we could perhaps do something similar today, though of course we can't make a habit of raiding the school supplies.' She paused, then added softly, 'Own your actions, dear child. And life will become much, much easier.'

'And stop falsely accusing others,' murmured Phoebe, under her breath but loud enough to be heard by Belinda and Rose and Edie, who were all standing near. Belinda and Rose moved pointedly into the biscuit queue, as if wishing to disassociate themselves from Phoebe's vendetta. Edie followed, feeling uncomfortable on Anastasia's behalf.

But she was baffled too. It was true that Anastasia didn't look hurt – but then why had she made such a fuss on the pitch?

'Now, girls,' said Miss Winifred, when everyone had got their rations. 'We've got an un-timetabled half-hour to play with. Who says yes to a game of Hangman?'

Several pairs of hands shot up into the air.

'Can I think of the word, please?' asked Sally, as Miss Winifred moved to the fold-up blackboard in the corner, and rubbed out a game of noughts and crosses that had been chalked up.

Miss Winifred cocked her head. 'Mmm,' she said. 'Have you already thought of one?'

'*I* have, Miss Winifred,' pleaded Rose. 'Can I be hangman?'

'No, let me!'

'I didn't have a turn last time!'

Edie supposed Hangman was a regular game among the first-years, for just about every hand was now raised.

'I think you should be hangman, Miss Winifred,' someone called out, and Miss Winifred inclined her head gracefully.

Edie had never played Hangman before but she learnt the rules quickly enough. The girls called out letters, and in response Miss Winifred either drew a line of the hangman picture on the board or filled in a blank of her chosen word. Miss Winifred seemed to be enjoying the game as much as the girls were, gaily filling in each blank as the letters were guessed correctly.

'O' and 'A' were called, and the mystery word started to take shape: '-a-a-o-a.' The hangman picture waited only for its arms and legs.

'Phoebe, give me a letter,' said Miss Winifred, her chalk poised over the blank spaces.

'P,' Phoebe said, smirking.

'Spot on,' Miss Winifred replied, chalking in the word's first letter.

Edie supposed Phoebe had only guessed it because it was the first letter of her own name. 'Z,' she said defiantly, when her turn came next. Miss Winifred tutted and gave an arm to the hanging man.

'Maybe instead of wasting another turn on a wrong letter, you should start thinking about the word. Come on. Surely one of you can guess?'

Everyone looked puzzled. But Edie, glancing at Anastasia, saw that the blood had drained from her face.

'Anastasia, is it hurting?' she whispered, touching her arm, but Anastasia's face was blank.

Miss Winifred appeared to have spotted her discomfort too. 'Anastasia, dear, why not try?'

'Paranoia,' Anastasia croaked, staring at the floor.

'Well done,' Miss Winifred murmured, filling in the gaps.

Phoebe let out a pointed laugh but several of the other girls looked baffled, clearly uncertain what the word meant.

Edie knew, and was amazed Miss Winifred could be so insensitive. For a moment Edie feared she would ask Anastasia to explain to everyone what paranoia was. But then the bell rang, and Miss Winifred wiped down the blackboard, smiling any queries away.

Anastasia left the room with a flounce, and Edie had to run down the corridor to catch up with her.

'Anastasia, wait,' she said, catching her by the arm, but Anastasia shook herself free.

'They can all think I'm paranoid if they want to, but I know Phoebe tried to hit me on purpose. She had the whole goal to shoot into, so why did she have to hit me? She obviously wanted to hurt me! It's just like her, she's so spiteful!'

'Did it hurt?' Edie asked, hesitant.

'Yes, it did!' Anastasia replied fiercely. 'I hate this English thing that everyone has to put a brave face on everything and never complain. Why shouldn't I shout if I'm hurt?'

'But I think you are brave, Anastasia,' Edie said quietly.

'I think there are lots of things you never complain about.'

They had reached the dormitory, and when they were inside she closed the door and turned to Edie with a crumpled face, from which all the anger had vanished. 'I'm not brave Edie, not like you,' she said, her voice choked by a sob. 'But I'm not mad either. Miss Winifred wants me to see a doctor. She thinks I need special help. But I'm not going to. I refuse to be a special case. The whole *point* of coming here was to show I could be normal.' Anastasia paused. When she spoke again her voice was low and determined: 'I *can* fit in, Edie, and I will!'

A Surprise Visit

'I don't understand where we're going.'

Charles Rodriquez smiled coldly as he put his foot on the accelerator. 'You, young man, are going wherever I take you. Your mother had no business dumping you on me for the day and I have no intention of changing my schedule.'

'Got the message,' Lyle said glumly. 'But you could still tell me where your schedule is taking us.'

'I could,' Charles agreed.

Just then the telephone rang through the car speaker and Lyle sat back, impressed, while his cousin conducted something he called 'business' with a man called Stolly.

Charles: 'Are you in the country? I had no idea.'

Stolly: 'I'm in the South of France. Filthy weather, filthy temper. I spoke to Anastasia again this morning and she was distraught.'

'What about?'

'She wouldn't say. I could hear that she was crying, but she insisted nothing was wrong. She's obviously in trouble of some sort and frightened of telling me – so I rang the dragon and she claimed Ansti was making things up about the other girls.'

Charles: 'That doesn't sound like Ansti.'

Stolly: 'Too right it doesn't. And the Ansti I spoke to didn't sound like Ansti either. My impression is that the trouble's got worse since your girl pitched up. Have you heard from her?'

Charles: 'She appears to have been parted from her mobile.'

Stolly: 'I could have told you that would happen. The school's run by maniacs.'

Charles: 'I hoped my girl would break the rules.'

Stolly: 'I hoped mine would settle in.'

Charles: 'I'm actually on my way there now. I think our little spy might need a bit of gentle encouragement. I'm afraid she's taken her eye off the job.'

Stolly: 'Get a result, Charles. I don't like not knowing what's going on.' This was followed by the sound of an engine revving, and the conversation ended as abruptly as it had begun.

'Who on earth was that?' asked Lyle.

'A prince,' said Charles. 'Out of your league.'

'What league?' asked the boy.

'Any league you might ever care to join,' his cousin replied.

'Are we going to see Edie?' Lyle asked slyly.

'I am,' Charles replied. 'You can stay in the car.'

'Come off it, coz. You sent me out to buy her chocolates – why can't I give them to her in person?'

'What a surprising boy you are. I never expected for a minute you would spend my money as I instructed. I assumed you'd blow it all on cigarettes.'

'I blew the change,' said the fox-like boy, with a wolfish grin.

'Why were you so horrid to her, out of interest?'

Lyle shrugged. 'It was a game. I was testing her.'

'You made her run away.'

'Girls,' Lyle said gloomily. 'They take everything so seriously. I mean, that prince geezer just now. Who was he talking about?'

'None of your business.'

'Well, I'm not stupid. He was talking about some girls being horrid to another girl. I mean, like, hello, Prince, grow up. Anyway, what's Edie got to do with whatever he was talking about?'

Charles threw him a sideways glance, as if weighing something up. 'She might tell you one day. Until then I suggest you keep out of it,' he replied.

'Boring,' Lyle murmured, making a face.

Miss Fotheringay was reading Edie's class a passage from *The Merchant of Venice* when they were interrupted by Miss Mannering.

'Please sit down,' the deputy said, catching Edie's eye as the class rose automatically to its feet. Edie watched, curious, as Miss Mannering walked over to Miss Fotheringay's desk. The headmistress's expression made clear that she did not welcome the interruption. But what Edie heard next made her heart quicken:

'I'm very sorry, Headmistress, but I have Edith's guardian, Mr Rodriguez, in reception to see her,' Miss Mannering explained in a hushed voice, just audible from Edie's desk in the front row.

Edie's first thought was that he had come to take her away. *'If you're not up to it, I'll send you back to Devon.'* That's what he had said. And she realised with a jolt that it was no longer just a question of not wanting to go back to Folly Farm. She *wanted* to stay at Knight's Haddon. Her new life of bells and lessons that had seemed so strange two weeks ago had become safe and familiar to her now, and as if in an act of unconscious protest, she clenched her hand round the rim of her chair and clung to it tightly.

'Perhaps you would be kind enough to remind him of the rules,' Miss Fotheringay replied, turning back to her text.

'You might have more luck. But I'm afraid he was rather insistent. Says he's going abroad next week and this is the last chance he has to see her for some considerable time.'

Miss Fotheringay sighed, and slapped her book on the desk. 'Very well,' she said, addressing the class. 'Miss Mannering, perhaps you could continue with Act One. The others will tell you where we've got to. Edith, come with me.

Edie followed Miss Fotheringay from the room. She wondered if she dare confide in her, and beg her to send Cousin Charles away, but Miss Fotheringay's expression was vexed. Neither spoke as they walked to the hall.

Cousin Charles was standing twirling his hat. He barely looked at Edie – it was to Miss Fotheringay that he flashed his cursory smile. 'I hope I haven't called at an inconvenient time. I didn't realise I would be interrupting a Shakespeare class.'

'By arriving unannounced you might have guessed you would be interrupting something. I'm sorry, Mr Rodriguez, but we have designated *exeat* weekends – we do not encourage family members to turn up as and when they please. *However*,' she went on, as Cousin Charles opened his mouth to protest, 'in the light of your travel arrangements we will make an exception today. Tea is at half past four. Perhaps you would like to take your guardian on a little tour, Edith, for the intervening half-hour.'

Edie nodded reluctantly, her eyes following Miss Fotheringay as she walked away. 'I didn't know you were going abroad,' she said, mildly curious.

'I am not, Edith. It was a lie. And it paid off,' Charles added smugly, 'because it got me what I wanted – an audience with you. Now, where are you going to take me?' Something in his voice made Edie nervous. She wondered where to go. There was nothing about her school life she wanted to share with Cousin Charles, not least because she knew that everything about it would make him sneer.

'We could look at the art room,' she said, thinking she could show him a vase she had made in pottery. But as soon as they were in the room he closed the door behind them and turned on her with smouldering eyes.

'You have been here nearly two weeks, Edith, and you've hardly been in touch. One letter! You're not here on holiday. Prince Stolonov wants results, and he's worried that Anastasia's in more trouble since you arrived.'

Edie was alarmed. She dared not tell him how little she had found out.

'It – it – *could* be that Phoebe's the one to blame.'

'Phoebe? Who's Phoebe?' Cousin Charles asked sharply.

'She's another girl in our dormitory, and she hates Anastasia and she might have tried to hit her on purpose during lacrosse but we can't prove it,' Edie explained, warming to her theme. 'That's the trouble. We can't actually prove anything. You see, Anastasia noticed her torch and a few other things missing from her bedside table on Tuesday evening . . . well, either she got in a muddle and forgot where she'd put them – which is what's happened before, like with her glass bird which she thought had been stolen from her desk . . . or someone must have taken them while we were at the play rehearsal. And Phoebe's only got a small part in the play – the gaoler – so she wasn't needed at the rehearsal on Tuesday, so that's why I think—'

'The glass bird? Did you say it had gone missing?'

'It *did*. But then she found it again, so I think that was

her being careless.'

'Careless of her father to give it to her in the first place,' Charles muttered. 'Has anything else gone walk-about?'

'Yes,' Edie volunteered. 'There was another rehearsal yesterday, and when we got back to the dormitory Anastasia couldn't find her English homework. She'd had to redo it because she can't spell for toffee and she *says* she left it on her bed, but—'

'*For toffee!*' Cousin Charles scoffed. 'I see you've picked up the boarding-school lingo quickly enough. But I've had about as much as I can stomach of this schoolgirl nonsense. I want it cleared up. You'll need to keep a watch on the dormitory during these rehearsals if that's when things are happening – which means you'll have to pull out of the play.'

'Pull out? But . . . I can't do that!'

'Don't argue with me, Edith. I've got a lot on. I don't want to waste any more of my time on eleven-year-olds who can't find their torches. Either Anastasia is being hysterical, or she's being victimized. It's one or the other and if you can't solve it I'll replace you with someone who can. When she loses something again search every wretched drawer until you find it.'

Replace me? Edie thought. She imagined her replacement taking the part of Nerissa in the first-year play, and sleeping in her bed, and sitting on Miss Fotheringay's sofa, learning Latin and eating marbled cake; and she clenched her fists. Cousin Charles had the power to take her away from Knight's Haddon. *I hate him*, she screamed silently, and the thought calmed her.

'Come back to the car with me,' Charles said in a warmer tone, opening the art-room door. 'I've got a surprise for you.'

'But I'll be late for tea,' Edie protested, as her cousin laid his arm around her shoulders, and propelled her back to the hall.

Charles had parked out of sight of the main entrance, round the first twist of the drive. 'In case I needed to make off with you,' he said playfully, tightening his grip.

'But . . . I'll be in trouble,' Edie said, seeing the chestnut Bentley looming in the dusk.

'Don't run off just yet,' Charles said, gripping her arm, 'I have something for you. Your favourite cousin—'

The word was barely out of his mouth before Edie uttered a scream as she caught sight of Lyle's face against the car window, pressed into a ghastly leer. The car door opened, and Lyle sprang out.

'How's it been, coz?' he said. 'Folly's not the same without you and Tilly.'

Edie stared at him balefully, but did not speak.

Charles regarded them with amusement, then he took the small package that Lyle was holding, and tucked it into the pocket of Edie's coat. 'Something for when you feel hungry in the dark reaches of the night. Now off you go, back to your other master.'

Edie needed no second bidding. As soon as Charles

released her from his grip she shot like an arrow from its bow, back up the drive and into the uncertain shelter of Knight's Haddon.

Lost for Words

Edie sat silently through supper that evening, haunted by Cousin Charles's threats. *'Prince Stolonov wants results . . . You'll have to pull out of the play, Edith . . .'* But she was enjoying the play more than anything else at Knight's Haddon – during rehearsals she could forget that she was different from the other girls, and although she knew she would never be as good an actress as Anastasia, she felt her confidence was growing. She and Anastasia shared most of their scenes, and always ran through their lines together between rehearsals. Edie remembered what Cousin Charles had said, and secretly laughed to think that playing Anastasia's servant should have brought them closer.

Why should she pull out of the play just because Cousin Charles said so? The next rehearsal was on

Tuesday. *And if I go*, Edie thought, *I needn't tell him.*

The next day was Saturday. The encounter still weighed heavily on Edie's mind, making her distracted in class, and when she was asked to stay behind after history, Edie expected a reprimand. But for once the Man did not look cross. She stood behind her desk, peering at Edie over her spectacles.

'In the light of your good homework, I have decided to repeal my ban on your going to the village,' she said in a voice that was almost friendly. 'Do you know what repeal means, Edith?'

'It means I can go with the others?'

'That is the short of it,' Miss Mannering replied. '*However*—' she added, seeing Edie's delighted smile, 'you will bear in mind that next time I am unlikely to be so lenient.'

'Funny definition of lenient,' Edie said to Anastasia when she told her the good news.

'Come with me and we can have tea at the Blue Kettle,' Anastasia said delightedly. 'They do the best doughnuts there.'

Edie resolved to waste no more time worrying about Cousin Charles. After lunch she hurried to collect her pocket money from Miss Winifred. The rules were clear: all pocket money had to be handed in at the beginning of term, and each girl could draw out a maximum of five pounds a week.

'Aren't you taking anything out?' she asked Anastasia, who had been waiting for her outside.

'I don't need any,' Anastasia said, patting her pocket slyly.

It was a pleasant walk to the village, across the park and then down a winding country lane. The village was quite large with several shops and a post office, and three tea rooms serving the tourists who came to see the famous Norman church. Edie bought some biscuits from the grocer, then they went to the Blue Kettle. Anastasia had tried out all the tea rooms, and this was her favourite. It was small and homely, with checked tablecloths and fogged windows. There was a group of fourth-years sitting at the central table who pointedly ignored the two first-years when they walked in, but it was the person in the corner who caught Edie's eye:

'*Anastasia, look!*' she hissed. She gestured with a nudge towards a single table beside the till, where Miss Winifred was sitting on her own, her head bent over a book.

Anastasia shrugged carelessly. 'I've seen her in here before,' she said, guiding Edie to a table on the other side of the room. 'I've even seen Fothy once – eating buns with the Man! It's the best tea room by far, so I suppose it's hardly surprising they come here too. I'd come every day if I could,' she went on dreamily, scouring the menu.

Edie murmured agreement. She had never been out to tea before with someone her own age and liked the feeling of independence; Anastasia ordered for them both as though she were quite used to it. 'You never see the lower school in here,' she said. 'We're allowed so little

~ 115 ~

pocket money, and most of them think it's a waste spending it on tea.'

'With one exception,' Edie said, nodding to the door.

Anastasia turned to see Phoebe appear. 'What's *she* doing here?' she whispered, keeping her head bowed as Phoebe walked past them and sat down on her own at a table in the opposite corner to Miss Winifred, tucked behind the coat stand.

'Having tea, like us, I suppose,' said Edie. 'But where's Irene? I saw them leaving school together.'

Anastasia shrugged. 'She must have given her the slip – wouldn't you? But Phoebe will be for it if Miss Winifred sees her on her own. She'll probably make her join up with us!'

Edie glanced round anxiously – she didn't want Phoebe spoiling their treat. But Miss Winifred had not looked up from her book.

'Anyway, I don't get it,' Anastasia said sourly. 'Phoebe knows I like to come here, so if she hates me so much why can't she choose a different tea room?' Anastasia shuffled her chair round so that she couldn't see Phoebe any more, and cheered up when they had ordered some hot chocolate and eclairs. 'I can't believe my godfather is your guardian,' she said suddenly. 'You must have such fun with him.'

Now it was Edie who looked unsettled. Cousin Charles had warned her that he was going to tell Anastasia of their connection. '*She'll find out soon enough*,' he had said. But Edie had been too awkward to mention it herself. She couldn't tell Anastasia the whole truth, so to mention it at all seemed like a lie.

'When Papa and I meet him in London we always go for tea at the Ritz,' Anastasia went on chattily. 'Papa likes the piano-player there. I bet Charles takes you for tea at the Ritz *all the time*.'

Edie shook her head. She and Babka had walked past the Ritz once, and peered inside. She remembered it being very pink, and full of tall pot plants and tinkling music. Having tea there with Cousin Charles was an unimaginable thought. 'I – I haven't really known him long enough,' she said.

'But I thought he was your guardian.'

'Not exactly – I mean, he's . . . he's only one of them,' Edie replied, confused, then quickly changed the subject by telling Anastasia about her other life with Aunt Sophia and Uncle Tony and her three cousins in Devon.

'Do you like them – the boys?' Anastasia asked.

Edie hesitated. She had noticed that the girls at Knight's Haddon always portrayed their home lives in a glowing light. No one seemed to have any relations they didn't like. It seemed to be an unspoken rule at school, this culture of brave pretence. But Edie sensed that Anastasia did not subscribe to it. She was different from the others; she would understand.

'I don't like the eldest one much,' she admitted. 'And then there are the twins. One of them's less horrid than the other, but when their older brother's around they're both pretty awful. He sort of eggs them on.'

Anastasia cocked her head enquiringly. There was something sympathetic in her expression, and Edie found herself telling Anastasia about the goldfish and about Lyle's visit to the school the day before. As she spoke of it she had a vision of Lyle's face at the car window, and felt her skin crawl.

'It was funny really, but seeing him made me realise how much I dread going back at the end of term,' Edie said, reflecting that this was probably Cousin Charles's intention. "There's just – oh, I don't know,' she said hurriedly, 'it's not only Lyle . . . it's Folly Farm, I just hate it there.'

'Your cousins sound *horrible*,' Anastasia said in a lowered voice. 'What about your aunt? Doesn't *she* take your side?'

Edie grimaced. 'She's *their* mother.'

'Oh, Edie,' Anastasia said, putting one of her small white hands over hers, 'it must be awful not having anyone who's really, you know – yours.'

'Oh, but I have. I've got a grandmother,' Edie said hastily, and she told Anastasia about Babka, and how they'd lived together before she went blind. 'She's in a nursing home near here now. I'd like to take you to see her one day.'

'I'd love to come,' Anastasia said eagerly. 'I wish I could take you home with me but it's a bit difficult with my father being abroad all the time and my mother not being well.'

'Not well?' Edie asked. Cousin Charles had told her that Anastasia's mother was 'difficult', but he hadn't mentioned her being ill.

'It's nothing really. She just gets tired sometimes and

she—' Anastasia took a sip of her hot chocolate, then stirred it slowly with her spoon. Edie waited. She sensed Anastasia was weighing up how much to tell her. 'She just gets a bit upset about things,' Anastasia said finally. 'About me, and being safe. If she'd had her way I wouldn't be allowed into the village without a police guard! And she gets stressed about other things too.'

'What sort of things?' Edie asked gently.

'Odd stuff. It's hard to explain really, but—' Anastasia looked at Edie cautiously, as if trying to weigh up the chances that she'd understand. 'She sort of thinks everyone's against her, oh, I don't know,' she broke off suddenly. 'She just worries a lot. Most of all she worries about my stepfather. He doesn't really like visitors.'

'Why not?' Edie asked curiously. Anastasia had shown her a photograph of her stepfather's house in Yorkshire, and it was huge.

Anastasia shrugged. 'He's just difficult, I suppose.' She did not volunteer anything else. Then: 'What about your parents, Edie?' she asked shyly. 'Did they—'

'They were journalists. They were killed by a bomb in Moscow when I was a baby.'

'In Moscow?' Anastasia said in surprise. 'That's where my father lives. Some of the time, anyway.'

Edie nodded. 'And my father's still there – I mean, not really of course, but . . .'

'What?' Anastasia asked, her eyes wide.

'Well, his body was never found. My mother's body was brought home, and buried here. But my father . . .'

'How awful for you,' Anastasia whispered.

'It was a long time ago,' Edie said hastily. 'I don't miss them, because I never knew them. I don't even know any of their friends. Babka never kept in touch with anyone.'

Anastasia looked sad and Edie was relieved when the waitress come to clear their plates. 'Have something else, Edie, I'll pay,' Anastasia urged. 'We might as well.'

As she spoke Anastasia sneaked a look over her shoulder to the corner table, where Miss Winifred had been sitting, and saw that the mistress had stood up and was putting on her coat, ready to go. The girls ducked their heads over their hot chocolate, giggling in conspiracy as Miss Winifred walked by. When the lower-school mistress had left the tea room Anastasia lowered her voice guiltily: '*Papa sent me a fifty-pound note last week!*'

Edie was astonished. 'Fifty pounds! Why did he give you so much?'

'Oh, I don't know,' Anastasia sighed. 'It's just what he's like. He says you're always safer with money. I did tell him we were only allowed five pounds pocket money a week but he thought it was silly.'

'Aren't you going to hand it in?'

'I can't hand it in; it would be too embarrassing. You can imagine what Fothy would say. Anyway, it's more fun to spend it here.'

Edie agreed. It felt very grand being taken out to tea on a smuggled fifty-pound note, and they ordered two more cakes to mark the occasion. They were still tucking in when Phoebe brushed past their table on her way out. Edie looked up and mumbled hello, but Phoebe looked straight ahead, as if she hadn't seen them.

'Good riddance,' Anastasia said mischievously, watching the door close behind her. A few minutes later she went to fetch her purse from her coat, which she had hung in the corner. But when she opened it her mouth fell. 'It – it's gone,' she stammered. 'I know I put it in here, the fifty-pound note, I know I did – but . . .'

'Are you *sure* you couldn't have left it somewhere else?'

'Positive. I remember opening the letter on my bed, and the money falling out from inside. *Don't lose it*, Papa wrote, and I swore to myself I wouldn't. I put it straight into my purse.'

Edie looked at her friend carefully. She had never really believed that Anastasia had been orchestrating all the unpleasant things that had been happening to her – her hurt had always seemed too genuine. And seeing her expression now, Edie was quite certain of her innocence. The waitress came back, but even when they put all their coins together they didn't have enough to pay and the manageress was called. Anastasia was one of her regulars, and she was very nice about it. 'That's all right, dear, you can pay us back next time,' she said; but Edie noticed all the fourth-years had turned to look at them.

She was glad at least that Miss Winifred was not there to witness Anastasia's latest humiliation. As they walked out of the tea room Edie saw the mistress a little further down the lane, talking to a tall and slightly stooped-looking man. Edie could not see his face, but was struck by his height, and his shock of jet-black hair.

'Look!' Edie whispered, nudging Anastasia as Miss Winifred and the man got into a shiny red sports car. 'Do you think that's her boyfriend?'

Anastasia watched the car drive off with a shrug, too tormented by her own problems to care. 'I just don't understand, Edie. I never lose things at home. But now everything seems to disappear. Sometimes I think I'm going mad.'

'You're not going mad,' Edie said firmly. 'Someone's stealing from you, or playing tricks. And I'm going to help you find out who it is.'

'Will you?' Anastasia asked, a look of helpless gratitude in her eyes.

Edie smiled, thinking suddenly of Babka – Babka asking her to do the shopping when she started going blind, asking her to read the bills, and sometimes even to forge her signature on the cheques. Edie liked to be needed; it made her feel she had a place in the world.

'Yes,' she said, in a determined voice. 'Of course I'll help you. And we may not have to look very far.' Anastasia looked at her blankly. 'Oh, come on, Anastasia,' Edie said impatiently. 'Phoebe was sitting right next to the coat stand. It would have been the easiest thing in the world for her to have reached into your pocket and taken money from your purse.'

Anastasia looked shocked. 'But . . .'

'I think you should tell Matron,' Edie said. 'If you tell her that you think Phoebe's taken your money she'll search her drawers – and then we'll know.'

Edie dreaded following Charles's instructions and

having to search Phoebe's belongings herself. If anyone saw her, they would think *she* was the thief; and she would certainly feel like one. And if Phoebe was harbouring the money, Edie was sure she would have found somewhere clever to hide it. Much better if she could recruit Matron to do the job for her.

But Anastasia seemed horrified by the idea. 'I can't accuse Phoebe – I might as well accuse one of the fourth-years, or Miss Winifred – they were all in the tea room too! And what if the money turns up again, like everything else? I've been made to look a fool enough times already. And if I tell Matron I had a fifty-pound note she'd tell Miss Fotheringay and I'd probably be gated for the whole year. You know how strict they are about money. No, I can't tell anyone, Edie, I just can't!'

Edie kept a very close eye on Phoebe. But Tuesday came and she still hadn't found anything concrete to report to Cousin Charles. That afternoon, when the post was laid out on the hall table, she found an envelope addressed to her in his handwriting, the contents of which gave her a jolt:

If we don't get some results by the end of term we might decide you're in the wrong job. I trust you've already pulled out of the play – the best servants remain invisible, and you weren't sent to Knight's Haddon to lark around onstage. I shall be telephoning your headmistress this week to keep myself informed.

It was written on a blank card, and signed in an impatient scrawl. He did not put 'love', as he usually did. Edie's hand shook as she read it. Then she saw Anastasia coming and hastily shoved the card into her book.

'Hurry up,' Anastasia said. 'The rehearsal's about to start and we can't be late – we're going through our new scene. And Helen's beginning to fuss. I heard her complaining to one of the other prefects at lunch that we've only got three weeks left and half the cast can't remember their lines. Don't *you* worry, though,' she added. 'You were perfect when I tested you this morning.'

'It's not that,' Edie said miserably, for it was true they had been testing each other all weekend. 'But I'm afraid . . .'

'Edith the Brave, afraid? Never!' said Anastasia, laughing as she pulled her friend down the corridor.

Moments later Edie found herself back in the lower-school common room. The other first-years were chatting by the tuck boxes, but Edie stood apart. She wondered if Cousin Charles would telephone Miss Fotheringay that evening. She could have kicked herself for telling him about her part in the play. He had clearly fixed on it as the reason she was failing in her job, and some instinct told her that this time, if she did not obey him, he really would take her away from the school.

The rehearsal began. Edie was not needed for the first scene, and stood in a world of her own.

'All right then,' Helen said finally. 'Let's run through Act Four, scene two.' The others hurried forward but Edie did not move. 'Edie, wake up!' Helen said amiably.

'Sorry,' Edie mumbled, taking her place. The scene got under way but Edie was hardly aware of what was being said.

'Edie!'

'. . . *Edie!*'

Edie gave a start. Helen was looking at her with a puzzled expression, and she realised she had missed her cue. She had no idea what the last person had said. She floundered wretchedly, stammering a hotchpotch of half-remembered lines.

Helen sighed. 'Let's try it again.'

But this time was even worse. Edie was so over-wrought she recited lines from a different scene entirely.

'We're rehearsing Act Four, Edie, not Act Three,' Helen said wearily. 'If you didn't have time to learn it you should have said so.'

'But I *did* learn it, I was practising all weekend!' Edie cried. But what was the point in telling Helen how hard she had tried? She would have to pull out of the play anyway.

She heard Helen's voice, as if from a distance. 'Come on, Edie, read from the script if you have to. You can't hold up the whole rehearsal just because you haven't done your prep.'

But all Edie could think of was Cousin Charles, telling her to pull out of the play so she could search the dormitory during rehearsals. In a terrified vision, she thought she saw him watching her from the corner. She struggled to stay calm but there was something burning inside her, a nettle being dragged in her throat. And when she spoke it was not her own voice she heard:

'Find someone else to play Nerissa if you want to! I don't care! I *hate* this stupid play anyway!' she cried, and ran from the room, slamming the door behind her.

The Head Strikes Back

Edie sat alone in the lower-school library, staring at the unopened book on her desk. She knew Anastasia would come looking for her, but it seemed a long time before she appeared.

'At least Helen will be pleased,' Edie said self-pityingly, as her friend sat down beside her. 'She only wanted me in the play to keep you happy. Now she can give my part to someone else.'

'That's rubbish, Edie,' Anastasia said, colouring at the imputation that she was Helen's favourite. 'She chose you because you're good. If you go and talk to her this evening and explain why you were so distracted then I'm sure she'll give you another chance.'

Edie glared at her. 'And why was I so distracted?'

'I don't know,' Anastasia said gravely. 'Tell me.'

Because I am working for you, Edie thought bitterly. *I'm your servant.* But she couldn't say it. She knew it wasn't Anastasia's fault; but she did not think she could bear to be told off by her all the same.

'You don't have to tell me the reason,' Anastasia said, 'but promise me, Edie, that you will go and talk to Helen.'

'I can't.'

'But you can't just walk out of the play in a fury—'

'I'm not in a fury!' Edie said furiously.

Anastasia smiled. 'Come on, Edie. You were the one who got cross, not Helen. Think how upset she'll be if you don't come back.'

Edie remembered how patient Helen had been in previous rehearsals, quietly explaining things when she didn't understand. 'I would talk to her, but – I . . . I just can't. Oh, Anastasia, please try and understand!'

But Anastasia couldn't. She sat there for a long time, trying to make Edie change her mind, and seemed baffled by her stubbornness. 'I think you're being an idiot,' she said finally.

Edie could see how selfish her behaviour must appear, and it came as no surprise that all the first-years took the same view.

'I don't understand what you're upset about,' Alice said in the dormitory that evening. 'Helen didn't say anything unkind.'

Edie was sitting on her bed writing a letter to Cousin Charles, reporting that his latest order had been carried out, and she felt a sense of helpless frustration welling: 'Oh, shut up!' she choked. 'Why does *everyone* keep going on about it?'

But it seemed the first-years could talk about nothing else, and whenever they saw Edie coming their conversations came to a muffled stop. Even Anastasia appeared to have lost faith in her.

'You are silly, Edie. If you don't come back, Helen will probably give your part to Belinda – she stood in for you after you stormed off and she was completely wooden. It will spoil things for everyone.'

'You can hardly expect me to care about that,' Edie snapped.

'Really, anyone would think you were being forced to give up your part,' Anastasia returned. 'But it was your decision.'

Edie took this in silence. And as if Anastasia's disapproval weren't bad enough, she still had to face Miss Fotheringay. Edie was sure the headmistress would have been informed about her outburst, and she dreaded another summons.

She found it difficult to concentrate on her job, but she knew she must use the rehearsal time next evening to her advantage. Anastasia's fifty-pound note was still missing, and she was more convinced than ever that Phoebe was responsible for this, and for all the other things that had happened to Anastasia. She knew that while Anastasia, Alice and Sally were all due to attend the next rehearsal, Phoebe would not be needed. Edie wondered if she might seize the chance for more thieving, and decided to keep watch on the dormitory in the hope of catching her red-handed.

When she knew the rehearsal had begun, she hid herself behind a cupboard at the far end of the corridor, peering out furtively at the dormitory door. Cousin Charles would have been proud of her, she thought grimly, but it was a lonely feeling, crouching there on her own, spying on an empty corridor.

After twenty minutes she was bored and stiff. But then she heard footsteps, and the Man hove into view. Edie watched with a volt of excitement as she walked as far as her own dormitory, and turned inside. Was the Man carrying out one of her famous drawer searches? Perhaps she would find Anastasia's fifty pounds and save Edie the trouble? She tiptoed out of her hiding place, meaning to spy on her through the door. But Edie had not reckoned on the eyes in the back of the Man's head.

'Ah, Edith,' she said sharply, spinning round. 'I was just coming to find you. Miss Fotheringay would like to see you. Immediately.'

Edie's heart sank. So much for being a spy – she seemed to be the one who was always being caught out. She guessed Helen must have reported her outburst during the rehearsal, and when she knocked on the headmistress's door she feared the worst.

Miss Fotheringay was sitting at her desk. This time she did not get up when Edie came in. 'Come here, Edith,' she said.

It was only six paces, but Edie felt as though she were wading through mud. There was a chair pulled up to the desk, but Miss Fotheringay did not invite her to sit on it, so Edie stood awkwardly in front of her.

Miss Fotheringay's face was calm, almost mask-like. 'I hear you have walked out of the play, Edith.'

'Yes,' Edie murmured.

'Why?'

No answer.

'I understand from Helen that she would be willing to let you carry on, if you would like to. It is not too late, Edith. In fact,' Miss Fotheringay added meaningfully, 'I understand that Helen is very reluctant to lose you.'

'I – I can't be in the play any more. I – I'm sorry . . .' Edie stammered.

'You can say sorry to me, so why not to Helen?' Miss Fotheringay asked.

'I don't know.'

'I can only suppose Helen must have upset you very much for you to take this stance. Perhaps you would like to tell me what it was all about – in confidence, of course.'

Edie stared at the floor. She thought of the Latin lesson, when she and Miss Fotheringay had sat on the sofa and talked about her mother and Cousin Charles, and had an impulse to tell her everything, but when she met her headmistress's eye something stopped her. Miss Fotheringay looked as though her mind was already made up. The silence became oppressive, and Edie felt self-conscious standing there being looked at, like an animal in a pen.

'You do realise how selfish you're being?' Miss

Fotheringay said finally. 'Helen has put a lot of time into directing the play, and now they will have to start rehearsing your scenes all over again. I would like you to think about this carefully, Edith. You have the chance to put things right.'

'But – I can't.'

When she summoned the courage to look up again she saw deep displeasure in Miss Fotheringay's face. But her headmistress's voice was expressionless. 'Very well, Edith, that will be all. I regret I shall not be able to take you for Latin on Friday. Something else has come up.'

Edie took a step back from the desk.

'I am not the Queen, Edith. You needn't walk out backwards,' Miss Fotheringay said coolly, picking up her pen and returning to the pile of papers in front of her.

'Don't run!' shouted a prefect in vain as Edie fled down the corridor. When she reached the dormitory she flung herself face down on her bed and gave in to a fit of passionate sobbing.

She felt broken. No one had ever shown such an interest in her as Miss Fotheringay had; and now Edie had lost everything. There had been something in the harshness of Miss Fotheringay's dismissal that made Edie certain she would be given no second chance. The only person she could imagine talking to now was Anastasia, but even she had turned against her. That at least would change, if Edie found out who was targeting her. All that remained was to solve the mystery of what was happening to Anastasia – and then Cousin Charles would take her away.

The thought steeled her, and she sat up on the bed and looked around with eyes washed clear by tears. It *had* to be Phoebe; there was no one else.

She stood up and walked slowly across the dormitory. If anyone came in and saw her she would be sent back to Miss Fotheringay in disgrace; but what did it matter now? A breeze from the window touched her arm and made her shiver as she crouched on the floor and opened the drawer of Phoebe's bedside table.

The Glass Bird

At first glance, the contents of Phoebe's drawer looked perfectly ordinary – a torch, a jumble of letters, half a contraband chocolate bar. But as Edie reached inside she felt like a criminal breaking into a safe. *I am only investigating*, she told herself, trying to stop her hands from shaking.

Her investigation had not got far when two voices in the corridor made her jump. Edie recognised them at once as belonging to Matron and Miss Winifred. She pushed the drawer shut and darted back to her own bed. At first she was too startled to register what was being said. But then she heard Anastasia's name mentioned, and listened attentively.

'She's a dreamy little thing, not at all practical,' Matron said in an affectionate tone. 'I suppose it can't be easy for her. I gather she's quite the princess back in Russia.'

'They are certainly rich,' Miss Winifred replied. 'Stupidly rich. And I'm afraid it shows.'

'Do you think so?' Matron asked in surprise. 'But of all the girls here I would say that Anastasia is unusually polite.'

'She would naturally be polite to you,' Miss Winifred said. 'She has clearly made a decision that you are a servant, and that good manners are therefore a must.'

'Is that so now?' Matron asked in a voice which gave nothing away.

'I wish I was afforded the same treatment,' Miss Winifred went on. 'Her behaviour in class has been so disruptive I hardly know what to do.'

'*Really?*'

'Oh yes, I see a very different side. At first I put her troublemaking down to being spoilt – the poor child has been fawned on and over-indulged all her life, I thought it was hardly surprising she found school such a challenge. I decided the kindest thing was to treat her with a firm hand, but I can see now I was being much too harsh.'

'Well, if she was being disruptive—'

'She needs sensitive handling, I feel,' Miss Winifred insisted. 'Her problems go quite deep, I'm afraid. You know about her mother?'

'Miss Fotheringay told me that she had recently been in hospital, which is why she couldn't have Anastasia home at half-term – I was told it was some infection.'

'An infection, hmm, that's one way of putting it.' There was a pause. When Miss Winifred spoke again her voice was lowered, so Edie had to strain to hear. 'Anastasia's mother is *mentally unstable*, and the hospital was a psychiatric one. Sadly it would appear that her daughter suffers from the same delusions. There is madness in the blood, Matron, though they'd sooner throw the family diamonds into the Black Sea than admit to it. The father can deny it all he likes, but as her form mistress I can tell you that I am extremely concerned.'

Edie stiffened.

'I see,' Matron replied slowly. 'That would be a worry now.'

'We must all be gentle with her,' Miss Winifred went on softly, 'and in the meantime if you notice anything disturbing, Matron, I would be grateful if you could inform me.'

'What sort of thing would you be looking for?' Matron asked in a puzzled tone.

'In class, one of her most distressing ruses is to accuse other girls of harming her. It's some sort of victimisation complex – there was the incident last week on the lacrosse pitch, when the poor child seemed to convince herself that Phoebe had tried to maim her. And she is forever hiding things, then accusing the other girls of stealing them. It's upsetting for everyone, and it doesn't help that everything she owns is so precious. That glass bird, for example – you know it's from one of the prince's old crystal collections? Imagine sending a child to school with such a treasure.'

'Perhaps I should offer to look after it for her until the end of term,' Matron said. 'I don't suppose the head would approve of such a valuable item in the dormitory.'

'Oh no, I shouldn't do that,' Miss Winifred replied quickly. 'The bird by itself is probably not worth so much and we mustn't deny the poor child her few comforts of home. But please do let me know of any upsets.'

'Well, since you ask, there is something . . .' Matron volunteered, sounding a little hesitant.

Edie listened, rigid. But at that moment the bell rang for supper. It seemed to clang even longer and louder than usual, and when it had finished she heard Miss Winifred and Matron's footsteps receding down the corridor.

She wondered what Matron had been about to confide. Could she have got wind of the missing money, even though Anastasia had resolved not to mention it? But it was what Miss Winifred had said that troubled Edie most. What did she mean about there being madness in the blood? Anastasia *wasn't* mad. Edie was sure of it.

Edie did not want to upset Anastasia by telling her what she had overheard, but she felt she must warn her against confiding in Matron. Edie supposed Miss Winifred was only trying to help, but she knew Anastasia would hate the thought that anything she told Matron would be passed on. They had hardly spoken since their conflict over the play, so Anastasia looked a little surprised to find Edie waiting for her outside the dining room after supper.

'Look, I've been thinking about it, and you're probably right not to tell Matron about the money,' Edie said. 'I promised to help you, Anastasia, and I will. Give me a day or two and I'm sure I can find out who took it.'

Anastasia's face fell. 'I wish you'd make up your mind, Edie. Yesterday you said I *should* tell Matron. And this afternoon she was being so friendly I decided I would. I told her Papa had sent it to me, and that someone must have stolen it, and she was very nice. She said she'd help me have a real look for it. Why, what's wrong?' she said nervously, seeing Edie's face.

'Oh, nothing,' Edie replied. She could guess now how Miss Winifred and Matron's conversation must have finished. And when the lower-school mistress swept into the dormitory just before lights out, she felt very apprehensive.

'Good evening, girls,' said Miss Winifred, greeting them with a smile.

'Good evening, Miss Winifred,' everyone replied.

'I am afraid I am here on unpleasant business,' the mistress said, looking sweetly concerned. 'Matron tells me there has been a theft in this dormitory – and the victim, you may not be surprised to learn, is Anastasia. Someone has stolen her pocket money. Rather more pocket money,' Miss Winifred added meaningfully, 'than is usually allowed.'

Anastasia looked shocked.

'I'm afraid I have no option but to search everyone's

drawers,' Miss Winifred continued. 'I do regret the inconvenience to you all, but I'm sure none of you would wish to remain under suspicion.'

The mood became anxious as every girl wondered if there was something in her drawer Miss Winifred shouldn't see. Edie suddenly remembered Lyle's chocolates. She had looked inside the box and seen they were dark, with violet icing, and she had buried them in her sock drawer, knowing she wouldn't like them. It would be just her luck to get in trouble for some sweets she didn't even want.

But it was Phoebe's bed that Miss Winifred approached first.

Edie kept a careful eye on the other girl, looking for signs of guilt. But as Miss Winifred opened the drawer of the bedside table, Phoebe's face gave nothing away. Even when Miss Winifred found her half-eaten chocolate bar, her expression remained impassive.

Edie watched avidly, secretly grateful to Miss Winifred for continuing where she'd had to leave off.

But then Anastasia let out a cry: 'Oh!'

Everyone stared.

'It – it's here . . . my fifty pounds,' Anastasia stammered, turning crimson. 'It's in my drawer . . . But I don't understand. It wasn't here earlier, I know it wasn't!'

The other girls looked astonished on learning how much money was at stake, but Miss Winifred did not seem at all surprised at Anastasia's finding the money in her own drawer.

'Anastasia's telling the truth,' Edie said earnestly. 'I

helped her look for it, earlier.'

'Please, girls,' Miss Winifred said, taking the note and briefly holding it up to the light before tucking it in her pocket. 'Let's not waste our time with excuses. What's done is done and I'm just relieved that poor Anastasia's money has been found. I shall keep it safe until the end of term and now let us hear no more about it.'

Miss Winifred was very calm about it. She waited until everyone had got into bed, then turned the lights out without another word. But a short time later, when she had done the rounds of the other first-year dormitories, she reappeared.

Edie lay very still, watching Miss Winifred's shadow loom across the ceiling as she moved silently to Anastasia's bed. She sat there for several minutes, talking to Anastasia in a low whisper, too softly for Edie to follow what was being said. She caught only the odd snippet of a sentence, in which she heard Miss Winifred use the word 'paranoia', repeated several times.

Anastasia was sitting up and hardly spoke, but Edie could see her across the dormitory, shaking her head.

'What was all that about?' Sally whispered when Miss Winifred had left.

'Nothing,' Anastasia replied.

'It didn't sound like nothing.'

'Nothing never does.'

The room fell silent. Edie waited until everyone else was sleeping, then slipped out from under her covers and tiptoed over to Anastasia's bed. She was awake too, and when Edie sat down she saw she had been crying.

'She was going on about the doctor again,' Anastasia said in a hoarse sob. 'She says she knows someone in Oxford who could help me. I told you, Edie – everyone thinks I'm mad!'

'No they don't,' Edie whispered, thinking uneasily of the earlier conversation she had overheard.

'Well, Miss Winifred does – she thinks I need *professional help*,' Anastasia said contemptuously. 'She asked me if I had "troubles at home", and maybe I do but I don't want to think about my stepfather when I'm at school. That was the whole point of coming away. And if it wasn't for stuff disappearing everything would be going so well. This half of term seemed so much better than last, with you, and the play, but now . . .'

'You should at least talk to Miss Fotheringay,' Edie said with sudden conviction. 'She's bound to ask to see you when Miss Winifred tells her about the money. You should say that someone's setting you up. I'll come with you and tell her—' Edie faltered. In her concern about Anastasia she had forgotten her own disgrace.

'Did she have a go at you about the play?' Anastasia guessed.

Edie nodded wretchedly, feeling she might have alienated their best ally. 'My word won't count for anything now.'

'I'm sorry,' Anastasia said in sympathy. 'Anyway, I don't want to talk to Fothy. I know she'll just say I'm making it all up. I'd much rather talk to Miss Mannering.'

'The Man!' Edie was horrified.

'Why not?' Anastasia asked. 'She sat with me in the

san when I got hurt during that lacrosse match and she turned out to be really easy to talk to. She didn't seem suspicious of me like everyone else.'

'Well, I'm suspicious of her!' Edie said, realising with a jolt that it was true. 'I promise you, Anastasia, there's something strange about her. I saw her coming in here earlier today, during the rehearsal – she was supposedly looking for me, but . . .' Edie hesitated. Her latest suspicion was only beginning to take shape.

'What?' Anastasia pressed.

'Well, you know,' Edie went on slowly, 'she was in here on her own for a minute – long enough to put the money back in your drawer.'

'Oh, Edie. Yesterday you were sure it was Phoebe. Now you seem to think the deputy headmistress is involved. It doesn't make sense.'

'Phoebe's still a suspect,' Edie said firmly. 'But if other people behave suspiciously, we have to suspect them too.'

Anastasia looked unconvinced. 'One thing is certain – if I tell Miss Fotheringay that I think Miss Mannering's plotting against me then she really *will* think I'm mad.'

Edie frowned. She could see it might look far-fetched; and Cousin Charles's instructions had simply been to keep watch on the other girls. He had never mentioned anything about the mistresses being under suspicion.

'It *must* be one of the girls, Edie, and it could be any of them – I bet we'll never find out who's doing it,' Anastasia said piteously. 'Oh God, you don't know what it's like – I just don't feel *safe* here any more.'

Edie was silent. She did not feel safe either, because of the threat of being taken away. But Anastasia had a deeper fear. 'I'll find out who's doing this, Anastasia – I promise,' Edie said, clutching her friend's hand.

'I hope you can, Edie. Otherwise . . .' Anastasia's voice trailed off.

'Otherwise what?'

'Otherwise I might have to run away.'

'Well, if you do I'm coming too – but I'd sooner wait for the summer term, when it's a bit warmer,' Edie teased.

Anastasia looked at her affectionately. 'Thanks, Edie. I don't know what I'd do if *you* didn't believe me.' She pushed back her covers, then got up and tiptoed over to fetch something from her chest of drawers. 'Here, have this,' she said, pressing a small object into Edie's hand.

Edie gave a little gasp of pleasure. It was the glass bird that she had been caught holding on the first day of term. Anastasia gave Edie her torch so she could look at it more closely. It was even prettier than Edie remembered.

'It used to be one of a pair, but the other one got broken.'

'I can't have this,' Edie said. 'It's yours.'

'But I want you to have it.' Anastasia smiled. 'You might as well. I'll only lose it.'

A Midnight Feast

Miss Fotheringay pushed back the brocade curtains and peered into the motionless October night. The study window was open but there was no breeze. A pale lantern glowed below in the courtyard, and the moon showed the drive twisting through the park, ghostly white.

Edith Wilson and Anastasia Stolonov. She sipped her whisky, murmuring the names as she walked slowly back to her desk. There she opened her ledger and read again her first impressions of Anastasia: *A confused home life has instilled an unusually heightened sense of order. She might need to be encouraged to let go.*

Miss Fotheringay smiled. The pensive child who had appeared in her study on that first afternoon of term had given no hint of the trouble she would cause.

Then she turned to the entry she had made two weeks ago under Edith's name: *A habit of defiant reserve . . . let the child be stripped free of time to think and she will have a chance of flourishing.*

'A record of my mistakes,' she murmured. She paused a moment, before starting a new entry underneath: *Wilful, stubborn, obstinate and secretive . . . like her mother.* Miss Fotheringay bit her lip, her pen poised over the page, when a knock on the study door made her jump. 'Ah, Diana,' she said, slipping the ledger into a drawer. 'I was hoping you might have sent me a cowering child you'd discovered in the wrong dormitory.'

'No such luck,' Miss Mannering said brightly, dumping a cardboard box on the desk. 'But it's been a bumper evening for confiscations. Eight books, as many torches, three packets of sweets, and' – Miss Mannering's face puckered in satisfied indignation – 'the beginnings of a midnight feast! The second-years were intending to celebrate a birthday but I pounced before the cake was cut.'

Miss Fotheringay tipped the box towards her, and peered inside. 'I can only admire your rigour, Diana, but your enthusiasm for confiscating books would be questioned in some quarters. There is a school of thought which says children should be encouraged to read.'

'Not after lights out.'

Miss Fotheringay smiled, and poured her a drink. Then she handed her a printed-out email. 'From Prince Stolonov,' she said, in a tone of weary displeasure. 'Wanting to know what happened to Ansti on the lacrosse pitch.'

Miss Mannering lowered herself into an armchair by the fire, and read it with arched brows. When she had finished she scrunched it up and threw it into the flames. Her face was flushed and indignant.

'I hope you told him—'

'I told him the truth, that it was an accident and that Anastasia was not hurt,' Miss Fotheringay said coolly. 'And I also told him that such incidents are best dealt with by the school.'

'Always best to keep the parents out of it,' Miss Mannering agreed, folding her spectacles back into her pocket.

'And you are my most useful ally when it comes to that,' Miss Fotheringay said, looking at her affectionately. 'When they say they only want to keep an eye on their darlings, I tell them that no one *could* keep a closer eye on them than my deputy.'

'Parents don't watch,' Miss Mannering mused, sipping her whisky. 'Some push and others worry, none watch. If they really wanted to keep an eye on their little darlings they wouldn't send them to us in the first place.'

'You sound disapproving, Diana.'

'Not disapproving, exactly, just . . .'

'Realistic?' said Miss Fotheringay, smiling.

'I do see that in some cases boarding is a child's best chance of a normal childhood, certainly in the case of someone as cosseted as Anastasia,' Miss Mannering conceded. 'Anyway,' she went on, looking at Miss Fotheringay with a mischievous glint, 'perhaps she'll be better able to stand up for herself now she's got the stalwart little Edith as a friend.'

Miss Fotheringay did not rise to the tease. 'Are they still friends? I wondered if they'd quarrelled after Edith walked out of the play—'

'No one knows what that's about,' Miss Mannering said, brushing the issue aside. 'But what I do know is that Edith Wilson is quite a promising historian. Look what I found *her* reading after lights out.' Miss Mannering delved into her confiscations box and held up a book for the headmistress to see. 'I must admit I felt a moment's hesitation before confiscating it. I don't suppose one would find many first-years reading such a book by torchlight.'

'Edith was reading this?' Miss Fotheringay took the book and looked at it curiously. It was a history of the Crusades: an old edition, with a faded green cover. Opening it, she saw the name *Anna Carter* inscribed in childish writing on the first yellowing page.

She put down her whisky and turned the book over in her hands, her eyes distant. But then something fell out – a plain postcard, covered in scrawled black writing. She saw the signature, Cousin Charles, and did not hesitate before reading the rest:

If we don't get some results by the end of term we might decide you're in the wrong job. I trust you've already pulled out of the play – the best servants remain invisible, and you weren't sent to Knight's Haddon to lark around onstage. I shall be telephoning your headmistress this week to keep myself informed.

'*Results?*' Miss Fotheringay murmured.

'Something of interest?' Miss Mannering enquired.

Miss Fotheringay replaced the card in the book and snapped it shut. 'No,' she lied. She was silent a moment. 'Are you on breakfast duty tomorrow?'

Miss Mannering nodded.

'Good. You will kindly tell Edith when you see her that I have changed my mind about tomorrow's Latin lesson. We shall have it after all.'

Alone in her study Miss Fotheringay's expression was like stone.

'Sophia? It's Caroline Fotheringay.'

It was ten years since they had last spoken, but the voice that answered had not changed: 'Caro Fo-th-er-in-gay. I was wondering when you'd call. When I looked up the school to which my niece had been spirited away and saw you were the headmistress, I knew it was only a matter of time before you put two and two together.'

'When you say spirited away—'

'Oh, never mind that. Tell me how you worked it out. Her peaky looks . . . her brilliant prose?'

Miss Fotheringay picked up a pen, and doodled the word 'drunk' on her blotter.

'I suppose you're waiting for me to ask how she is?' Sophia continued.

'I was ringing to talk about her, yes.'

'If she's in trouble you should speak to Charles. She's his responsibility now.'

'It is her relationship with Mr Rodriguez that I wanted

to speak to you about.'

'Don't you trust him?'

'Do you?'

There was a peal of laughter, followed by the sound of something being splashed into a glass. 'So – what's he been up to now?'

'I'd like to know why he sent Edith here. Under the circumstances it seems unusually generous of him to undertake to pay the child's fees.'

'He's doing it for Edie, not for Anna. He's always been fond of her.'

'He hadn't met her until a month ago.'

'And what else has she told you?'

'Very little,' Miss Fotheringay replied. 'But I think he's frightened her into pulling out of the school play. At Knight's Haddon we demand a free hand with the children. In my experience, outside interference—'

'*Please*, Caroline. I have three children of my own, a leaking roof and two thousand acres to look after. I really can't be expected to take an interest in your school drama club.'

'Nor, it seems, in your niece's welfare.'

'That's rich, coming from you. I didn't see you taking any interest in Edie when she was orphaned.'

There was a brief silence before Miss Fotheringay hung up.

Midnight, and on the other side of the school, Edie's dormitory was waking up.

The feast had been Sally's idea after she had spotted

Lyle's chocolates hidden in Edie's sock drawer, and at first Edie had looked hesitant.

'It's all right, Edie, we know you don't like sharing,' Phoebe said sarcastically.

'It's not that. It's just that they're probably disgusting. There's nothing on the box to say what they are, but they look like violet creams.'

'I *love* violet creams!' Sally said, her eyes shining.

Everyone else agreed that the feast was an excellent idea – even Alice seemed up for a bit of mischief. 'It's only fair that we should have at least one midnight feast each term,' she said in a measured voice.

'OK,' Sally said, taking charge, 'the drill is I set my alarm for five to midnight and we all wake up and start eating on the stroke of twelve. And if you don't like violet creams, Edie, then all the more for us – but since you're providing the feast you'll be part of it, anyway. And if we're caught we're all in it together.'

Edie smiled. There was something comic about Sally's determination to have fun according to some rule book in her head.

At five to midnight, five sleepy girls congregated around Edie's bed. 'Four each,' Edie said, counting out the chocolates and handing them round.

'Not sure I'll manage more than one,' Alice said, examining her ration with a yawn.

'Ready . . . steady . . . eat!' Sally whispered in a gleeful voice, as the school clock began to strike.

Edie watched sleepily as the others tucked in. But then Phoebe gave a strangled shriek, and Edie saw with horror that her lips and tongue had turned pitch black. Her face seemed frozen, her mouth forced open in a silent scream.

Edie looked to the others for help but they had the same ghastly expression. 'Wh-what is it?' she stammered, looking at the four blackened mouths in dismay.

Alice was feeling around her lips with her fingers. Then: 'Water,' she gasped, sicking something into her hand.

Edie ran to the sink while the other girls all sat spluttering on the bed, coughing the swollen sweets out of their mouths.

'Eugh,' Phoebe croaked, clutching her throat. 'What . . . what was it . . . they . . . they sort of *exploded*!'

'I'm so sorry,' said Edie, shaken. 'It . . . it must have been a trick . . . I didn't know.'

'Of course you knew!' Phoebe said furiously. 'Don't tell me it was just a coincidence that you didn't eat one yourself! You might think it was funny but you nearly choked us. And what's everyone going to say tomorrow when we go down to breakfast with black lips?'

Edie stared stupidly at the empty chocolate box. She saw a bit of paper poking from beneath the scrunched foil wrappers, and pulled out a smudged note:

'*Happy Trouble, coz!*' it said in Lyle's familiar, spiky hand.

'It's all right, it comes off,' Anastasia said, washing her face in the mirror above the sink. 'And anyway, it wasn't Edie's fault – her cousin gave them to her.'

Alice and Sally looked sympathetic, but Phoebe's face

was screwed with spite. 'I'm going to tell Miss Winifred you tried to poison us.'

'Don't be mad,' Alice said sensibly. 'Then we'll all be in trouble.'

'You're all in trouble anyway,' came a familiar voice, and Edie looked up to see Matron standing in the doorway, her arms folded across her chest.

The Plot Thickens

The black box lay open on Miss Fotheringay's desk. It was not a letter she took out this time, but a newspaper cutting stiff and yellowed with age. She unfolded it, and stared once again at the faded headline: 'JOURNALIST ANNA CARTER KILLED IN MOSCOW' and at the greying photograph of a young woman smiling at the camera.

Miss Fotheringay lay the page on top of her Latin primer, and traced her finger over the ghost-like face. 'I punished her,' she whispered slowly, 'like you punished me. And now I am going to win her back.'

'I am returning this,' Miss Fotheringay said, handing Edie the confiscated book with Cousin Charles's postcard tucked inside.

Edie looked up from the sofa, trying not to show her disquiet.

'I have been thinking about your behaviour over the play, Edith, and it occurs to me that you may have been under pressure to act as you did,' the headmistress said, looking at her calmly.

Edie said nothing, her eyes shifting as Miss Fotheringay pushed Black Puss out of the way and sat down beside her.

'Look at me, Edith, when I am speaking to you.'

Edie looked, but Miss Fotheringay didn't see the way she pinched the palm of her hand to keep the tears at bay.

'Are you all right, Edith?'

'Yes,' Edie replied, and found that it was true.

'I saw that your cousin's visit last week upset you and I suspect that you are, for some reason, afraid of him.'

'I'm not afraid of anyone,' Edie said quickly. It was like a religion with her, to state this as fact.

Miss Fotheringay smiled. 'Let me rephrase that. You are not afraid of anyone, but your cousin is your guardian and this puts him in a position of power over you. It may be that on his visit here he used that power to make you give up your part in the school play. Why he should do this, I have no idea, but I do know that some adults have a foolish, ignorant belief that everything outside the classroom is an unnecessary distraction.'

Edie's eyes flashed agreement. Miss Fotheringay had echoed Charles's words exactly: *It's a distraction, Edith, cut it out.'*

'Does your Cousin Charles have no idea how strong you are, academically?'

Edie coloured with pleasure. This was the first such praise she had ever received from Miss Fotheringay. 'He thinks that I must have some catching up to do,' she replied carefully.

'Mmm. Nothing that Shakespeare won't teach you,' Miss Fotheringay mused. Then – 'Would you *like* to go on with *Merchant*?' she asked suddenly, as if the thought had just struck her.

'*Yes!*' Edie said, nodding her head energetically.

'Then I shall fix it,' Miss Fotheringay said, her voice brisk. 'I'll tell him you have no choice in the matter. You are under orders – *my* orders – and as long as you are in my care those are the only orders that count.'

Edie looked at her gratefully. She felt the peculiar force of Miss Fotheringay's personality, and was exhilarated to think that this time the headmistress was on her side.

'You will apologise to Helen?' Miss Fotheringay enquired, pressing her advantage.

Edie nodded. She wondered if Miss Fotheringay would refer to the incident with Phoebe, and point out that this was not the first time she had been made to say sorry as a result of losing her temper – but it was not mentioned.

'I imagine Portia will be pleased to have her maid back.' The headmistress smiled. 'Miss Winifred tells me that you and Anastasia are now inseparable.'

'Sort of,' Edie replied. Then, after a pause, 'Something funny's going on with Anastasia. Everyone thinks she tries to get other girls in trouble but I know it's not like that. I think someone's trying to get *her* into trouble all the time, by taking her things and putting them back again as soon as she reports them missing.'

'I see,' Miss Fotheringay said slowly. 'And have you any evidence of this?'

'Well, no, but . . .' Edie faltered. She could not accuse Phoebe without proof. And as for telling Miss Fotheringay her suspicions about Miss Mannering . . . she didn't dare. 'I just meant that . . . well, Anastasia's not a troublemaker, and – and she's not mad,' she finished clumsily, wishing she had never begun.

'Is there anything else you would like to tell me, Edith?' Miss Fotheringay asked.

'No,' Edie said uneasily, shaking her head.

Miss Fotheringay waited, as if hoping she might change her mind, then stood up abruptly and walked to her desk.

'I gather your dormitory had a midnight feast last night,' she said brusquely, retrieving something from a drawer. She returned holding the box of chocolates, which she placed on the table in front of them. 'Well?'

Edie shifted uncomfortably. So she *was* in disgrace, after all.

'Did you not feel you had been in enough trouble this term already, Edith, without involving your friends in such a childish prank?'

'It – it wasn't my prank exactly,' Edie said, and told

her about the encounter with Lyle.

Miss Fotheringay nodded. It was as though she already knew the story, but had needed to hear it from Edie's lips. 'The world is full of danger, Edith. I can only make Knight's Haddon a place of refuge if my pupils abide by the rules, and one of my rules is that no pupil is to accept gifts from outside without them being seen by me first. I am the one who decides who and what enters this school, Edith, you would do well to remember that. And now we had better turn our minds to Latin.'

The following morning Anastasia was summoned to see the headmistress. As she left the common room Edie detected something knowing in Miss Winifred's expression, as though she expected that Anastasia's meeting would not be a pleasant one.

But when Anastasia returned, she looked happier than before. Edie could tell that she had been crying but it was as if the anxiety had been washed from her face.

'I said that we – I – thought someone was hiding my things, trying to get me into trouble, and Miss Fotheringay – well, she didn't actually *say* that she believed me, but she sort of looked like she did,' Anastasia explained. 'I was wrong about her, Edie. She was so nice about it all. She wasn't even cross about the money.'

'I told you she wouldn't be,' Edie smiled. 'And what about the – you know,' she said hesitantly, 'the doctor?'

'We did discuss it,' Anastasia said, sounding much

calmer on the subject than before. 'And she just said the option was there.'

Edie looked concerned. If Miss Fotheringay believed Anastasia's story, then why had she mentioned seeing a doctor? 'What did she say she'd do – about all the things being taken, I mean? Did she say she'd look into it?'

'She said that if anything else happens I'm to tell her or Miss Mannering. She didn't *say* not to tell Miss Winifred, but she sort of made it clear. *You must speak either to me or Miss Mannering.* I think she knows how upset Miss Winifred's getting about it, and she thinks Miss Mannering will be more sympathetic.'

'But, Anastasia, you can't talk to Miss Mannering, I told you she—'

'Oh come on, Edie. You can't still think that. Just because she does drawer searches it doesn't make her a thief.'

Edie looked doubtful. She had been watching Phoebe like a hawk, but to no avail, and Edie feared that her case against her was starting to wear thin. But her suspicions about Miss Mannering were mounting. Her drawer searches would provide her with the perfect opportunity to meddle with Anastasia's things, and it was unsettling to think Miss Fotheringay wanted to encourage Anastasia to confide in her. It was almost as though the head was in her deputy's power, but why? And why didn't she want Anastasia to talk to Miss Winifred?

'I think Miss Mannering's much nicer than she pretends,' Anastasia went on. 'You know she spends her weekends going to see people in prison?'

'*Prison?*'

Anastasia nodded. 'Alice told me. Alice's godfather's on the board of a prison somewhere not far from Oxford, and apparently Miss Mannering visits every Sunday.'

'But – but why?' Anastasia spoke as though it were perfectly natural for a history mistress to know people in prison, but Edie thought it very odd.

'I don't know,' Anastasia shrugged. 'It's just a good thing to do, I suppose. It must be pretty lonely being in prison. Perhaps Miss Mannering cheers the prisoners up.' Edie looked incredulous at this suggestion. 'Oh well, I agree she's not a patch on Fothy,' Anastasia smiled. 'Miss Fotheringay's so easy to talk to. I can tell her things I wouldn't discuss with any other mistress.'

'What sort of things?' Edie wondered.

'Oh, you know, about my mother and the divorce and my stepfather and your cousin Charles—'

'What did she want to know about *him*?'

'Nothing really, she just asked if I'd spoken to him much this term – I don't know why. And when I said Mummy was taking me to London for the *exeat* she asked if we'd be seeing him, and I said no because he was more Papa's friend now.'

Edie was alarmed by Miss Fotheringay's interest in Cousin Charles. She sensed she distrusted him, and she feared her finding out too much. If she discovered he was using her as a spy, Edie was sure she'd be expelled immediately.

'It would have been fun if Mummy and me could have come and seen Charles in London, then we could have spent some of the *exeat* together,' Anastasia said.

'We're not going to London,' Edie said gloomily. 'In his last letter Charles said he was going to take me back to Aunt Sophia's for the night.'

'I wish you could come out with us,' Anastasia said kindly.

'Maybe next time,' Edie replied – but she was dreading the *exeat* much more than Anastasia could have guessed. Since coming to Knight's Haddon, her short stay at Folly Farm had taken on the quality of a bad dream. The chocolates had been a reminder of Lyle's horridness. But it was seeing Cousin Charles that worried her most – he would be furious that she still had nothing firm to report.

Edie was glad that Anastasia seemed reassured by her meeting with Miss Fotheringay, and for the next few days the girls made the most of the respite from trouble, and threw themselves into the play with more vigour than ever. It impressed Edie that when Anastasia was rehearsing she never seemed distracted by her other concerns. Whenever something upsetting happened her acting seemed to become even more convincing.

'That's what I like about acting,' Anastasia said suddenly, as if to herself, when she and Edie had been running through their lines in the common room after supper. 'You can be a strong person when you're not, and you can be a popular person when you're not, and you can be happy . . . completely happy, even when . . .

even when you're not,' she finished, laughing.

Edie smiled. The play offered her an escape too. She had been frightened that Helen might not be convinced by her apology, but when Edie had sought her out the head girl had simply dismissed the whole incident with one of her bewitching smiles. Edie had thought nothing could spoil her pleasure at being in the play again. But she couldn't help noticing that however hard she tried, it was always Anastasia who was singled out for praise.

'I am lucky having you as Portia,' Helen said one evening, catching up with Edie and Anastasia in the corridor after a weekend rehearsal. 'Miss Winifred said I was a fool trying to do Shakespeare with the first-years, but she'll take it back when she sees you.'

Anastasia glowed, but Edie felt a stab of envy. She longed for a shard of Helen's attention, and hated having to keep her admiration to herself, as if it were a guilty secret. She wished she could confide in Anastasia, and make a joke of it, but they had both become shy of the subject and Edie suspected Anastasia might be even more enamoured of Helen than she herself was.

On Tuesday morning, Edie suggested that they went through their lines together before lunch, but Anastasia looked embarrassed. 'Helen wants to go through my soliloquy in Act Three – we're going to rehearse in the tower with a picnic,' she said, failing to hide her excitement. 'But perhaps we can go through them tonight?'

'Whatever,' Edie shrugged. She had never seen the tower; it was at the edge of the park, beyond the woods. It wasn't very far – only ten minutes at a run – but that whole patch was considered the prefects' territory, and none of the junior girls dared go near it. 'I thought only prefects were allowed in the tower,' she said, trying to sound indifferent.

'Prefects and their guests,' Anastasia replied, her eyes shining.

When Anastasia came hurrying back to the classroom just in time for the first afternoon lesson, her flushed face told Edie that the picnic had gone very well. This time she did not even try to hide her pleasure.

'Oh, Edie, it was wonderful! You should see the tower – it's quite tall, three storeys, with a little gallery at the top – and it's so pretty, the brick's sort of pink. And if you look out of the gallery window you can see the top of the school over the trees. Helen says that if you look through her telescope you can see into Miss Fotheringay's bedroom window!'

'Did you?' Edie asked.

'Of course not,' Anastasia giggled. 'We were too busy rehearsing. But she showed me around. There are bunk beds and a little sink with running water, and a cupboard full of food – tins of cake and things. Helen even keeps a change of clothes in a trunk upstairs. She lets the other prefects use it too – they sometimes camp there in the summer. But she's the only prefect with a key.'

Anastasia's face was glowing; Edie felt very left out.

'Oh, Edie, the tower feels so remote and peaceful. I couldn't help wishing . . .' Anastasia hesitated, seeming to think better of it. 'I do like Helen. She's not like the other sixth-formers. She talked to me as though we were friends.' She looked wistful. 'Helen's home does sound fun. They live in a farmhouse on the other side of Oxford and ride all the time. Have you ever jumped cross-country fences, like out on an English hunt?'

'No. And I would *never* hunt,' Edie said passionately.

Anastasia shrugged. 'It's illegal now anyway. But I'd love to go drag-hunting – that's when you follow a pretend trail. I nearly did once, in Yorkshire, but then Papa got wind, and said just because it wasn't cruel it was still dangerous and he forbade it. But Helen wants to take me home for Sunday lunch one day – she says her father would like to meet me – so maybe at least I'll get a ride.'

'Is her father a farmer?' Edie asked.

'I don't know,' Anastasia said. 'But he owns a lot of land. Her mother's a doctor in Oxford – a psy . . . psy – you know,' she said, smiling, 'like one of those people Miss Winifred wanted me to go and see.'

'A psychiatrist,' Edie said, struck by how cheerfully Anastasia now dismissed the matter.

'That's right, and I'll tell you something interesting, Edie,' she went on, lowering her voice conspiratorially. '*Helen's parents are friends of Fothy's!* Fothy's been to stay with them in the holidays!'

Edie tried to look pleased, but the idea of Helen and Anastasia and Miss Fotheringay all having links outside school and meeting in the holidays made her feel even more excluded. It was a world she would never belong to. And she didn't belong to Babka either, not any more.

She felt like a tree pulled up by a storm, with nowhere to replant its roots.

'*Self-pity corrodes the soul, Editha,*' her grandmother used to say, whenever Edie showed signs of feeling any. *Perhaps my soul is corroded already*, she reflected gloomily, on her way to sleep. She determined to stop minding about Anastasia and Helen. As if it mattered, anyway. But her indifference was tested the next morning, when her friend came dancing up to her before assembly:

'Edie, would you like to come with me to the tower?' she whispered. 'Helen's given me the key and she's asked me to run over there after lunch and fetch her copy of *The Merchant of Venice* – she left it behind yesterday and she hasn't got time to go herself.' Anastasia was clearly delighted to be able to offer Edie a share in this privilege. '*Please* say you'll come,' she urged. 'Helen says I've got to go with someone else – you know we're not allowed beyond the woods on our own.'

Edie scowled. Helen hadn't suggested Anastasia take her; she was just being used as a walking partner. 'Actually I'm busy,' she said, hating herself.

Anastasia looked hurt. 'That's a shame. Oh well, don't worry, I'll find someone else.'

But at the end of the lunch hour, as the bell was ringing to summon everyone back to class, Edie saw a breathless Anastasia running back into school on her own.

'Did you go alone?' Edie whispered.

Anastasia looked furtive.

'You are an idiot,' Edie said, grudgingly admiring of her friend's daring. 'If the Man finds out you've been in the woods on your own you'll be gated for a month!'

'Well, she won't, will she?' Anastasia smiled.

Edie noted the way Anastasia carried Helen's copy of the play around all afternoon as if it were a rare manuscript, until proudly returning it to her after their last lesson. But her happiness was short-lived.

'Look!' Sally shrieked, bursting into the common room after tea, and flying to the window. 'Helen's tower's on fire! Look – you can see it from here!'

Alice, Phoebe and Edie all sprang from their beds, but Anastasia remained standing by her chest of drawers, as if frozen. And when Edie looked from the window she felt a throb of fear. Across the park, on the crest of the low, wooded hill, there was black smoke belching from the trees, billowing up into the still, moonlit skyline, and through it she could see the tip of Helen's tower, lit by a thin dance of flame. An excited crowd of pupils had gathered outside, pointing excitedly as the flashing lights of a fire engine appeared at the bottom of the drive.

'It was Belinda and Rose who spotted it,' Sally said dramatically. 'They'd gone to look for a jersey Rose had left behind on the lacrosse pitch and Rose saw the smoke so they ran back and raised the alarm. Helen hasn't been to the tower today so she doesn't know how it could have started. But they reckon the most likely is that some idiot tried to light a fire to warm the place up a bit – it's freezing in there, there's no electricity – but the chimney was blocked, so that's how it started. And I suppose the culprit was too frightened to tell anyone.'

'How do you know all this?' Edie asked, with deep foreboding.

'Belinda told me,' Sally said importantly. Belinda had a sister in the sixth form which made her a good source of information. 'Whoever it was had quite a nerve. Imagine trespassing in Helen's tower!'

'But – but how did they get in?' Anastasia stammered. 'Helen always keeps the door locked.'

'That's just it,' Sally said. 'They let themselves in! Helen lent the key to someone this morning, and asked them to do an errand for her – and now this! Well, Helen obviously knows who she gave the key to, but she's not saying – she's not like the other prefects, she doesn't enjoy getting people into trouble.'

Edie saw Anastasia's face drain of colour.

'Well, I wouldn't mind getting them into trouble if I were her,' Phoebe said. 'What a stupid thing to do!' Edie looked at her avidly, searching her expression for the slightest flicker of guilt. But she could see none. Phoebe seemed as rapt by the drama as everyone else.

'But who would *want* to do something like that?' Alice asked, mystified. 'It's just so—'

'I know; it's weird, isn't it,' Sally agreed, suddenly looking apprehensive. 'And to Helen, of all people. If you ask me, it must have been someone pretty mad.'

19

KNIGHT'S HADDON

A Chronic Case of
Schoolgirl Crush

The fire was soon put out, but the smoke lingered. 'Who started it?' was the question on everyone's lips. Instead of the usual chattering and clattering of plates at supper there was a choked hush, with everyone talking in whispers and stealing furtive glances around the room.

Edie's eyes kept returning to Miss Mannering, who was sitting at the head of her table, serving the food with brisk precision. She did not speak, and though her face gave little away, Edie sensed something agitated in her manner. She wished she could talk to Anastasia, but she was at a table on the other side of the room. When Edie swivelled round she could see her, sitting silent and ashen-faced.

Edie was in no doubt of her friend's innocence. Whoever lit the fire in Helen's tower had been trying to frame her. But why?

She waited for Anastasia after supper, but as they were walking back to the dormitory Helen caught up with them. 'Anastasia, can I have a word?' she asked sweetly, leading her away.

Anastasia was gone for ages. Edie eventually found her in a music room, playing one of her mournful Russian piano pieces accompanied by low, shuddering sobs. When Edie drew up a chair Anastasia turned and looked at her wildly, then carried on.

'Oh, Anastasia, tell me what happened,' Edie asked. 'Did Helen really think . . . ?'

Anastasia gave no sign of having heard her. She went on until she had finished her piece, then gently closed the piano lid. 'She wanted me to confess that I had lit the fire,' she said in a low voice. 'As I hadn't, I wouldn't. But of course I was tempted. Because if I had . . . you know, Edie, this is how you send people mad. It's what they used to do, in Russia. And probably, in the end, I *shall* go mad. People do.'

Edie was frightened. Anastasia's voice was unnaturally calm.

'Of course, by the time I *am* mad everyone else will have been writing me off as mad for ages. No one will tell the difference.'

'Nonsense,' Edie said earnestly, but she could hear how thin her protest sounded. 'Listen, Anastasia, let *me* talk to Helen. *I'll* tell her you didn't do it!'

But Anastasia shook her head fiercely. 'It will only make it worse. You can see how it looks, Edie. I had the key all day – who else could have done it?'

Miss Mannering, Edie thought. Somehow she felt certain the deputy headmistress must have been involved. But without proof how would she make Anastasia believe her?

'Oh, Edie, it's so *embarrassing,*' Anastasia said with sudden disgust. 'It's not only the fire – it would be bad enough if she thought I had just tried to burn the place down but it's even worse than that. She thinks I went and made myself at home there, sitting in her chair and trying on her clothes . . . as if – as if I was pretending to *be* her. But I wasn't, Edie, I wasn't!'

'Was Helen very angry?'

'No!' Anastasia said bitterly, launching into a tearful imitation of the prefect's serene, smiling voice: *"It's all right, Anastasia . . . I know how difficult things have been for you . . . I want to help . . . everybody will understand . . ."* She talked to me as though I were one of her mother's patients.'

'Her mother's patients?'

'I told you before. Her mother is a psychiatrist. Giving pills to people like my mother when she has one of her fits. *Fits,*' Anastasia repeated bitterly. 'That's what my stepfather calls them, *fits*. Oh God, Edie, I thought I'd be able to get away from all that stuff by coming here – but now they think I need to see a doctor too!' She started crying again and Edie put a hand on her arm, trying to soothe her.

'Is Helen going to tell Miss Fotheringay?'

'I'm sure she knows already,' Anastasia hiccoughed. 'I thought Miss Fotheringay might have believed me about the tricks, but she doesn't, Edie – she's been talking to Papa.'

'When?' Edie asked sharply.

'After I went to see her, I spoke to him on the phone the next day and his voice was different from how it normally is. He said that I was to get on with my work and concentrate on the play and *stop worrying about things*. Fothy must have spoken to him, and told him I was making stuff up. So now I can't even talk to him. I'm all alone.'

'But you're seeing your mother at the weekend,' Edie said.

'Well, I'm certainly not going to talk about all this to her!' Anastasia said furiously. 'Whatever I tell her she repeats to my stepfather, and whenever he interferes he makes everything worse. She told him once that my dog was chasing sheep and he – he . . .'

'What?' Edie asked gently.

'He had him shot!' Anastasia said grimly. 'I'm terrified of my mother taking me back to Yorkshire. Oh, Edie, I know you think, *"Huh! At least she's got a family!"* But one day you'll meet my mother and stepfather and then you'll understand that it's not . . . not—'

'Not what?'

Anastasia turned her head, and ran her fingers silently along the piano. 'It doesn't matter what it's not. I mean, it does matter but I – I can't explain. I can't explain

~ 170 ~

anything any more, Edie. I think, perhaps, that I *am* making things up, but then I can't admit that I am . . . so confusion becomes sort of . . . a choice . . .' She trailed into silence. 'Am I making sense?' she said eventually, throwing Edie a pleading look.

'No,' said Edie firmly. 'Be specific, Anastasia. What, exactly, do you think you've made up?'

Anastasia bowed her head. 'It's not what I think. But I know it's what other people think – and perhaps they're right.'

Edie felt afraid for Anastasia, and out of her depth. But she could not give up, not yet. 'Listen, Anastasia. Did you or did you not have anything to do with the fire in Helen's tower? Did you at any time light a match or do anything, leave a magnifying glass glinting in the sunlight, *anything*, that could be used as evidence against you?'

The sudden fierceness in Edie's tone appeared to calm Anastasia. 'No,' she replied, shaking her head. 'I just went in, collected the play and went out again. And then I locked the door behind me. I didn't touch anything else, and I gave the key back to Helen when I gave her the script.'

'So, you didn't start the fire, but what about the other stuff?' Edie demanded. 'The glass bird, the fifty pounds? Done *to* you or done *by* you? It's one or the other.'

Anastasia did not flinch. 'Not done by me,' she said, with another shake of her head. 'Oh, Edie, you make everything so clear. I'm sorry for not being like you. It's just that I'm afraid.'

'What are you afraid of?'

'I sometimes feel that I have to agree to other people's versions of what's going on, in order to be left alone.'

'Whose versions?' Edie asked, frustrated. 'You talk in such riddles sometimes, I want to follow you, Anastasia, I really do, but sometimes I can't.'

Anastasia looked away. 'I know. I'm sorry. It's not complicated really. All I want, you see, is for the horrible things to stop happening. I want to be able to stay here – *and feel safe.*'

'You will, but first you've got to help me,' Edie said. 'Now listen, Anastasia, who knew you went to the tower today – did you tell anyone, other than me?'

'I – well, yes, when you said you couldn't come I asked Alice; but she couldn't come either because she had lacrosse practice . . . then I didn't ask anyone else. I just went on my own.'

'And you're sure no one saw you?'

'I don't think so,' Anastasia said. 'The only person I saw outside was Miss Mannering – Helen says she often goes out at lunchtime to look for sixth-formers smoking in the woods – but she can't have seen me because if she had she'd have asked what I was doing.'

Edie tensed. 'Anastasia, is there any way the Man could have known that Helen took you to the tower yesterday for a picnic?'

'She definitely knew,' Anastasia said, surprised. 'I had to ask her permission to have lunch with Helen. I was worried she'd say no, but she was fine about it. She . . . Oh, Edie, you don't really think?'

'Does the Man have a key to the tower?'

'Yes. Helen said Miss Mannering had a spare key and—'

'Then it *was* her!' Edie cried, jumping from her chair.

'But . . . but what about Phoebe—?'

'Yes, yes, I know, that's what I thought,' Edie replied impatiently, 'but don't you see? It couldn't have been her! I was in the same classes as her all day, and I know she didn't go anywhere during the lunch hour, I was watching her – so there's no way she'd have had time to get to the tower. But Miss Mannering – oh, Anastasia, you must believe me, everything fits! Now listen,' she went on, before Anastasia had a chance to protest. 'From now on I want you to make a note of everything that happens, anything you lose, however small, and anything odd that the Man says, and if you *ever* see her snooping—'

'But, Edie, I have been!' Anastasia groaned. 'When the trouble first started Papa told me to do just that so I've been writing everything down in my diary. He told me to keep the record-keeping a secret, so I didn't even tell *you*. And now it's gone.'

'*Gone?*'

'Yes. I thought I lost it once before, near the beginning of term, but then it turned up under my pillow and I've kept it there ever since. But I found it had gone missing again just after Sally came in and told us about the fire.' Anastasia turned very red. 'Oh, Edie, I'll *die* if anyone reads it. I'd tucked all my poems and things inside it – there . . . there was even a poem about Helen!'

'It must have been the Man who took it,' Edie said darkly. 'The Man's our suspect now, not Phoebe, and if I can only prove she's the one who's taken your book then we'll know for sure. I'm going to sneak down to the staff cloakroom tonight and look in her confiscations box, and if I don't find it there I'll search her office!'

Anastasia looked hesitant. They both knew there would be serious trouble if Edie was caught. 'Edie, you will watch out?' she whispered.

'It's the Man who had better watch out,' Edie said boldly.

It was as the school clock struck ten that Edie crept to the end of the pitch-black corridor and fumbled blindly for the handle of the door. It was only when she was inside the cloakroom that she dared to turn on her torch. She flashed it around the walls and saw Miss Mannering's famous box on a shelf perched high up above a rail of oilskin coats.

She hurriedly pulled up a chair, and when she stood on it on tiptoe, she found her arms could just reach. But as she started to pull the box towards her a light came on in the corridor, then Edie heard voices that made her rigid. It was Miss Fotheringay and Miss Mannering.

'Can we be *sure* that it was Anastasia who started the fire?' Miss Fotheringay asked.

'I don't see who else it could be,' Miss Mannering replied. 'Helen gave her the key to the tower this morning and asked her to run up there at lunchtime and fetch something for her—'

'Anastasia went *on her own*?' Miss Fotheringay asked sharply.

'Yes, Caroline, on her own. Strictly against the regulations, I know, but it's her behaviour on reaching the tower that concerns me.'

'The fire was an accident.' Miss Fotheringay sounded firm. 'Anastasia couldn't have known that the chimney was blocked. She would have had no idea of the damage she'd cause.'

'That may be, but it was mighty odd of her to light the fire in the first place. She had no right to loiter there. Helen went to inspect the damage, and she says that whoever it was had been trying on her clothes! I'm afraid, Caroline, we have a chronic case of schoolgirl crush.'

'It looks like that, I agree. I'm beginning to think Winifred's suggestion Anastasia should see a doctor might not be such a bad idea,' Miss Fotheringay said cautiously.

'A *doctor*?'

'A head doctor, Diana. A shrink. There's someone in Oxford who's been recommended to her. Winifred thinks the child is mentally disturbed.'

'Have you spoken to her parents?' Miss Mannering asked.

'The prince called a few days ago and I downplayed everything. Anastasia, of course, had told him she was being set up. She's convinced that someone in the school is trying to discredit her.'

Miss Mannering gave one of her unmistakeable snorts. 'I see. And is there any evidence?'

Edie was so gripped by the conversation she forgot the danger she was in. Miss Mannering's trenchant tone struck her as highly suspicious. Anastasia was clearly being framed.

'There is one thing I should tell you,' Miss Fotheringay began.

Edie waited, breathless, but just then she felt the confiscations box slipping towards her. She tried to push it back, but it was too heavy and next moment she found herself watching with a stifled cry as it tumbled over her head and crashed to the floor.

'*Edith Wilson!*' Miss Mannering exclaimed, bursting in at the door.

Miss Fotheringay followed, looking in silence at the confiscated sweets and books and torches lying strewn about the floor. Edie remained standing on her chair, her eyes darting from one woman to the other.

'Get down!' Miss Mannering shouted, addressing her like a disobedient dog. 'What on earth is this about?'

'I – I came to get my torch.'

Miss Mannering looked incredulous. 'You came and entered the staff cloakroom at ten o'clock at night and took my box from the shelf in order to *get your torch*?'

'Yes,' Edie whispered. Miss Mannering's eyes were protruding ominously. But when Edie dared look at Miss Fotheringay she saw to her surprise that there was no anger in her face, rather an impish glint.

Miss Mannering took a deep breath. 'Well, Edith Wilson, this time you have gone too far. What do you think, Headmistress? I suggest—'

'Let's gate her,' Miss Fotheringay said, her lips pursed into a teasing smile. 'Instead of going out with her guardian this weekend she can stay here, with me. That will make her think twice about stealing into the staff cloakroom at night.'

Curiosity Not A Crime

'Bye, Edie – I hope you don't have too awful a time,' Sally said. 'Daddy, this is Edie, the girl who joined late, remember? I wrote to you about her. She's been gated, poor thing!'

Edie smiled politely for what felt like the hundredth time that day. The school was crawling with other girls' parents and not even the dormitory was safe to hide in. Too late she'd learnt that this was the traditional time for parents to inspect their daughters' sleeping quarters.

'I'm sorry to hear you've been gated.' Sally's father was short and jovial-looking, with thick spectacles and thinning hair. 'Did you do something very bad?'

'She's so funny, Daddy, she's, like, addicted to reading,' Sally chimed. 'She can't stop at lights out so then she reads by torchlight and then her book gets confiscated and then she goes marching off looking for it in the confiscations box in the middle of the night! I said she should use sleepwalking as a defence – they can't punish her for what she can't help, can they?'

'*Do* you sleepwalk?' Sally's father asked Edie, with a concerned look.

'I – no . . . I don't think so,' Edie answered stupidly. *You've only had all morning to get your story straight*, she told herself crossly. *Why haven't you thought of something?*

When Sally and her father had gone Edie hunched herself up on the windowsill, hoping she would be left alone. Looking down, she saw Miss Winifred standing in the middle of the courtyard, ticking names off a clipboard as each child came up to say goodbye before being driven away. She spotted Alice, walking arm in arm with her father to his car, and Phoebe, weaving through the crowd with an unfamiliar spring in her step. Anastasia had already gone; Edie had not met her friend's mother – she had come early and had whisked her daughter away ahead of the rush.

Before long only a shiny red sports car remained. Edie saw Miss Winifred bend over to speak to the person in the driving seat, then the door of the car opened and a man got out. Edie peered down curiously, her knees hugged to her chin. She could not see the man's face, but noted the shock of jet-black hair and the tall, angular frame that unravelled from the car like a coil. She chewed her cheeks in quiet pleasure – he was the same man as the one she had seen with Miss Winifred in the village. He *must* be her boyfriend! That would be something to talk about to the others, when they came back to school bubbling over with tales of home treats.

The man loaded a suitcase into the back seat, then he and Miss Winifred got into the car and drove off at a slight skid. No one else appeared, and Edie felt strange thinking of herself left behind in the empty school, though she did not actually care about being gated – anything was better than going back to Folly Farm.

As far as she knew all the staff except Miss Fotheringay had gone, and she wondered shyly if the two of them would eat supper together in the huge school dining room, and if it would be Miss Fotheringay who appeared at eight o'clock to turn out the dormitory light. Edie supposed that for the most part she would be left to amuse herself, and she determined to make the most of her time. Perhaps she would have a chance to search Miss Mannering's study?

'Well, have you solved it?' asked a quiet voice, and Edie looked up in fright to see Miss Fotheringay standing over her.

'S-solved what?' she asked, wondering how long her headmistress had been there.

'I don't know. You just had the look of someone thinking something through.' Edie blushed, feeling caught out. 'I shall have plenty of time to unravel your secrets, Edith,' Miss Fotheringay continued, handing her a small canvas bag. 'Pack up what you need for the night. You're coming to stay with me.'

'With you?'

'I'm afraid you've got no choice,' Miss Fotheringay

said, looking at her with an amused expression. 'There are usually one or two girls left behind during *exeats*, but it so happens that on this occasion all those with families abroad have found friends to take pity on them. We're the only ones left. And you surely didn't imagine I'd leave you in an abandoned dormitory for the weekend? I've had a bed made up for you in my spare room – you can hide in there all weekend if you want to.'

Edie gathered her things in a daze. Miss Fotheringay lived above her study, in the West Tower, but Edie had only ever heard of prefects being invited there.

'Toothbrush?' Miss Fotheringay prompted, as Edie was zipping up the bag. 'Slippers?'

Edie felt shy as she walked beside her headmistress through the silent school. When they reached the hall Miss Fotheringay reached down and took her hand, as if guessing how strange she must feel. 'I'm glad you've disgraced yourself,' she said, putting this small awkwardness behind them. 'I sometimes find it lonely here when everyone's gone.'

They went out into the courtyard, and entered the West Tower through a pointed wooden door that Edie had never noticed before. *So much for my being a spy*, she thought guiltily.

Miss Fotheringay took the narrow stairs two at a time and led Edie into a large, curved drawing room with vaulted ceilings and windows on both sides. In one corner there was a tall gold birdcage with its door swinging open ('I had budgerigars once, but Black Puss ate them,' Miss Fotheringay explained, sheepishly); and beside the fire was a wooden jukebox with an old brass amplifier on top.

Edie thought it was one of the loveliest rooms she had ever seen – there was an atmosphere of friendly untidiness, with overflowing bookshelves, and rugs draped carelessly over the chairs. On one side stood a long oak table, where the day's newspapers lay unfolded next to a coffee pot and an unwashed cup and saucer.

'Now, Edith, you must make yourself at home,' Miss Fotheringay said, tossing her scarf over a chair.

Edie wondered how to go about this. She saw Black Puss curled on the sofa and went to sit by him, but he jumped to the floor, arching his back in disdain. When the phone rang, she watched self-consciously as Miss Fotheringay walked to the desk by the window and frowned into the receiver.

'No, Mummy, I'm not a machine. I *am* here . . . No. I'm staying at school for the night. I've got a pupil with me . . . You want to come *here*? With Dad? I suppose that would be all right.' Miss Fotheringay looked up, and gave Edie a doubtful glance. 'What sort of time? . . . Lovely. See you both later then.' She put the phone down. 'Well,' she said to Edie, 'I had been hoping we might have a quiet supper and watch a film together, but I'm afraid my parents have just invited themselves to stay.'

Edie's disappointment in not having Miss Fotheringay to herself was outweighed by curiosity. She had sometimes wondered, secretly, what it would be like to have Miss Fotheringay as a mother – but she had never considered that Miss Fotheringay might have parents of her own.

'Do they live nearby?' she asked.

'In Oxford,' Miss Fotheringay replied. 'They still live in the house where I grew up.'

Edie tried to imagine Miss Fotheringay growing up, but couldn't. 'Are they very old?' she ventured.

'Pretty old,' Miss Fotheringay said. 'Old and deaf in my father's case, and old and cross in my mother's.'

'Why is she cross?'

'Because she wanted one sort of daughter and got another.'

'But – but what doesn't she like about you?' Edie asked, shocked.

'There's plenty not to like about me, Edith.' Miss Fotheringay smiled. She picked up the cat from the floor and placed it in Edie's lap. This time it did not protest, but settled and purred. 'You will never know what it is to disappoint a parent,' Miss Fotheringay said, perching on the arm of the sofa. 'Perhaps that is one small thing you have to be grateful for. But what about your grandmother? She must have high hopes for you. Do you ever disappoint her?'

'I think,' Edie said thoughtfully, 'that sometimes she wishes I was more like her.'

'How funny. That is exactly what my mother feels about me.' Miss Fotheringay seemed to reflect on this coincidence. 'Would you like me to drive you over tomorrow to see your grandmother?' she asked after a pause. 'She's in a home just outside Oxford, isn't she?'

Edie was taken aback. She had not expected to see Babka again until the end of term. 'Yes – please . . . I mean, maybe, I—'

'You don't know what sort of state she'll be in?' Miss Fotheringay suggested.

Edie nodded.

'Well, it's up to you,' Miss Fotheringay said. 'But if you would like it, just say. My parents will be gone after breakfast, so we'll have the day to ourselves.'

'I would like it,' Edie decided, with sudden resolution.

'That's settled then,' Miss Fotheringay said, giving an affectionate ruffle to Edie's hair.

That afternoon was the happiest Edie could remember. First she helped Miss Fotheringay make a kedgeree for supper, in her funny rickety kitchen up a little twist of stone stairs, then they toasted muffins by the fire, and when it stopped raining Miss Fotheringay took her to her private garden to see if the hens had laid any eggs.

'This garden is a secret,' Miss Fotheringay said, pushing open a painted green door. 'Are you good at keeping secrets, Edith?'

Edie nodded fervently.

'Good,' Miss Fotheringay said. The door opened into a small, overgrown hideaway of shrubs and fruit trees, enclosed by a falling down red wall.

Edie found two eggs in the hen hutch, and put them in Miss Fotheringay's basket. 'Are you really the only person who comes here?' she asked, looking about her solemnly.

'Not quite,' Miss Fotheringay replied. 'I'm not much of a gardener, so Miss Mannering helps.'

'*Miss Mannering?*' Edie said, returned to her job with a jolt.

Miss Fotheringay looked intrigued. 'Are you frightened of her, Edith?'

'No!' Edie said emphatically. 'No, I mean, I . . . where has Miss Mannering gone this weekend?' she asked in a sudden rush.

'She's gone to her parents. They're even older than mine. She's very good to them.'

'And – and is it true she . . . has friends in prison?' Edie persevered.

'Well, I suppose that's one way of putting it. What have you heard exactly?'

'Only that she has . . . *connections*,' Edie replied carefully.

Miss Fotheringay smiled. 'Miss Mannering works as a volunteer teacher in an open prison not far from here. She has been doing it for years; she gives up most of her Sundays.'

Edie felt briefly deflated. This information did not suit her theory that Miss Mannering was up to no good.

'Really, Edith, you are a very curious child,' Miss Fotheringay said. Edie looked embarrassed. 'It's not a crime,' the headmistress went on, stooping to shut the hens back in their hutch. 'I'm also curious. I'm particularly curious about you.'

Edie's heart quickened, wondering if she had aroused suspicion. When Miss Fotheringay stood up she looked at her even more intently than usual.

'You remind me of someone I knew when I was a child,' she said quietly.

'Someone you liked?' Edie asked.

Miss Fotheringay frowned, as though weighing something up in her mind. 'Too many questions,' she said.

Ten miles away in Oxford, Miss Winifred and her mystery companion sat deep in mystery conversation at the bar of the Old Stoke Hotel.

'We should have done it yesterday, when we had the chance. I had her in my room, I'm telling you, May, we should have—'

'Hush, Vlady. You know we've got to wait for the passport. They told me yesterday it would be here within three days.'

'It had better be. This waiting is killing me. I wish I'd just snatched her when she was coming out of that teashop.'

'You're the one who's mad, Vladimir. The police helicopters would have been out before we'd even got to the M40. I tell you, if you want this to succeed we need time. We can't go until you've won her trust – how else are we going to keep her quiet on the ferry?'

'I have my ways. Anyway, I don't think my bedside manner's fooled her so far.'

'I'm not so sure,' Miss Winifred said softly. 'I think she's coming round to you. Time, Vlady, give it time.'

Thrillingly Private

Edie had her supper early and then she went upstairs to have a bath. Miss Fotheringay explained that as her parents were coming she was going to put Edie in the little room off hers, rather than in the spare bedroom as had been planned. Edie was glad as this meant she was able to see Miss Fotheringay's bedroom. It had a thrillingly private atmosphere, with books scattered on the unmade bed, and an armchair strewn with clothes. On the windowsill was a pair of binoculars, and what looked like a rusty metal camping lamp.

'That's an old Navy flashlight – it belonged to my grandfather,' Miss Fotheringay said, seeing Edie looking at it. She walked towards it, and on the way Edie saw her take a small photograph from the mirror on her dressing table and slip it into the pocket of her cardigan.

'Do you know how to the make the SOS signal, Edith?' she asked unexpectedly.

Edie shook her head.

'Three short flashes,' Miss Fotheringay said, picking up the flashlight to show her. 'Then three long ones, followed by three short again. Always useful to know.'

Edie blinked, for the light was almost blinding. Miss Fotheringay put the flashlight down, and turned to the window. 'This room has the best view in the whole school,' she said. 'On a clear day I can see the spires of Oxford.'

'Is it true you can see into this bedroom from the top window of Helen's tower?' Edie asked impetuously, remembering what Anastasia had told her. 'I mean . . .' She hesitated, worried that she had given away the prefect's secret.

'I had not heard that theory,' Miss Fotheringay said delicately. 'I shall have to remember to close my curtains in the summer. But you can certainly see the tower from here. Look.'

Edie peered out. There was a clear moon, and she found she could just define the black point of the tower looming over the silvery treetops. She thought of the fire, and wondered for a moment if she should tell Miss Fotheringay how certain she was that Anastasia hadn't caused it – and how nearly certain she was that the Man had. But she pushed the thought away. She needed proof – and besides, she did not want to let anything spoil tonight.

Next to Edie's bedroom there was a small bathroom

with green tiles. Miss Fotheringay set the bath running while Edie unpacked her bag.

'That's for you,' Miss Fotheringay said matter-of-factly, seeing Edie looking in surprise at a pale blue nightdress laid out on her pillow. 'There you are,' she said, handing her a towel, 'you won't be disturbed,' and she left before Edie could thank her.

Edie unfolded the nightdress and sat on the bed holding it for a long time. It was new, with its label still attached, and she wondered if Miss Fotheringay had been into a shop and chosen it specially for her, or whether the headmistress stockpiled pale blue nightdresses for stray gated girls. Then she remembered that her bath was running and jumped up just in time to turn off the taps.

If only Miss Fotheringay was a suspect, Edie thought happily, as she made a neat pile of her clothes, *then I could have a really good spy all round her bedroom*. She did not really wish it. She did not wish for anything except that the weekend should go on for ever. Her mind flickered, briefly, over the image of Miss Fotheringay removing the photograph from the mirror. She wondered if the headmistress had a boyfriend, like Miss Winifred, but she could not imagine what sort of man he might be.

When she went back downstairs to say goodnight, Miss Fotheringay's parents had arrived and were sitting round the table.

'It's not a comfortable place to live,' a large, forceful-looking old lady was saying. 'Really, Caroline, wouldn't you be better getting somewhere in Oxford?'

'I like it here,' Miss Fotheringay said firmly. Then, seeing Edie in the doorway, she beckoned her over to be introduced.

Edie thought Miss Fotheringay's father had the kindest face and the bluest eyes she had ever seen. 'I'm an awful bore, I'm afraid,' he said, waving his glass in the air. 'Can't hear a thing.'

Edie smiled, thinking how unlike Babka he was – her grandmother always talked as though her age and loss of sight made her more interesting than other people. She noticed that Miss Fotheringay was very tender with her father, and that he caught hold of her hand and held it for a moment as she bent over the back of his chair to fill up his drink.

'Everything all right with you, old girl?' he asked her. 'Mad school still suiting you?'

'Ssh,' Miss Fotheringay smiled. 'Mad school has left behind a spy.'

Miss Fotheringay's tone was flippant, but Edie felt her stomach lurch at the mention of spying. If the head teacher ever found out her reason for coming to Knight's Haddon . . .

'*Amplius postea*,' the headmistress added and Edie looked up, surprised. The words sounded Latin but Miss Fotheringay had told her that no one spoke Latin any more.

'*Expectabo*,' the old man replied.

'Come and sit down, dear,' Miss Fotheringay's mother interrupted, patting the chair beside her. 'That's a pretty nightdress you're wearing.'

'Miss Fotheringay gave it to me,' Edie said shyly.

'Did she now?' Mrs Fotheringay said, glancing at her daughter approvingly.

'Edith only came down to say hello and goodnight,' Miss Fotheringay said briskly. 'It's actually her bedtime.'

Edie found herself shepherded upstairs to her room. She climbed into bed and Miss Fotheringay pulled up the blankets to her chin.

'Thank you for your help this afternoon,' she said, smiling down at her. 'Having you made it easier having them. Now will you read or will you go straight to sleep?'

Edie did not think she would be able to concentrate on her book so Miss Fotheringay leant down to kiss her before turning out the light. Edie could not remember the last time anyone had kissed her goodnight. Babka did not like kissing, and Aunt Sophia never climbed the three flights of stairs to Edie's room at Folly Farm. 'If you want anything just call,' Miss Fotheringay said, but Edie knew she would not dare.

She couldn't sleep. There was a pipe spluttering and the small room felt warm and airless, so she turned on the light and slipped out of bed to open the window. A murmur of voices came up to her and she realised that she was sleeping directly above where the others were sitting. She listened carefully to hear if she could make out any words and found that old Mrs Fotheringay was the clearest. Her voice was almost trumpet-like – a result, Edie supposed, of having always to shout at her deaf husband.

'I hope you're still coming to France for Christmas, dear . . . have you booked your ticket?'

'Yes, yes, I'm coming,' Edie heard her headmistress reply. 'I must chase my new passport, it still hasn't arrived. When I rang last week they said it had been signed for so there's obviously been a mix-up.'

'Well, you'd better sort it out . . . your brother won't want to come if you're not there. You know how bored he gets with us.'

Edie leant against the window, greedily gathering these little snippets about Miss Fotheringay's life. Then suddenly she heard a name that made her stand completely still.

'Michael, this will interest you. You remember Caroline's friend – Anna Carter? That awkward-looking child is her daughter. Arrived here quite by chance a few weeks ago. Isn't that amusing, dear?'

Mr Fotheringay's response, if it came, was not audible. But Edie could hear her headmistress's voice, urgent and pleading: 'Please, Mummy, Edith doesn't know . . .' and the sound of a window being pulled shut.

Edie heard nothing more. *Caroline's friend, Anna . . .* The words echoed in her head as she went back to bed and lay there in a state of fearful elation, trying to make sense of what she had heard. Edie's mother, the mother she had never known, had been Miss Fotheringay's friend. *You remind me of someone I used to know . . .*

Edie thought back in a daze on all their conversations – on the gentle interrogations, when Miss Fotheringay herself had so often seemed on the brink of confiding something. And now she knew. Miss Fotheringay and her mother had been friends! She wriggled under the heavy blankets, her mind filled with magnificent possibilities. Perhaps Miss Fotheringay would offer to adopt her! For as long as she could remember, Edie had dreamt of a long-lost friend of her mother's turning up and laying claim to her. It had always been a guilty dream, for it seemed ungrateful to Babka, but now that Babka had retreated into a home what harm could there be?

A small, needling voice in her head asked why Miss Fotheringay had not told her of their connection – but Edie silenced it. She was sure to tell her soon enough, she was probably just waiting for the right time. Edie tried to imagine how Miss Fotheringay might present such an intimate revelation, but couldn't.

She lay very still, smiling in the darkness. She did not know how late it was when she finally heard her headmistress come upstairs to bed. But long after Miss Fotheringay's light had gone out Edie was still pinching herself to stay awake, fearing as her eyes grew heavy that it was all a dream, and that if she fell asleep the dream would end.

The Fact of a Deception

Edie was very quiet at breakfast, bursting with questions she dared not ask. She knew so little about her mother, although she had thought about her so much, and the knowledge that Miss Fotheringay had been her friend pushed everything else from her mind. Even Anastasia's problems, she realised guiltily, seemed less vital than before. But she felt impatient. If only everything were out in the open . . .

'Not very well, I'd say. She's in a complete dream,' mused old Mrs Fotheringay, touching Edie gently on the arm.

Edie looked up, confused, to see the headmistress's mother smiling at her kindly. 'My husband was just wondering whether you slept well, or did we keep you up with our talking?'

Edie felt her face burn. 'I slept very well, thank you.'

'So well that you're still half asleep this morning, eh?' Miss Fotheringay's father said in a teasing voice. 'She should have been allowed a lie-in,' he added in mock indignation to his daughter.

'She's too young for lie-ins,' Miss Fotheringay replied firmly.

'Are you?' Mr Fotheringay asked, looking at Edie with a mischievous expression. 'Or is it possible your head-mistress doesn't know you as well as she thinks?'

'I . . . I don't know,' Edie stammered, wishing she could think of some light-hearted reply. Everyone was laughing, but she felt too seized up inside to make any pretence at joining in.

After Mr and Mrs Fotheringay left, Edie and her head-mistress set off to visit Babka in St Benedict's Nursing Home. Edie sat in the front of the car, staring nervously through the window. She felt she could not bear to wait much longer, and wondered if she dare confront Miss Fotheringay with what she had overheard last night. That way, Edie calculated, she would be spared the awkwardness of having to pretend to be surprised when Miss Fotheringay finally chose to raise the matter herself. *Now is the time*, she thought, feeling her chest tighten – but the words would not come.

'I expect you would like to see your grandmother on your own,' Miss Fotheringay said, breaking the silence.

Edie frowned, unsure. Babka could be very rude, but Edie found herself wanting to share every part of her life with Miss Fotheringay, even if it meant subjecting her to Babka's scathing tongue. Then suddenly she understood. Of course Miss Fotheringay did not want to see Babka – Babka might remember her and give the secret away. Miss Fotheringay clearly wanted to tell Edie in her own time, and if that meant keeping the pretence alive a little longer, then Edie would have to swallow her impatience.

'It might be best,' she agreed.

'Will you talk to your grandmother about school?' Miss Fotheringay asked.

Edie shrugged. 'She's not interested in school. We'll probably talk about chess.'

'She won't want to hear horrid stories about all your teachers?'

Edie hid a smile. *I'll ask her about you!* she thought. If Miss Fotheringay had been a friend of her mother, then Babka would probably have met her. Edie could hardly wait.

It was only eleven o'clock when they arrived at St Benedict's but it looked as though lunch had already been served. Babka was sitting with several other old people in a room dominated by a large television playing an antiques show – at full volume. She was in a wheelchair, her empty plate on the plastic table that trapped her in. When Edie tapped her arm she looked up angrily, but on seeing Edie she greeted her with a tired smile.

She raised a withered arm and a young male nurse came over. 'I would like to talk to my granddaughter in my room,' she said in an imperious tone.

'Why is she in a wheelchair?' Edie asked, running to keep up as the nurse wheeled Babka away.

The nurse looked at her in surprise: 'Ah, sure she cannae see very well,' he said.

'She doesn't need a—' Edie began, but her grandmother silenced her with an irritable shake of her head.

'How many times did I teach you *not* to fight battles you can't win, Editha?' she said sharply when the nurse had gone.

'But you don't have to do everything they say!' Edie protested. 'If you tell them you don't need a wheelchair then they can't make you use one.'

'Can't they?' Babka laughed scathingly. 'There is a lot you don't understand, Editha.'

'Like what?' Edie asked, alarmed by the bitterness in her grandmother's tone.

When Babka spoke again her face was twisted, and her voice little more than a hiss. 'I can say what I like to them: "Wheelchair, no wheelchair, pills, no pills, bath, no bath . . ." but they won't listen, not to an old fool like me. They say I'm senile!'

'*Senile?*'

'Oh yes, Editha! You had better believe it. Crazy old lady! That is what they call me.'

'But you're not!' Edie pleaded.

Babka waved a hand impatiently. 'I am to them. It suits their methods. If I'm mad they don't have to take notice of what I say. It gets me out of the way. In the end, I agree. It suits me to agree. It gets me my lunch.'

Edie started, struck by a sudden recall of her

conversation at the piano with Anastasia . . . *'You know, Edie, this is how you send people mad. It's what they used to do, in Russia. And probably, in the end, I shall go mad. People do . . .'*

Then Edie remembered the strange expression on Anastasia's face as she had spoken the words, and she looked at Babka fearfully. Could it be true that someone was trying to get Anastasia out of the way, by showing her to be mad?

'Don't fret about me, Editha, I don't forget who I am,' Babka said, assuming Edie's concern was for her.

Edie shook herself, trying to shut her mind to the echo of Anastasia's stricken voice. 'Babka,' she said gently, taking one of the old lady's hands and pressing it between her own, 'don't you want to hear about my school?'

Babka sniffed. 'A school chosen by your English relations. The decision was nothing to do with me.'

'But *I'm* to do with you.'

'Are you? Then show it. Show me your game.' She nodded to the plastic trolley, on which the chessboard was laid out. Edie wheeled it over and Babka mechanically returned the pieces to their starting positions, feeling each one in her fingers.

Edie started badly and Babka tapped her hand in rebuke. 'I don't want to play!' she cried, surprising herself by her sudden rebellion. 'Why won't you let us talk, ever?'

Babka moved her rook and looked at her through pale, unfocused eyes. 'What do you want us to say?'

'Why don't I know any of my mother's friends?'

'You know her sister,' Babka replied.

'*They* weren't friends. You know they didn't like each other – Aunt Sophia never talks about her.'

Babka shrugged. 'Perhaps,' she said, 'your mother was not such an easy person. Perhaps she had no friends.'

'Of course she had friends,' Edie said furiously. 'You've just kept them away from me. But now I know one of them!'

'So,' said Babka. 'What is their name? Eh? Tell me that, little girl.'

'C-Caroline Fotheringay,' Edie said, stumbling on her headmistress's Christian name which she had learnt only the day before. Babka burst into an ugly cackle.

'*Caroline Fotheringay?* Now that takes the biscuit. Oh, my dear Editha, is that the best you can do? What is the saying in your language? With friends like those, who needs enemies? Caroline Fotheringay, indeed.'

Edie felt as though she had been struck in her stomach. She put her hand to her mouth and threw her grandmother a pleading look.

Babka stared back, cat-with-creamy. *She is loving this*, Edie thought, hating her suddenly. *She is enjoying my distress.* 'Tell me what you mean, Babka,' she begged, her voice rising through a sting of tears. 'I need to know . . .'

'Why?' Babka asked suspiciously. 'Where do you find this name anyway, *Caroline Fotheringay*?' Edie made no answer. 'So,' said Babka, waving a hand in dismissal, 'you give me nothing, I give you nothing. It is even-steven.'

'I don't have anything,' Edie protested weakly. 'I just heard someone say they were friends.'

'It is the same with me,' said Babka, shrugging. 'I cannot tell you what I never knew. She told me nothing, your mother. Just black brows around the name of Caroline Fotheringay. Anna was a good hater, Editha. Oh yes, she did not forgive a quarrel.'

'What did they quarrel about?'

Babka cocked her head, frowning as if in deep concentration, but when she spoke her tone was impatient. 'She said that Caroline Fotheringay was a dangerous woman. That her urge to control was out of control. Something like that. It was not interesting to me, Editha – your mother had too many passions. But your father was not like that and he also hate this woman. They were joined against her.'

'But why?' Edie asked, her voice trembling.

Babka shook her head. 'Enough is enough,' she announced grandly. 'It is the past. There is no more to say. Now you tell me something, Editha, something about your new life. What is the play you mentioned in your letter?'

'*The Merchant of Venice*,' Edie replied flatly.

Babka smiled. '*All that glisters is not gold*. Remember that, Editha, with your English relations. And now I am tired of talking. Ring the bell, please.'

When Edie returned to the hall Miss Fotheringay greeted her with her warmest smile. Edie looked back at her helplessly. Every part of her longed to trust her headmistress. Perhaps, she thought wildly, her grandmother had been playing games, in some desperate attempt to claw back power. Perhaps it was Babka, not Miss Fotheringay whose urge to control was out of control . . . ?

But why hadn't Miss Fotheringay been open with her? If she had been her mother's enemy, as Babka claimed, then her secrecy made sense. She must have done something terrible. What? Edie followed her in silence to the car, Cousin Charles's words ringing in her ears: '*Sometimes the only thing you have to go on is the fact of a deception . . . You have to work backwards from there . . .*'

And there *was* a deception. Miss Fotheringay had been deceiving her from the start.

Edie had neglected her mission all weekend but now a new suspicion began to grow on her: could it be that Miss Fotheringay had some part to play in the persecution of Anastasia? She scrunched her eyes tight, recoiling at the very idea of it – but the seed, once planted, took root at an alarming rate.

She knew – from Cousin Charles – that Miss Fotheringay had been dismissive of Anastasia's problems when Prince Stolonov had raised them with her. And Anastasia was convinced that Miss Fotheringay had told the prince she was making things up. The headmistress seemed determined to make out that everything was Anastasia's fault. But why? The working backwards, Edie resolved, should begin at once.

'Well, how was she?' Miss Fotheringay asked, as they pulled out of the car park.

'They make her sit in a wheelchair,' Edie said dully.

Miss Fotheringay threw her a sympathetic glance. 'It often happens, in homes. It's upsetting, I know. How was her mood?'

Edie shrugged.

'I have a feeling you don't want to talk,' Miss Fotheringay speculated correctly, and reached to turn on the news.

When they got home Miss Fotheringay produced a delicious lunch of ham and pâté and soft round cheeses, and little tarts and biscuits and sweet cakes, all pulled from the fridge in their brown paper bags and spread like a picnic on the kitchen table. Edie sat down, resolving neither to eat nor speak. She saw something perplexed in her headmistress's expression, as though she were wondering what she had done to hurt her.

'Eat up, Edith,' Miss Fotheringay said quietly, putting food on her plate.

Edie lowered her eyes, hearing another unwelcome echo of Cousin Charles's voice: *It often turns out that the person deceiving you is someone you have grown to trust . . . to be good at this work you must detach . . . Are you capable of that, Edith? I have a hunch you might be . . .*

After lunch the headmistress went into the garden to plant some bulbs, leaving Edie to do her maths homework. But she was very far from being able to settle down to her sums. She walked over to the window, and waited until she could see Miss Fotheringay in the garden below. Then she picked up the telephone on the desk and dialled Cousin Charles's number.

It was answered at once. 'Rodriguez.'

'It's Edith.'

'Edith! Do you know, I was about to write to you.'

'You – you said to ring if anything was ever . . . urgent.'

'Of course. You have something to report?'

'Y-yes.'

'About Anastasia's recent troubles?'

Edie heard something oddly detached in his voice. 'It's about Miss Fotheringay,' she said nervously.

'I thought it might be. Has she guessed you've been up to something?'

'No, I don't think so.'

'Really? She seemed awfully interested in you.'

'I think there's another reason for that.'

'What would that be, my dear?' Cousin Charles asked, sounding amused.

'I think she knew my mother.'

'Yes. I was aware of that.'

Edie tightened her grip on the receiver. Her hand was shaking. 'But . . . but then why didn't you tell me?'

'I didn't know the connection when I sent you to Knight's Haddon. Sophia let it slip when we met the other day. But what of it? I thought you didn't remember your mother?'

'I don't,' Edie said flatly.

'But you believe this coincidence is significant?'

Edie watched as Miss Fotheringay knelt by a bed on the far side of the garden, and started digging with her trowel. 'Why did she hide it from me?' she asked, her voice quavering.

Cousin Charles sounded impatient. 'People hide things all the time, Edith. Usually because they don't want to deal with the consequences of the truth.'

'But you told me—'

'I told you to keep your eyes open and your mouth shut. You have discovered that your headmistress had a link with your family that she was not open about, and that was clever of you. It just so happens not to be relevant to the case.'

'How do you know it's *not relevant*?'

'No one will take you seriously, Edith, if you whine. I know it's not relevant because the case is closed. Prince Stolonov has spoken to Miss Fotheringay and she has convinced him that Anastasia's problems are of her own making. As you have no doubt discovered, she is an actress of no mean talent. The poor girl seems to have been engaged in an elaborate bid for attention – but your headmistress is confident she's found a new outlet for her dramatics in the school play. Most thoughtful of her to cast Ansti in the lead role . . . quite inspired.'

Edie felt sick. Cousin Charles and Prince Stolonov were abandoning Anastasia just when she needed them most.

'Anyway, you're off the job,' her cousin said casually. 'Enjoy your last few weeks at boarding school – you won't be needed there next term.'

'But you don't understand – the job *isn't* over. I've found out all sorts of things!'

'I'm sorry, Edith, but Prince Stolonov has not been

paying your fees in order for you to investigate the relationship between Miss Fotheringay and your mother.'

'No! I don't mean that! I mean things about Anastasia. The problem isn't solved, it's got bigger. There was a fire, you see, and—'

'And?'

But suddenly Edie noticed Miss Fotheringay was gone from the garden; then she heard a door bang downstairs.

'I can't talk any more. She's coming—'

'Put it on paper,' said Cousin Charles in a bored voice. 'If you dare.'

A Disturbing Date

On Tuesday afternoon Miss Mannering divided her Norman history class into stitchers and builders – the first group were sent to the library to piece together the story of the Bayeux Tapestry, while the second remained behind in class to learn what to look for in a twelfth-century church. But Miss Mannering had not got very far with this presentation when an idea seemed to take hold of her with sudden force.

'Hands up anyone who hasn't yet been inside the village church of St Bede's.'

Five pairs of hands rose sheepishly into the air. 'Shame on all of you,' said Miss Mannering gaily. 'Buildings must be read as well as books if we are to understand the past.'

'She's in a good mood,' Edie said to Anastasia as they

walked down the drive. She still wished she'd had a chance to search Miss Mannering's office over the *exeat*, but Miss Fotheringay had hardly let her out of her sight. Now Edie had two mistresses under suspicion.

'I like Miss Mannering,' said Anastasia. 'I know you don't.'

Only because I'm looking out for you, Edie thought with a sudden flash of irritation. Edie had felt more alone than ever since the *exeat*. Anastasia hadn't seemed to notice her misery when everyone returned to school on Sunday night. Instead she had told Edie all about the sumptuous teas she had shared with her mother in their hotel without once asking what Edie had got up to with Miss Fotheringay. And now here she was tossing her head and insisting on the Man being a good sort, irrespective of any insights Edie might bring to a discussion of the history mistress's character. *She expects me to help her, but she's not actually interested in what I think*, Edie reflected crossly.

And yet even Edie had to admit that the Man revealed a very different side in the church. Her high spirits seemed to increase in the damp gloom of the interior, which was lit only by the jewelled blue-and-red glass in the windows. *It's as though it's her natural habitat*, Edie thought, watching as the history mistress weaved about, pointing out all the inscriptions and carvings.

'Feel this,' Miss Mannering said to Edie and Anastasia, giving the column near which they were standing an appreciative stroke. 'It's worn smooth as skin by the hands of centuries. Time, you see, has brought it closer to its original condition.'

'What do you mean?' asked Anastasia.

'The Normans filled their walls and pillars with rubble,' replied Miss Mannering, looking delighted to be asked. 'The stone on the outside is quite literally a skin.'

After a bit Miss Mannering left the girls to explore for themselves and told them to meet up at the church gate in fifteen minutes.

'Shall we slip away and have tea at the Blue Kettle?' whispered Anastasia, touching Edie on the sleeve as they emerged into the bright winter sunshine. 'They know me so well there now – I'm sure they'll let me come back and pay on Saturday.'

'Are you mad?' Edie asked, looking at her in astonishment. Anastasia flushed, and Edie winced at her clumsiness – ever since the fire in the tower, there had been rumours among the other girls about Anastasia's 'mental state', as it was coyly referred to.

'Anastasia, I'm so sorry – I didn't mean that.'

'I know you didn't,' Anastasia replied, affecting a look of indifference. 'I suppose I just thought it might be fun to get into trouble for something I *have* done for a change—' But then she stopped, an expression of incredulity on her face.

'What is it?' Edie asked, shaking her arm.

Anastasia had her mouth open in a look of dumb startle. Miss Mannering, emerging from a bend in the lane carrying a bag of buns, also noticed her surprise. She and Edie followed Anastasia's gaze in time to see Miss Winifred disappear inside the Blue Kettle accompanied by a tall man with black hair. Edie recognised him at once as the man who had driven Miss Winifred away in his car.

'Well, Anastasia, welcome to the shocking realisation that members of staff also have private lives,' Miss Mannering said briskly. Anastasia appeared not to have heard her. The other girls, meanwhile, had congregated at the gate. 'I seem to have misjudged you, Anastasia,' said Miss Mannering, seeming amused by her dreaminess. 'Your mind was perhaps on higher things?'

'My mind?' Anastasia asked in a faraway voice, turning to face her teacher.

'Oh dear, have you lost that now?' Phoebe called out spitefully. 'Chances are it'll turn up inside your pencil case tomorrow.'

There was an appreciative titter from several girls before Miss Mannering silenced them with a cold stare. 'What a very unpleasant thing to say, Phoebe. What can you have been thinking of?'

'It was just a joke,' Phoebe said mulishly.

'Then you will walk along with me and explain it,' Miss Mannering replied.

The party made its way back to school, with Edie and Anastasia bringing up the rear.

'Pitied even by the Man,' Anastasia said bitterly. 'She must think I'm disturbed in some way or she wouldn't have come down so hard on Phoebe.'

'It doesn't matter what she thinks,' Edie said, though she was secretly puzzled by Miss Mannering's behaviour. If she was trying to persecute Anastasia, then why was she so quick to defend her? Edie tried to think of an instance when Miss Mannering had been openly mean to Anastasia – but couldn't. On the face of things at least, her behaviour was always sympathetic.

'It matters to me. I *hate* people thinking I'm mad,' Anastasia said.

'*I* never think it,' Edie said stoutly.

'I know you don't,' Anastasia replied, taking her arm. 'But nor can you listen to everything in my head. That's why I agreed to talk to him.'

'Who?'

'Dr Browning. Miss Winifred's date in the Blue Kettle. He's the doctor she wanted me to see and I have. Miss Winifred said it would be better not to talk about it. Now I suppose he's debriefing her about my problems.'

Edie looked at her aghast.

'Now you're cross with me,' Anastasia said flatly.

'No,' said Edie, in a low panicked voice as her mind worked furiously on this new information. 'It's just . . .' She paused, uncertain how much to reveal. 'I can't help you if you keep things secret from me.'

'You can help by not getting cross. Miss Winifred talked to me again about seeing someone, and I know I was against it before but I changed my mind. I think for once she was trying to be nice. She talked to me again just after the fire, said it might make things better. I saw him last week.'

Edie remembered with alarm how Miss Winifred had sat whispering on Anastasia's bed when she had first suggested it. Now she was learning that the teacher hadn't given up the idea after Anastasia's earlier refusals. 'And what happened?' she asked.

'I don't know. We just talked. He was quite funny — and I could tell from his accent that he was Russian. Maybe that was why Miss Winifred thought we'd get on.'

'Russian? But then why's he called Dr Browning?'

Anastasia shrugged. 'Lots of Russians working in England use English names. His real name's Britianov — I noticed it on a letter on his desk.'

'So did he ask you all about your parents? Isn't that what those sorts of doctors are meant to do?'

'He didn't ask much about Mummy. But he wanted to know everything about Papa — I told him how much I minded him not believing me.'

'What else?'

'Oh, you know, how well we got on, and how often he comes to see me, and when we last spoke. He wanted to know all sorts of funny things too, about how I feel about having so many houses and things. I told him that it was just what I was used to, but he seemed very interested in it all. He even asked me about Papa's art collection. But mainly we just talked about my problems. I told him that Papa had always been the one who's understood, but that he seems to have stopped caring.'

I think your father does care,' Edie said slowly.

'He's got a fine way of showing it,' Anastasia replied, with a signature toss of her head.

'So what did Dr Browning say?' Edie asked, feeling increasingly uneasy.

'He said I shouldn't blame myself about anything – he said it wasn't fair on me, that I must be under a lot of strain. I felt I could talk to him. I would have told him lots more, but we ran out of time. Anyway, I'm seeing him again the day after tomorrow—'

'The day after tomorrow,' Edie repeated, frowning.

'Yes, why?'

'Anastasia, you *have* to talk to your father,' Edie pleaded. 'You don't need a doctor. You're not mad! Someone's just—'

'No!' Anastasia broke away from the hand which Edie had placed on her arm. 'Why do you take Papa's side? You don't even know him. I liked the doctor. Stop trying to turn me against everyone!'

Edie remembered the conversation in the music room, when Anastasia had been at her most distraught . . . Someone, Edie felt certain, was trying to make it look as though Anastasia were unstable. And now Anastasia was behaving as though she believed it herself. And the fact that the doctor was so closely involved with a mistress made Edie even more certain that something wasn't right. Now Miss Winifred was a suspect too, and Edie's instinct was to put her name at the top of the list.

She had an impulse to take her friend by the shoulders, and shake some sense into her. But by the time they had reached the school, she had said nothing in response to Anastasia's outburst.

'I'm sorry if I seem ungrateful,' her friend said, breaking the silence. 'I know you want to help. But maybe you just . . . can't?'

Edie smiled, and Anastasia looked relieved, as if all their talk about the doctor had been forgotten. Edie was baffled how quickly Anastasia's moods could change. She watched her across the table at tea, smiling at some madcap pony story of Rose's, as if she had no sense of the danger she was in. But Edie had seen the fear in her face in the music room, and wondered where it had gone. It was as though she had now decided to place her trust in the doctor, and not to consider any information which might shake that resolution.

She knew she had to persuade her friend that her father – the prince – was not her enemy, and that the doctor might be. But how should she do this? The answer, when it occurred, made her light-headed with relief. She should tell Anastasia everything she knew – not only about Miss Winifred and the doctor, but also her own role in the affair. If she confided in Anastasia they could work together, and if Anastasia knew her father had placed someone in the school to look out for her, it would surely convince her that he was on her side.

It was Cousin Charles who had made Edie promise to keep her spying work a secret from Anastasia. But now she was her own master.

Edie seized her chance after supper, when she found herself alone with Anastasia in the dormitory. Her friend was lying on her bed, flicking through her photograph album.

'Look, Anastasia, we need to talk,' Edie said, sitting

down beside her, hardly knowing where to begin. 'The thing is . . . you're wrong, you know, about your father not caring . . . the truth is— Oh, Anastasia, I know it will sound mad—'

That word again! It was all much harder to explain than Edie had expected. But she persevered, telling as best she could the tangled story of how Prince Stolonov and Cousin Charles had recruited her to work secretly on Anastasia's behalf.

'Don't you see, Anastasia, I'm only here because your father wanted someone to look after you! He *does* care, you know he does. The problem is that the teachers have persuaded him there's nothing to worry about.'

Edie looked at Anastasia helplessly, hoping for some reaction, but her friend's expression was blank.

'The doctor that you liked so much isn't who you think he is. I mean, he may be a doctor – I don't know – but he is also Miss Winifred's boyfriend!'

Anastasia said nothing.

Edie persevered, telling Anastasia how she had seen him driving Miss Winifred away for the weekend. Then she moved on to Miss Fotheringay, and her fears that even she was not to be trusted. Slowly, painfully, she explained about the secret link she had discovered between Miss Fotheringay and her mother, and the mysterious betrayal that Babka had implied.

'So you see I haven't ruled out the Man, but now there are three mistresses under suspicion! It could be any one of them!'

Anastasia listened in silence, showing no emotion at all.

'I'm sorry for not telling you sooner,' Edie said, unnerved. 'It's just—'

'Yes,' Anastasia said coldly. 'It is a great pity that you didn't. I don't know, now, what to think.'

Join the club, Edie thought, suddenly impatient. So much for her notion that they would solve this mystery together! Perhaps it was better for her to work alone. Anastasia was too selfish to be any help.

She left the dormitory and walked back to the common room. Alice was helping Sally with her homework, Belinda and Rose were playing a raucous card game and giggling uncontrollably. Some other girls were sitting cross-legged on the floor playing jacks. Several glanced at Edie when she came into the room, but none said anything to her and no wonder – she looked, at that moment, as though she would bite off the head of anyone who dared!

Red-handed!

Edie slept badly. Her throat was sore, and when she woke up next morning her forehead felt clammy. She was worried – it would be just her luck to get ill now, and be ordered to bed. But once she had got dressed she felt a little better, and went down to breakfast grimly determined not to let the row with Anastasia get in the way of her detective work.

Last night Anastasia's behaviour had seemed so spoilt Edie had almost given up on her. But she knew she couldn't. Somehow the fact Anastasia had seen Dr Browning made Edie certain that her friend was in real danger, and now that Cousin Charles had turned his back on the case she felt that Anastasia needed her more than ever.

She was still suspicious of Miss Mannering, but it

was Dr Browning who worried her more. Everything she had heard about him made her uneasy. Why was he so interested in Prince Stolonov? And as for his having a Russian accent, and enjoying secret meetings with Miss Winifred in the Blue Kettle . . . it was all highly suspicious.

Cousin Charles was no longer her master, but Edie had not forgotten his advice: '*If you can't get at your suspect, look at the people close to them.*' Dr Browning was out of Edie's reach, but she could still investigate Miss Winifred – and she would start by searching her office.

She bided her time until tea, when Miss Winifred was on duty in the dining room, then slipped off alone to the North Tower. It was already dark, and though the corridors were deserted Edie found herself walking on tiptoe, her heart beating faster with every step. She passed Miss Mannering's study, which was a short way down the corridor from Miss Winifred's. The door was closed, and there was no light coming from inside. Miss Winifred's door was the same. Edie feared it might be locked, but when she turned the handle the door swung open.

She crept inside, and found herself in a large, low-ceilinged room, with an oak desk facing her in the centre of it, and two armchairs crouched, phantom-like, on either side of an unlit fire. The curtains had been left open to the moonless sky and the only light was the dim yellow glow from the corridor.

She decided to leave the door ajar, so she would hear if anyone approached, but as she walked to Miss Winifred's desk the only sound was the thumping in her chest. She had borrowed Sally's torch, giving her a half-baked story about wanting to go and look for a book she thought she had left behind on the lacrosse pitch, and she turned it on now and flashed it over the desk. It was tidy, arranged with several stacks of books and two piles of marking covered in Miss Winifred's thin, spidery red pen. There was also a large black diary. Edith opened it, and started skimming hurriedly through the entries for the last few weeks, but they contained only details of Miss Winifred's school timetable.

Then she started work on the drawers. There were six on either side of the desk, each containing thick bundles of letters and papers, and Edie wondered where to begin. She started randomly pulling out documents, scouring them for any mention of Anastasia or Dr Browning's name. But all she found were school reports . . . a bill from Miss Winifred's dentist . . . a listing of the term's lacrosse fixtures. There was also a watch with the name *May Senior* engraved on the back. Edie was puzzled. She did not recognise the name.

Then, in the last drawer but one, she noticed a blue book poking from beneath a jumble of postcards. She pulled it out, and saw the name ANASTASIA STOLONOV engraved in thin gold letters on the cover. It was the missing notebook! She felt a shock of triumph. So it wasn't the Man who had been stealing Anastasia's things – it was Miss Winifred. But it made no sense. Could it be that Miss Winifred was setting out to make Anastasia appear unstable, so that she could be passed into the hands of Dr Browning . . . ? If so, why? Edie's mind started to somersault wildly as she tried to imagine what they were plotting.

Then something else in the drawer caught her eye – a red plastic folder, which had been lying underneath Anastasia's notebook. She took it out. The folder was not labelled and there were only a few loose documents inside. Edie emptied them onto the desk. One was a map, which seemed to be showing the inside of a large building complex – a train station, perhaps, or an airport – but the print was too faint to make out. She glanced at the door, then sat down on Miss Winifred's chair and pored over the map with her torch. It was covered with strange markings and words she did not understand, but she recognised from Anastasia's books that the language was Russian.

She turned hurriedly to the next document. This page bore the logo of a ferry company, and was the confirmation of a booking for a car and three passengers to travel on a night crossing from Ramsgate to Ostend. But it was the passengers' names that made Edie's pulse quicken.

One was Miss Caroline Fotheringay.

The second was Mr Vladimir Britianov. *Britianov . . .* Edith whispered the name out loud, as suddenly Anastasia's casual remark about Dr Browning echoed through her mind . . . '*Lots of Russians working in England use English names . . . his real name's Britianov – I noticed it on a letter on his desk.*'

So Miss Fotheringay knew Dr Browning too.

Edie felt a sudden foreboding. She looked down the page and saw that the crossing was booked for 28

November – tomorrow night; and the ticket was only one-way. Surely Miss Fotheringay didn't intend to abandon the school in the middle of term?

The last passenger was Miss Darya Britianov, who was listed as a child. Edie supposed it must Mr Britianov's daughter. But then she noticed one more item inside the folder – a passport – and when she opened it she saw that it was Darya Britianov who was named inside. But it was the photograph that made Edie's heart stop.

The photograph was of Anastasia.

Edie stared at it wildly, then with a trembling hand she took a piece of paper and copied down the details of the ferry crossing and the registration number of the car, and scrunched the note into her pocket. She returned all the documents to the red folder and replaced it in the drawer, so engrossed she did not hear the door opening behind her. It was not until the lights plunged on that she looked up and saw the tall, grass-like figure of Miss Winifred moving soundlessly towards the desk. Edie sprang from her chair in terror.

'Edith Wilson. What a surprise . . .'

Edie grabbed Anastasia's diary from the desk and staggered backwards.

'Give that to me,' Miss Winifred said. Her voice was quiet, but her face wore the flicker of a violent smile.

Edie knocked into a filing case, and as she stumbled to the floor Miss Winifred snatched the book from her hand.

'What . . . what are you doing? I don't understand . . . what are you doing to her?' Edie cried, her voice choked by fear.

'You are hysterical, Edith,' Miss Winifred said coldly. She reached down and pulled her roughly to her feet, marching her to the desk with her arm twisted tight behind her back.

Edie gasped in pain. Miss Winifred returned the book to its drawer then, with a look of brutal intent, took out a pile of papers and placed them on her desk.

'Miss Fotheringay?' she said, picking up the telephone and talking in a low dramatic voice. 'I'd be grateful if you could come and assist me . . . I have found Edith Wilson in my study – stealing examination papers.'

Uncrackable?

'Of course the child must be expelled,' said Miss Winifred, standing by the window of Miss Fotheringay's study with a wild look on her face.

Miss Fotheringay sat very still behind her desk. 'Diana? What is your view?'

That Miss Mannering had a view could hardly be in doubt. She had arrived in the study shortly after Miss Winifred, not waiting for an invitation before marching in and sitting down stiffly on the sofa. 'There needs to be an investigation, clearly, but we should not be hasty in jumping to conclusions,' she said, without looking in Miss Winifred's direction.

'Don't be ridiculous,' spat Miss Winifred. 'She has been caught red-handed sneaking a peek at examination papers. The girls are all talking about it. We have to make an example of her.'

'How do the girls *know* what she's done?' Miss Mannering asked quietly.

'I-I didn't tell them,' Miss Winifred answered, with an air of sudden confusion. 'But I see that you are determined to play this matter down and I won't stand for it. There has been a great deal of upset in the first-years this term, and I have good reason to believe that Edith Wilson has been behind it all. She's not merely a cheat; she's become obsessed by the poor Stolonov girl, and has been persecuting her under the guise of friendship. It is imperative we have her removed from the school this afternoon. If you won't support me I must offer you my resignation – and I shall file a full report to the governors,' she added breathlessly.

'Please believe me,' Miss Fotheringay said calmly, 'that the last thing I want is to question your judgement—'

'Then perhaps you'll think twice before doing so,' Miss Winifred replied, and abruptly left the room.

'What an extraordinary display,' Miss Mannering said, staring at the slammed door.

Miss Fotheringay's expression was pained. 'She is angry, Diana, and so am I. We have given that child every chance and now for her to reveal herself as a low-grade cheat—'

Miss Mannering snorted. 'I don't believe any of it.'

'What can you mean?'

'I mean, Caroline, that whatever Edith Wilson was doing in Celia's office, she wasn't looking for examination papers. I called in to speak to her in the sickroom on my way here—'

'You—?'

'Yes, Caroline,' Miss Mannering replied sharply. 'I'm afraid I cannot respect your decision to place an unhappy child in solitary confinement.'

'I put her in the sickroom because she had a temperature,' Miss Fotheringay replied defensively. 'Anyway, did you get anywhere?'

'She wouldn't talk to me, if that's what you mean – she doesn't like me,' Miss Mannering said matter-of-factly. 'But when I mentioned the examination papers her expression changed from caginess to confusion. She doesn't seem to understand what she's been accused of. The only thing she seemed interested in was talking to Anastasia. She kept saying her name, begging me to let her see her. There was something in her face, something—' Miss Mannering paused, thoughtful. 'All I can say for certain, Caroline, is that Edith Wilson is a very frightened child.'

'As most children would be, after being caught with exam papers in their hand,' Miss Fotheringay said bluntly. 'As for wanting to see Anastasia, I'm afraid this rather supports Celia's contention that she's obsessed by her.'

'Celia has no proof.'

'She believes she does. Before you arrived she told me she had found something belonging to Anastasia in Edith's bedside table – a glass bird or some such. Edith must have taken it – not to mention all the other things which have been going missing.'

'Anastasia's "losses" pre-date Edith's arrival at the

~ 224 ~

school,' Miss Mannering replied.

'What are you suggesting, Diana?'

'I don't know, Caroline. Only that something isn't right and that you should look into it.'

'But if the child won't talk?'

'She'll talk to you,' Miss Mannering said firmly.

'You're wrong about that. When I took her to the sickbay she wouldn't even look at me. She is an unusually secretive child, Diana.'

'So having failed to subdue her you now wish to wash your hands of her?'

'I didn't say that,' Miss Fotheringay replied. She sat with her hands clasped together to form a church and tapped her lips with the steeple. 'I am simply suggesting that Edith Wilson may be uncrackable.'

Miss Mannering snorted. 'And what about Anastasia?' she demanded, her tone suddenly impatient. 'Do we reckon she's cracked? I gather you've put her in the hands of a shrink.'

'How do you know?' Miss Fotheringay asked sharply.

'Everybody's talking about it. She's being teased for being demented on top of everything else.'

'As I understand it Anastasia specifically requested to see the doctor.'

'*As you understand it?*' Miss Mannering retorted. 'Do you mean that you were not directly involved in her going to see him?'

Miss Fotheringay appeared flustered. 'Not exactly. Celia recommended him. She arranged it all.'

'And have you checked him out?'

'No. But Celia seemed to think very highly of him. Why would she . . . ?' Miss Fotheringay frowned, then let out an exasperated sigh. 'Really, Diana, don't you think I've got enough on my plate.'

'I think you've had Edith Wilson on your plate!' Miss Mannering returned in a stinging tone. 'You have been so preoccupied with that child, it's made you neglect your duties to others. I think it is very peculiar of you, Caroline, to send a disturbed pupil – if she is disturbed – to see a stranger without first checking on his credentials. The mental health world is chock-a-block with cranks and charlatans. Surely *you* don't need *me* to tell you that.'

Miss Fotheringay was silent.

'The least you could do is speak to Helen's mother,' Miss Mannering went on crisply. 'Doesn't she oversee all child psychiatric services in the county?'

'Yes, indeed,' Miss Fotheringay said, a note of irritation in her voice. 'Thank you, Diana. I will call her.'

Miss Mannering looked as though she would like to stay and make sure it was done. Then she seemed to change her mind, and left the room abruptly.

Miss Fotheringay had been standing by her desk, her hand poised on the telephone, but as the door closed she crossed to the sofa, and sat caressing her cat. 'Well, Black Puss,' she murmured, placing a hand under his chin, and turning his face to hers, 'in future we shall have to be more careful.'

'They told me not to let anyone see you,' Matron said, putting down a cup of tea on Edie's bedside table. 'Now why was that, I wonder?'

Edie, who was lying crouched on the pillow, with her knees drawn up to her chin, rolled over and looked at her with the furtive air of a trapped animal.

'Well, it must be something pretty bad,' Matron went on, watching her curiously. 'But between you and me, Edith Wilson, I've never known a school with so many rules. It's a wonder you're not all breaking them all the time.'

Edie pulled herself up, her face clouded with fear. 'Will you help me?' she whispered.

'If I can,' Matron said casually, 'though the chances are—'

'I need to talk to Anastasia. Please – please find her for me.'

Matron shook her head. 'I'm sorry, but I'm under strict instructions. You know what they're like here, love – I don't want to be on the wrong side of those mistresses any more than you do.'

Edie looked at her flatly, before burying her face back in the pillow.

'I could fetch you a book from the library if you tell me what you'd like,' Matron said, but Edie lay motionless.

Matron retreated to her adjoining room, and sank into her rocking chair with a sigh. On the table beside her, resting on a pile of crossword puzzles, was an old Navy flashlight Miss Fotheringay had given her to mend. She picked it up now and turned it on, screwing her eyes with pleasure as its glare filled the dimly lit room. '*I know there's nothing you can't fix*,' Miss Fotheringay had said, smiling, when she had brought it to Matron's room last night.

Torches were one thing. Unhappy children were harder to fix.

She was still deep in thought when the pale, tearful face of Anastasia appeared at the door. 'Hello, dear. What can I do for you?' Matron asked, welcoming her with a smile.

'Have you got Edie in there?' Anastasia asked, nodding towards the sickroom.

'No visitors,' Matron said wearily.

'Oh, please let me, Matron,' Anastasia implored. 'She's been accused of something she didn't do and they're going to send her away and it's all my fault.' Anastasia moved towards the door, but Matron stood up to block her.

'If she's been accused of something she didn't do, then it's Miss Fotheringay you should talk to,' she said firmly.

'Miss Fotheringay won't believe me,' Anastasia said. 'No one believes me in this school, no one—'

'Diddums,' Matron said, producing a tube of toffees from her bulging apron pocket. 'Get out the violins, shall we?'

Anastasia smiled wanly. Then she tried a different tack. 'Darling Matron, *please* let me just say goodbye to Edie,' she began, with a beseeching expression. 'I won't tell anyone you've let me in – please . . . you've always been so kind to me, you're the only one who ever understands . . .'

'Flattery gets you nowhere,' Matron replied, looking amused.

'What about bribery?' Anastasia ventured. 'I'll bring

you the biggest pot of caviar you've ever seen.'

'What sort of fool do you mistake me for? Bribery curdles into blackmail sooner than milk into cream.'

'Not with me,' Anastasia promised.

Matron wrinkled her nose. 'Caviar – revolting stuff. You can leave your over-priced fish eggs at the bottom of your Black Sea. But go on, then. Be quick and then get back where you came from, before you're missed.'

Anastasia threw her arms around her, before slipping into the sickroom and closing the door.

Edie lay curled on the bed, turned to the wall. She had been drifting in and out of sleep, and had no idea how much time had passed when she felt the feather-like touch on her arm.

'Anastasia? Who – who saw you . . . careful, they—'

'Sssh, it's all right, Matron let me through,' Anastasia said, sitting and clutching her hand. 'But I haven't got long. Edie, I'm so sorry – I was horrid yesterday. I—' She stopped. Edie had said nothing, but something in her eyes seemed to tell Anastasia that there was no need of apologies now. 'Oh, Edie, tell me what happened – everyone's saying such awful things.'

'What things?'

'They're saying that you were caught stealing maths papers and that you're going to be expelled – and it's all my fault, Edie, all of it! I should never have let you risk all that just to try and find my notebook.'

Edie shook her head impatiently, lowering her voice to a whisper. 'It wasn't just the notebook I found. Oh,

Anastasia, everything's much worse than we had any idea of. You were right about running away . . . we've got to . . .' Edie had a sudden vision of Anastasia's pale, expressionless face staring from the stranger's passport, and glanced wildly at the door.

'Quick, Edie, tell me what you found.'

Edie swallowed hard, and told her first about the ferry tickets.

Anastasia frowned. 'Britianov? That's Dr Browning's other name.'

Edie nodded.

'Tell me, Edie, what else did you find?' Anastasia asked quietly.

When Edie told her about seeing her photograph inside Darya Britianov's passport, the blood drained from Anastasia's face.

'Kidnap,' she said flatly. She was silent for a moment as the information sank in. 'They all said Mama was paranoid to be so frightened about kidnap, and I thought it too. But now it's happening – and it's Mama's worst nightmare coming true.'

'It won't happen, Anastasia!' Edie said, clutching her arm. 'I won't let it!'

'I'm supposed to be seeing the doctor tomorrow. Miss Winifred's meant to be taking me there after breakfast. I must run away, tonight.'

'We,' Edie said firmly. 'I'm coming too. But where can we go?'

Anastasia looked at her doubtfully. 'Are you sure you want to come? They said— Oh, Edie, you don't look well.'

'I'm fine,' Edie said impatiently, pulling herself up on the pillows. 'Anyway, I can't stay here . . . Miss Winifred knows I'm on to her – though no one will believe me now she's labelled me a cheat.'

Anastasia squeezed her hand. 'Thank you, Edie,' she whispered. 'Now listen,' she went on hurriedly, hearing Matron moving about on the other side of the door. 'There's a barn beyond Helen's tower, I saw it from the top window – it's not far, about half a mile further on. We can sleep there tonight, then tomorrow—' She stopped, seeing Matron's heavy brogue shoe protrude around the edge of the door.

'Plotting your escape?' she asked cheerfully, looking from one to the other. 'What's it to be, rope of sheets out of the window?'

Edie shrank bank into the bed, but Anastasia smiled. 'We thought we'd knock you out with a sleeping draught, Matron, then slip out down the back stairs.'

Matron chortled. 'This one's too worn out to get far,' she said, walking over to the bed and feeling Edie's forehead. 'If you ask me she's coming down with a fever.'

'That'll ruin everything,' Anastasia wailed playfully. 'Pull yourself together, Edie, and make sure to meet me in the hall just when the clock strikes nine.' As she spoke, she stood behind Matron and held up her hands to Edie, showing first nine fingers, then shaking her head vigorously and replacing them with ten.

'Get away with you and all your nonsense,' Matron said fondly, turning round and shooing Anastasia from the room.

Fevered Flight

Edie heard the first rumbling of the storm shortly after nine. It was only hesitant at first – a low growl of thunder and a soft sighing in the trees. But soon the rain was lashing down like gunfire, and the wind rattled the sickroom window in its frame. She lay curled under the bedcovers, wondering if Anastasia would remember to fetch her coat and Wellington boots from the cloakroom, and how long it would take them to reach the barn.

The fields would be turned to bog, and chances were that the barn would be flooded. But the only thing that mattered was escape. As long as they could get away from Knight's Haddon they would be all right . . . they could make for London . . . or the sea . . . they could hide in a train . . . stow away on a ship . . . anything, *anywhere* would be safer than here.

At a quarter to ten she slipped out of bed and silently pulled her school uniform over her nightdress – but not her shoes. Shoes would make too much noise. She would put on her boots when she reached the hall.

When she was dressed she twitched back the curtain and saw a great volt of lightning tear across the sky. For a moment the whole park was lit up like a blasted landscape, its trees bowed against the gale. She drew the curtain shut in fright and stood with her back to the window, drinking in the details of the room. She would never sleep at Knight's Haddon again. She remembered the first night of term, when Miss Fotheringay had appeared in the dormitory . . . and the *exeat* . . . and finding the nightdress on her pillow, and felt a sudden well of grief, not for what she was leaving, but for what she thought she had found.

Another flash of lightning jolted her to her senses. She carefully placed her pillows to resemble a sleeping body and pulled up the covers, standing back to admire her handiwork before letting herself out.

There was a light coming from Matron's room, but Edie heard no sound as she tiptoed past the door. Then she saw the flashlight on the table in the corridor. Remembering the fierce yellow beam it had made when Miss Fotheringay had shone it for her in the bedroom, she took it with her, though she was too afraid switch it on as she fumbled her way down the twisting stone staircase in the pitch darkness. When she reached the corridor she saw a tiny torchlight dancing ahead in the hallway.

She crept on and found Anastasia waiting for her outside the staff cloakroom. She was already dressed in her outdoor clothes, and was holding Edie's coat and boots. 'Quick, put these on,' she whispered urgently. 'The front door's locked, but I've found a window we can undo from the inside. Hey, what's that?'

'Miss Fotheringay's torch,' Edie replied. 'But it's blinding; we can't use it until we're out of sight of the school or someone might see us.' She hurriedly pulled on her clothes, then followed Anastasia into the cloakroom and watched as her friend unbolted the little casement window and pushed it open into the gale.

Edie pulled up a chair and clambered out first. The window was only a couple of metres from the ground, but as she lowered herself into the flower bed below she could feel the storm raging all around, as if she were at the summit of a cliff.

She did not hear Anastasia drop down to the ground behind her; she could only hear the high, howling wind and the rain battering against her hood. She reached out blindly for her friend's arm – talk was impossible. They kept their heads ducked, screwing up their faces against the storm as they staggered across the drive. Anastasia flashed her small torch in front of them, but all they could see was the lashing silver rain.

They found their way across the field and eventually reached the woods, but the bare trees offered little shelter. It was only when she stopped moving that Edie realised her hands were numb, and her body was shaking. She could feel the fever taking its grip.

'How far is the barn?' she asked, as another bolt of lightning shot through the woods.

'We must hurry, Edie,' Anastasia urged. 'The lightning might strike one of the trees.'

'How far . . . the barn?' said Edie again, who could think only of the need to find somewhere to rest.

Anastasia looked at her anxiously. 'We'll go to the tower,' she said suddenly, prising the heavy flashlight from Edie's hands. 'Come on, Edie, it's not far. We can shelter there until the storm's died down – we can get in somehow, we can break a window if we have to.'

'It's too obvious – the tower's the first place they'll think of looking for us.'

'But they won't notice we're gone until the morning, and by that time we'll have moved on,' Anastasia said firmly. 'There's no point trying to reach the barn in this storm. We'll never find it.'

Edie gave in. She felt dead with exhaustion, and was glad to let Anastasia take control.

They tramped on in silence, using the flashlight now to guide them through the sodden woods. Eventually they came to a narrow path, weaving through two thick banks of brambles. Anastasia shone the light upwards and Edie saw the tall stone tower rising through the rain.

Anastasia ran up and rattled the front door. It was locked, and the windows were boarded with wooden shutters. But when they followed the wall around, they saw a small window at the back of the tower whose shutters had been flung open by the storm. Anastasia found a stone and smashed one of the thin glass panes, then carefully reached in her hand and opened the window from inside.

'Wait here,' she shouted. Still clutching the light, she scrambled up, then reappeared at the window and passed out a stool for Edie to climb onto.

Edie heaved herself inside, into a large round room, with chairs and a sofa, all blackened with soot, and a huge stone fireplace with a kettle and some rusty frying pans hanging above it. She looked longingly at the two bunk beds pressed against the wall, covered with charred grey blankets.

Anastasia took in the damage caused by the fire with a small intake of breath, then quickly took charge. 'Change into these,' she said, pulling a damp jersey from a cupboard. 'There are some more blankets in the chest upstairs; I'm going to get some, then we can lie down for a bit before we move on.'

'I'll get them. I'm all right,' Edie protested, but her teeth were chattering.

'Just do what I tell you for once,' Anastasia said, running upstairs.

'You should turn out that light, someone might see it,' Edie called after her feebly. She hardly had the strength to pull on the jersey, and sat on the sofa, burying her hands in it for warmth. She heard Anastasia's footsteps crashing on the stairs, then the creak of a door above.

'Edie, I've found another torch here,' Anastasia shouted down. 'We can take it with us. Now get into bed, and I'll bring you some blankets.'

'I told you, I'm all right,' Edie protested, but her eyes were growing heavy; and while her body was shivering her head felt boiling hot. Then she heard a noise that made her start. She looked about her, confused. It was not the storm she could hear now, but something else . . . a car door slamming . . . voices . . . the sound of a key rattling in a lock . . .

She stood up in fear and stumbled onto the stairs, looking back just in time to see the door of the tower fling open and two tall, raven-like figures lurch into the room.

'Anastasia, come down – it's all right, we're here to help you . . .'

Edie slunk back against the wall in terror. It was Miss Winifred's voice she could hear. Peering from the narrow staircase, she saw the other figure push back the hood of his coat, and fling open his briefcase on the table. It was Dr Browning.

'It's all right, I'll deal with her,' he said calmly, drawing a white packet from his case. 'She won't give us any trouble after this.'

Hide-and-seek

The two girls stood at the top of the stairway, looking at each other in terror.

'Anastasia . . . *Ana – staaa – sia* . . .' Miss Winifred's melodious voice travelled like an icy breeze up the stairs. 'Come down, Anastasia dear . . . Don't be frightened . . . Dr Browning's here . . .'

The doctor called out after her, 'You poor child, you've had a terrible fright. Now you will come down and be a good girl. I am your friend, Anastasia . . . your friend . . .' His voice was heavy and foreign, and menacingly calm.

Edie's eyes spun round the bare stone room in a daze of panic.

'Here, Edie,' Anastasia hissed, tugging her towards the wooden chest beside the window. Its lid was raised, and

Anastasia was still clutching one of the coarse grey blankets she had pulled from it. But there was only room for one of them inside.

'Get in,' Edie mouthed frantically, pushing her from behind.

'What about you?' Anastasia whispered as Edie silently lowered the lid on her.

Edie looked about her helplessly; but there was nowhere else to hide.

'Anastasia . . . come down, dear . . . it's only us . . .'

Edie stood paralysed, listening to the two pairs of footsteps rising up the stairs. Then she saw the stone fireplace, and the chimney gaping above it, pitch black.

She staggered towards it, and hoisted herself up by the jutting bricks. Her hands and feet were stiff with cold, and she could feel the freezing wind whistling down from above, the soot biting her eyes. She struggled higher, stopping only as the voices filled the room below.

'Anastasia . . . come out . . .'

'It's only us, don't be afraid . . .'

Edie clung to the blackened bricks, praying her feet could not be seen. The voices were more urgent now; they had shed their coaxing pretence.

'Where the devil is she?' the doctor snarled.

'She must be here somewhere. Look downstairs again . . . hurry, up can't you . . . if she runs out into that storm we'll never find her. If only you'd come quicker.'

'Don't blame me, woman . . . this was your fault for letting them get away.'

'My fault! If I hadn't checked Anastasia's bed we wouldn't have known that she'd gone at all.'

'It was stupid of us to think we'd find them here – it would have been too easy, they'd have been mad to come.'

'You forget, Vladimir, one of them *is* mad.'

'No, *you* forget,' the doctor said, his voice flat with anger. 'You forget what is true, and what is part of the story you have made up. I am afraid, I am very afraid, that you are the one who is mad.'

Edie swallowed hard. The soot was cloying in her throat, and she feared she would give herself away by choking. Miss Winifred, mad! That would finally make sense of some of what was happening.

'They'll be here,' Miss Winifred said, her voice dreamy, as if talking to herself. 'Little Ansti loved this tower. She loved coming here . . .'

The doctor snorted. 'Her friend would never have let her come.'

'The friend is an irrelevance,' Miss Winifred said. 'It's Ansti who matters . . . poor, rich little Ansti. And I know she's here, Vladimir, I can smell her . . . I know she's here . . .'

The friend is an irrelevance.

'The chest! Look in the chest!' Edie heard Dr Browning cry.

There was a creak, and a muffled shriek, then Miss Winifred's sweet, nightmarish voice fluted up the chimney:

'It's all right, dear, it's only us . . . only us . . .'

*

When at last Edie crawled down into the room she saw that the storm had stopped. Everything was calm and still. There was no sound save for the smooth rush of water overflowing from the gutters on the roof, and the wind moving softly in the treetops.

Miss Fotheringay's flashlight was lying on the floor. She picked it up and staggered downstairs where she found the door to the tower swinging open into the night – they had obviously left in a hurry. She went to shut it, and then it was that her eye fell on a small pigskin handbag lying next to the door. She recognised it as belonging to Miss Winifred and opened it at once, smearing soot marks all over its pale pink lining as she scrabbled inside.

She saw a plastic envelope and seized it, prising it open with shaking hands. When she saw the tickets for the ferry crossing her heart gave a beat of triumph. She slipped them into the pocket of her overcoat before shoving the envelope back into the bag. She was just continuing her search when she heard the sound of a car outside. She leapt up, dropping the bag on the floor where she had found it, and crouched behind an armchair, trembling.

There was a rush of cold air as the door flung open, then a hurried click of heels on the stone floor.

'Here it is!' Miss Winifred's voice sounded relieved. 'It's all right, Vlad, I'm coming. It's . . . *What the—*'

The voice went silent as the footsteps came closer. Edie closed her eyes against the horror, then felt her ankle being lifted off the ground.

'Edith Wilson! We meet again.'

Edie looked up to see Miss Winifred staring down at her, dressed in a mackintosh of lurid green. In a moment of terrified delirium, Edie saw again the pretty young mistress standing over her desk on the first day of term, and the delicate white hand tracing across the page of her exercise book as she helped her with her sums. Now that same woman's features were alight with frenzied malice.

'Deserted your friend at the last minute, I see. What a bore. You'll have to come with us now. What a pity you didn't keep your nose out of what isn't really your business.'

'Where is she?' Edie demanded, in a voice that sounded braver than she felt.

'Anastasia? Don't you think it's a little late to be asking that now?' Miss Winifred spat.

'What have you done with her?'

'I've chopped her up into dainty morsels and left her to marinate in a cooking pot in the boot of the car. I could feed you little bits of her as we speed along. You'd like that, wouldn't you, Edith Wilson? I've watched you watching her. You're obsessed with her. You'd like to eat her and then become her.' Miss Winifred arched her back, her mackintosh shimmering. She was like a garish snake, leaking poison, and Edie saw she had passed some invisible point of control.

'Why are you doing this? What's it about?'

'It's about to make me very rich,' Miss Winifred replied, playing with the tips of her long, thin fingers.

Then, without taking her eyes from Edie's face, she called out, throwing her voice behind her, 'Vlad, I'm afraid there's a hitch. Nothing that one of your little injections won't sort . . .'

'No!' Edie cried.

Miss Winifred laughed. 'Ah! At last I have found your weak spot. I knew you would have one. So, Edith the Brave doesn't like needles.'

Edie stood up, and edged away from her.

'Vlad! Come in here, at once.'

Edie looked up and saw that the doctor had appeared in the doorway. He said nothing, but stood there stooped and motionless, sunken eyes staring from a hatchet face.

'It's Ansti's little friend. She's hysterical. Deal with her, Vladimir,' Miss Winifred said, her voice high and trembling.

Edie saw as if in slow motion the doctor lift his briefcase, and lay it on the chest by the door. He drew a transparent packet from within and ripped it open. She moved her lips to form a cry of protest – 'No!' – but the sound that emerged was a strangled yelp.

'Come here, Edith, don't mess about or this could get nasty,' Miss Winifred said, stepping towards her with her hand outstretched.

'*No!*' This time Edie's voice was clear, a terrified, splintering shriek.

'Get her!'

Edie heard the alarm in the doctor's voice, the hissed warning, and something in it gave her strength. Miss

Winifred made to grab her but Edie sprang sideways, then picked up a wooden stool and hurled it at her wildly. Miss Winifred gave a startled cry, ducking as the stool veered past her and crashed against the wall.

'It's all right, I've got her,' the doctor said, his voice heavy as a stone.

Edie was aware of him advancing towards her, and for a split second stood immobile, mesmerised by the needle in his hand. Then she had a vision of Anastasia, lying unconscious in the back of the car, and as the doctor held up his needle she hurtled past him with a cry.

'Come here!' he shouted, lunging after her as she flew like a dervish through the open door.

Edie heard a crash behind her, but kept her head bent and ran on, sprinting round the side of the tower and into the woods. It was pitch black, and she could feel the fever seizing her body as she tore on, wet branches slashing at her face. Then she saw torchlight dancing in the trees, and heard voices rising behind her:

'Look on the road!'

'Shut up, for Christ's sake!'

'Here!'

Edie ran faster, but the trees were thinning, and in the moonlight she could see a field opening out ahead. She didn't dare leave the cover of the woods, and in her confusion she turned and ran left then right.

'Quick, over there!'

It was Miss Winifred's voice this time, and now there were two torch beams slipping after her, making silver, ghost-like circles in the trees. One of them shone along the ground just metres from where Edie was standing, showing a ditch with a steep bank grown thick with brambles, veering down into a black pit.

'Edith, come here. Stop this nonsense at once and we won't hurt you . . . *we won't hurt you . . .*'

Miss Winifred's voice was the last thing Edie heard as she flung herself down in the ditch. A wall of soft earth collapsed underneath her as she rolled down the bank, then she stifled a shriek as she plummeted down into a squelch of mud. She could hear footsteps rustling in the leaves above her, and Miss Winifred's thin voice calling into the wind:

'Edith . . . Where *a-rrrrre* you? Where *a-rrrrrre* you?'

Edie lay motionless in the ditch, and held her breath in terror. There were more footsteps, heavier this time, then she saw a stick smack down into the mud, tossed from the bank above.

'Find her.' The doctor's voice was so close Edie could hear his breath – then to her horror she saw a torch beam slip over the opposite bank. She waited, rigid, almost expecting him to come tumbling on top of her. 'Look along the ditch, I'll see if she's gone back to the road.'

'What if she's got into the field?'

'I don't care where she's gone. Just get her back.'

There was more scuffling, and the torch beam slipped along the bank again, circling so close it almost touched Edie's foot, then it vanished and the voices became muffled, as if they'd moved away. Edie lay very still, straining to hear, but soon the footsteps and the voices had faded entirely, and the only sound was the low murmur of the wind. She could not move. But then she saw the woods flood with light and heard a car starting, and a will tore through her like a scream. She scrambled from the ditch, clawing frantically through the brambles – she would hurl herself on the bonnet, she would scratch out their eyes . . . *It won't happen, Anastasia! I won't let it!* That's what she'd promised.

But by the time she staggered into the wood the doctor's car had gone.

A Piece of the Puzzle

Edie stood staring at the empty road, soaked and shivering. Edith the Brave, who wasn't afraid of anyone, had saved herself and let Anastasia down.

An owl screeched through her despair. She could not afford to give up now. She alone knew where the kidnap party was headed. For a moment she thought wildly of trying to hitch a lift to the ferry, but she knew she would never get there in time. The ferry they were booked to travel on was leaving that night. She must get to the village and alert the police, but her strength was ebbing.

She didn't dare go along the lane, imagining that the car might be lying in wait for her round a bend. She would have to double back through the wood, past the tower, then skirt along the edge of the park. She stumbled on, stopping only now and again to catch her breath, slumped against a tree. She wondered how long it would take a search party to find her in the woods, and how far, by then, Anastasia would have been taken. It was Miss Fotheringay who was booked to travel with her to Ostend; Edie wondered, vaguely, whether Miss Winifred would be going too.

Thinking of Miss Fotheringay she had a sudden, delirious vision of the little bedroom in the West Tower, where she had slept under a warm duvet. She closed her eyes as other memories crowded her mind . . . of the hot water running in the bath . . . of Miss Fotheringay's mother, of her father, and of their voices floating up to her through the open window.

Christmas, Edie remembered confusedly . . . they had been talking about Christmas.

'*I hope you're still coming to France, dear . . . have you booked your ticket?*'

Edie had an image of the Fotheringays sitting around a long table, with candles and presents, and holly, and light flickering from the fire. She thought of Mr Fotheringay's kind, wrinkled face, and wondered if he knew his daughter was a kidnapper.

The voices rang on, hazily . . .

'*Yes, yes, I'm coming . . . I must check my new passport . . . it still hasn't arrived . . . they said it had been signed for . . . there must have been some mistake . . . some mistake . . .*'

Edie was in sight of the tower now, but she stopped as a thought flashed with sudden clarity through her fevered brain. *Some mistake . . .* Could Edie have been the one mistaken? Could Miss Winifred have intercepted

Miss Fotheringay's passport? Her mind raced wildly through the fragments of evidence she had found, the strange conversations she had overheard. Her mother . . . what had Miss Fotheringay done to her mother? She was too weak to make sense of it all, but whichever turn her thoughts took, her mind kept veering back to Miss Fotheringay's passport. Why hadn't Edie seen it before? Miss Fotheringay had been duped.

She must reach her. But how? Her legs were buckling beneath her, and she knew she would never make it back to the school.

As she stood peering through the trees another muddled image played before her, of Miss Fotheringay standing by her bedroom window, pointing to the tower over the treetops, and showing her the old ship's light. *'Do you know how to make the SOS signal, Edith? Always useful to know. Three short flashes . . .'* Edie knew what she must do.

She dragged herself inside the tower and up the stairs. Miss Fotheringay's flashlight was lying where Anastasia had left it, on the floor beside the chest. It felt as heavy as a concrete slab when Edie picked it up.

She could no longer stand. She dropped to her knees and crawled up the final flight of stairs until she reached the small wooden gallery at the top of the tower. When she pushed open the shutters the sky had cleared. She peered beyond the woods, across the park, and in the moonlight saw the dim silhouette of the school and a prick of light coming from a window in the West Tower.

Miss Fotheringay must be awake – but would she see? With a shaking hand, she pushed the light out of the window, and flashed it three times . . . three short, three long, three short . . .

Miss Fotheringay slept through her alarm. She was woken at half past seven by the telephone ringing beside her bed.

'Caroline? It's Janet Greyling here. I'm sorry to call so early but I wanted to fill you in on Doctor Browning. I'm in the hospital all day and thought I might not get a chance.'

'Not early at all,' Miss Fotheringay said blearily, getting out of bed with the telephone clutched under her chin.

'Did Miss Winifred say where she picked him up?'

'N-no,' Miss Fotheringay replied cagily, detecting something ominous in her friend's enquiry. 'But she assured me he was highly regarded in his field—'

'Well, I don't know where she got that from. I can find no record of a Doctor Browning on the medical register and the clinic you mentioned was closed two years ago.'

Miss Fotheringay turned, frowning, to the window, as the memory of her disturbed night came back to her. She had drifted in and out of sleep, her anxieties about Edith Wilson accompanied by the sound of a raging storm. But then something else had woken her . . . she remembered walking to the window and peering out into a black, motionless night. The storm, she supposed, had been a dream . . . there had been nothing stirring in the deep void of darkness, only the distant, rhythmic flicker of a light . . .

'Thank you, Janet,' she said, her mouth hardening. 'I will follow this up with Miss Winifred.'

Miss Fotheringay dressed quickly, driven by a confused sense of urgency. She must find Miss Winifred at once, and challenge her about Dr Browning. And then Edith, she must deal with Edith.

As she emerged into the corridor she saw Matron hurrying towards her, looking unusually harassed. 'And how is your charge this morning?' Miss Fotheringay asked, trying to sound calmer than she felt.

'She isn't,' Matron replied.

'What?'

'I mean, she's gone. Vamoosed. I looked in on her at seven and thought I'd let her sleep on, but when I went back a few minutes ago I found the bed was empty – pillows under the blankets, Headmistress, oldest trick in the book.'

'You mean—'

'She won't have gone far. She was coming down with a fever last night, wasn't fit to walk across the courtyard when I tucked her in. I'll get the doctor out as soon as we find her. It's the flu, or worse if you ask me.'

'Worse?'

Matron nodded. 'She dozed off for a bit before supper and when she woke she was all in a muddle – rambling on about this and that. Delirious, I'd say, though she was better when she'd had some soup.'

'What was she saying?' Miss Fotheringay asked.

Matron looked vague. 'Just repeating names for the most of it . . . Babka, that's her grandmother, I think. And her mother . . . *She knew my mother* – that's what she kept saying, but I couldn't get out of her what she meant.

'Then she started off on a madcap kidnap story. Must have been some book she'd been reading, but she woke up thinking Anastasia was in danger. *Don't let them take her away* . . . Poor child. She didn't know if she was coming or going.'

They were interrupted by Miss Mannering, looking unusually flushed.

'Anastasia's gone,' she said.

'*Anastasia?*' Matron repeated stupidly.

'Run away, by the looks of it,' Miss Mannering confirmed.

Miss Fotheringay looked momentarily blank, as if struggling to take this in. 'Have you seen Miss Winifred?' she asked.

'No show,' Miss Mannering replied. 'And she hasn't rung in. I'd better go and take charge of the lower school. But meanwhile—'

'Wait – Diana,' Miss Fotheringay said. 'Matron says Edith is missing too.'

Miss Mannering's face froze.

'So they weren't joking after all,' Matron murmured – then coloured as both mistresses turned to her sharply.

'What do you mean exactly?' Miss Fotheringay asked.

Matron shifted uncomfortably. 'Nothing . . . it's just . . . well, I don't know, do I, but it is true that Anastasia came to see Edith last night—'

'Came to see her?' Miss Mannering demanded. 'Why didn't you tell us?'

'I'm telling you now,' Matron said tartly, but her tone changed when she saw the headmistress's expression. 'Anastasia said to Edith to meet in the hall when the clock struck nine, which I took to be a joke,' she volunteered, 'but in the light of current developments perhaps it wasn't.'

'We'd better call the police straightaway,' Miss Mannering said briskly. 'They will want to talk to you—'

'I'll thank you for not treating me like a criminal,' Matron retorted. 'It's Miss Winifred they should talk to, she's the one—' Matron stopped.

'The one who what?' Miss Fotheringay asked, throwing her deputy a warning glance.

Matron shrugged. 'She's the one who likes to go through other people's post.'

Miss Winifred's rooms in the East Tower had been deserted, drawers left open, coat hangers slung in haste across the unmade bed. The head of Lower School would not be coming back.

It was Miss Mannering who called the police and assisted as the search began, first pointing out the gaping window in the staff cloakroom.

Miss Fotheringay meanwhile had set out by herself for Helen's tower. As she hurried across the frosted courtyard she thought again of the rhythmic flashing of the light in the night, and her pace quickened.

The day had dawned clear and still. There was no breath of wind, and a pale cloak of white sunlight had spread across the park. But there was debris in the drive – some bits of broken boarding and tarpaulin sheets, flung out by the gale; and a rowan tree had been uprooted in the field. Miss Fotheringay had not dreamt it; the storm had been real.

As she entered the woods she broke into a run, haunted by a sudden image of Edith and Anastasia sitting in the back of a featureless car, being driven across an unknown landscape, towards an unknown place.

The tower door was swinging open when she arrived. When she entered she saw the shattered glass from the broken window and a sodden overcoat flung across the sofa. Then she saw muddy black footprints, and followed them up the stairs.

She found Edie lying on the floor of the gallery, curled up in a filthy, shivering ball. When Miss Fotheringay knelt down beside her the child started and raised a face blackened with soot, fever-bright eyes wild with fear. Miss Fotheringay took off her coat and tried to wrap it round her, but Edie pushed her away with a shriek.

'It's all right, Edith, I'm—' Miss Fotheringay began, but Edie was shaking her head, her eyes darting violently.

'The ship . . .' she said, through chattering teeth. 'They're taking her on a ship . . . from Ramsgate . . .' Trembling, she reached into her pocket and pressed the ferry tickets into Miss Fotheringay's hand.

Matron Takes Charge

'You should take a break, Headmistress,' Matron said, busying herself around the bed.

Miss Fotheringay continued to gaze at the patient, and made no reply.

'Temperature's gone down a little,' Matron muttered, holding the thermometer up to the light.

Miss Fotheringay raised an exhausted, enquiring face. Her expression had none of its usual authority – in the sickroom, Matron's rule was absolute.

'Thirty-nine,' Matron announced, making a note on her chart. 'I reckon she'll live another day. But as for you . . .' Matron stretched out a fat arm to replace the file on the shelf above the bed, then turned to Miss Fotheringay and looked at her critically. 'You'll forgive my saying it, Headmistress, but you have a duty to look after yourself.

I've got enough on my plate nursing young Miss Wilson here – I don't want a second invalid on my hands.'

Miss Fotheringay accepted this rebuke with a weak smile. It was three days since Edith had been discovered, feverish, in the tower. She had pneumonia. Every night since the girl had come back from hospital, the headmistress had kept a vigil by her bed, holding the thin hand that lay pale and motionless on the stiff cotton covers, snatching fitful bursts of sleep in the high-backed chair.

This morning she had gone straight from the sick-room to assembly, without even changing her clothes. At first she had tried to delegate the running of the school to Miss Mannering. But the deputy headmistress had been firm: 'Edith Wilson is not dying, and nor is she the only pupil in this school. The girls are over-excited, Caroline. They need you to steer them back to normality.'

But Miss Fotheringay sensed she was no longer at the helm. Since the news of Miss Winifred's arrest at Ramsgate it seemed as though every girl had become part of a secretive, whispering huddle. Caroline Fotheringay walked among her pupils with a feeling of eerie detachment, as though she herself were the object of their curiosity. She was always glad when evening came and she could return to Edie's bedside.

'You don't think she'll wake up again soon?' she asked anxiously.

'If she does I'll call you,' Matron replied.

'Do you know what happened at the deathbed of

Lenin's mother-in-law?' Miss Fotheringay asked, slowly gathering her things.

'I don't think I do,' Matron replied.

'His wife had sat up with her mother for several nights and Lenin offered to relieve her. The wife agreed to sleep, so long as Lenin promised to wake her if her mother should need her. The next morning the wife woke up and said, "How's Mother?" and Lenin said, "Mother's dead". The wife said, "Why didn't you wake me?" and Lenin said, "She didn't need you."'

Matron looked bemused. 'That's a funny story to bring up now,' she said.

'It's just a funny story full stop. Forget I told it.'

But Matron would not forget. She had always been rather in awe of the head. Now she was coming to see her as something of a card.

Miss Fotheringay stood up and walked a little stiffly to the door. But as she was letting herself out she heard a croak from the bed and turned round to see that Edie had opened her eyes.

'What day is it?' the child asked weakly, looking about her in surprise.

Miss Fotheringay made to return to her chair, but Matron raised a cautioning hand. 'Let me talk to her,' she murmured. 'You know how confused she becomes around you.'

Miss Fotheringay could not deny it. Several times already Edie had opened her eyes to find her sitting by the bed, and her pale face had flooded with apparent relief before she had turned away, in seeming remembrance of some shadow.

'It's Sunday,' Matron said, leaning over to straighten her sheets. 'Now what would you be after me getting you, dear?'

'Sunday!' Edie repeated, jerking herself upright and looking around her wildly. 'But Anastasia . . .'

She did not appear to take in Miss Fotheringay, who was standing inside the door, biting her finger, willing herself not to speak.

'I'm after telling you that already, dear, Anastasia's here, back at school, safe and well – and all thanks to you,' Matron said cheerfully, as if reporting on the weather.

'But . . . if she's here, then why . . . why *isn't* she here?' Edie stammered.

'Are we saying that we would like to *see* Anastasia?'

'But that *is* what I said,' murmured Edie in a confused, querulous voice. 'Isn't it?'

'She's out having lunch with her father but I'll make sure she comes to see you as soon as she's back.'

Edie looked momentarily reassured.

'Now then,' Matron went on, encouraged, 'if you're up to it, I've got Miss Fotheringay here to see you.' She gestured to Miss Fotheringay as she spoke. But Edie sank back on the pillow and pulled the covers over her head.

When Miss Fotheringay returned to her study her telephone was flashing with messages. She listened to them with her pen idle in her hand; there was nothing that couldn't wait. But then a familiar drawl made her fist clench.

'Caro? Is it naughty to call you that? . . . Your secretary didn't seem to like it – Miss Fotheringay this, Miss Fotheringay that – but I'm afraid I can't get all trembly about a headmistress at my age. I understand my niece is in bed but out of danger. Good . . . I just wanted to say that I've talked to my doctor and he advised that she's much better off staying at school . . . madness to move her, he said, until she's completely—'

Miss Fotheringay stabbed the machine into silence. She knew that she would have to deal with Sophia Fairlight sooner rather than later. First, though, she had to persuade Edith to talk to her. She was interrupted by a knock on the door, followed by the tall, upright form of Prince Stolonov.

'I took the liberty . . .' he began, with a slight bow.

'Please,' Miss Fotheringay said, rising from her desk with an apprehensive smile. The prince had already phoned her angrily. Had the school vetted Miss Winifred's job application more closely, he had said, they would have discovered that she was going under an assumed identity. Her real name was May Senior, and she had once briefly been employed in Prince Stolonov's Paris office, before one of his security team had discovered that she had a previous conviction for fraud. Miss Fotheringay's contrition had been sincere. But even so, she was in no mood for another reprimand. 'Is Anastasia well?'

The prince gave a wry smile. 'She seems completely

recovered from her adventure – well enough to harangue her old papa over lunch. I have come to you, Miss Fotheringay, with an apology. Anastasia was horrified to hear that I had accused you of carelessness. She points out that I was the negligent one, not believing my own daughter's story.'

Miss Fotheringay looked relieved. 'Your anger was perfectly understandable. I am sure that in your position I—'

The prince waved his hand dismissively. 'Anastasia and Edith are safe. Miss Winifred and her accomplice are in the hands of the police. And you have assured me that you will never again send a girl to see a doctor, real or so-called, without informing her parents. For now there is no more to be said. But I think we are at least agreed on one thing – that the girl Edith deserves a medal.'

Miss Fotheringay looked at him questioningly. Charles had arrived with the prince on the day Anastasia was found, and they had explained to her how Edith had come to be placed in the school. They had told the story without apology – like two proud schoolboys recounting how they had won a game. They seemed to feel vindicated by the fact that Edith had done such a good job. 'I'd employ her again,' Charles had joked. Miss Fotheringay had said nothing.

'But I suspect she is not especially interested in medals,' the prince went on ponderously, 'and while I believe that Ansti has made her a present of a little trinket I left with her – a glass bird – I would like to give some more practical mark of my appreciation.

'Anastasia, of course, never thinks of the practical details of school fees. She is not aware that I am responsible for Edith's.'

'Nor was I until this week,' said Miss Fotheringay. 'The funds were transferred from Mr Rodriguez's bank account.'

The prince shrugged, showing a hint of impatience. 'It's a small matter, but the point is I should like to make it a permanent arrangement. We can't have her leaving now – Anastasia would be distraught.'

Miss Fotheringay had been privately concerned that the prince might insist Anastasia return to Knight's Haddon next term with a private bodyguard – an arrangement she felt all the girls would find unsettling. But so far he had made no mention of it. And when Anastasia's mother had descended on the school a few days earlier, the subject of future security arrangements had not arisen. She had stayed long enough only to take her daughter out to tea and cross swords with the prince, before hurtling back to Yorkshire in a storm of accusations.

'You can't keep Edith here as Anastasia's bodyguard,' she said bluntly.

The prince laughed. 'I don't think either of them would want that. I have no hidden agenda, Miss Fotheringay – just a desire to keep Edith here as Anastasia's friend. And I am hoping that there won't be any further need for private arrangements of that kind.' He paused, and looked at her with a hint of challenge:

'My security team has had all your remaining staff thoroughly vetted. Including yourself.'

Miss Fotheringay inclined her head. Her expression was inscrutable. 'It is a generous offer,' she said after a pause.

'It is the least I can do,' the prince insisted. 'And you will ensure that I remain anonymous as her benefactor?'

'I think that can be arranged.'

'But you still seem uncertain. You think her guardian might not agree?'

'Sophia Fairlight? Oh, no – she'll be delighted,' Miss Fotheringay said. 'It's more—'

The prince looked at her expectantly. 'More?'

'It's Edith,' she said. 'First I have to make sure that she wants to stay.'

30
KNIGHT'S HADDON

Behind the Headlines

Edie woke to the familiar sound of a bell. Startled, she pushed back the covers, looking about her in surprise. It was dark outside, and in the thin orange glow of the bedside lamp the furniture looked eerie and unfamiliar.

She saw the plastic trolley by her bed and wondered if she was in Babka's room at the nursing home. 'Babka,' she croaked – but it was Anastasia's voice she heard:

'You can't keep me from her any longer. You can't, you can't! I know she's better because Helen heard Miss Mannering say so.'

'Just wait—' Matron protested, as the door opened and Anastasia ran in. Her face was flushed and excited, but seeing Edie her expression turned to dismay.

'Oh, Edie,' she gasped, sinking into the chair by the

bed and clutching her hand. 'You look awful.'

'Not dead yet,' Edie smiled.

The two friends sat in silence, looking at one another as if noticing things they had never seen before.

'Water,' Edie whispered at last, pointing to the bedside table where there was a jug and a glass. There was also a forest of get well cards, and the little glass bird perched among them, its violet eyes gleaming.

Anastasia filled a glass, and gently raised Edie's head on the pillow, then held it to her lips. 'Tell me what happened after they took you from the tower,' Edie asked finally, waving the glass away.

'I can't really – not all of it, anyway,' Anastasia said simply. 'They say I was unconscious for nearly three hours. And when I woke up the first thing I heard was your name. They were arguing – Miss Winifred and the doctor – and it was all about you, Edie, they were talking about you.' A shadow passed over Anastasia's face. 'Actually, Papa says it's best if I don't talk about it. Do you mind?'

Edie thought that perhaps she did mind, but lacked the strength to say so.

'Thank you for not making me,' Anastasia said. 'Papa said it was better if I didn't think about it. That I would forget quicker. Papa thinks the world of you, by the way.'

'He doesn't know me,' said Edie quietly.

'He knows that it was *you* who saved me. Do you remember anything? Like Miss Fotheringay finding you in the tower, and you giving her the ferry tickets – that's how the police caught up with us.'

Edie frowned, wishing she could find a way through the haze of images which kept returning to her . . . She remembered the storm, and the voices floating up the narrow stairway, and the soot choking her in the chimney. Then she remembered lying in a freezing ball by the window, and the relief when she had looked up into Miss Fotheringay's eyes.

But today Edie had buried herself under the covers, and driven Miss Fotheringay away. She tried to push the rush of confused thoughts from her mind, listening as Anastasia told her how her father had arrived at the school by helicopter and tried to take her away at once.

'He was on a plane to Mexico when it happened. He got the news as soon as he landed, then he had to turn round and fly all the way back again, and by the time he got back to England I'd left the hospital and was back at school. But I refused to go with him. I wasn't going to leave you here and the doctor said you couldn't be moved. So then Papa took rooms at the Old Stoke in Oxford because he said he couldn't bear to let me out of his sight. Charles stayed a night and we all had supper together – and honestly, Edie, from the way he was talking, anyone would have thought he'd masterminded the whole rescue himself. I had to remind him that he'd called you off the job.'

'What did he say?'

'He just laughed and said that I was a minx, and you were his blood relation, so of course you didn't give up.'

'But that's so . . .' said Edie in a choked voice.

'I know,' Anastasia said cheerfully. 'Grown-ups, eh? Papa's also trying to claim some credit. He says that people always laugh at him for being over-protective, but wasn't it just as well that he'd employed a spy to keep an eye on me because if he hadn't . . .' Anastasia looked at Edie with a grateful smile. 'Well, he says it doesn't bear thinking about.'

'But he stopped believing in you.'

'I know, and you wouldn't believe how sorry he is. He's promised he'll never doubt me again. Oh, Edie, just think of the tricks we can play. We can start as soon as you're better. Papa's going to stay in Oxford until the end of term!'

Edie looked at her friend sadly. Her own mind was still in chaos, but Anastasia seemed to have put all the trouble behind her, as if it had just been a scene in a play.

'You've been *so* ill, Edie, we had to pray for you in assembly. Even Phoebe looked quite solemn about it. And then in history Miss Mannering wrote "pneumonia" on the blackboard, and only half the class knew what it was. I'd heard of it – Mummy had it once – but I thought it was spelt like "new money", with an "a" on the end. We were allowed to spend the whole lesson writing cards to you, and then I was allowed to bring them up to the sickroom – Birdy came too, making her a sort of carrier-pigeon – and when I got here I found Helen was dropping off a card of her own.'

'Has the play happened?'

Anastasia shook her head. 'It's been cancelled until

next term. I said Portia couldn't possibly go on without her maid.'

'*Next* term,' Edie murmured.

'That's right, in the second or third week . . . that's what Helen said,' Anastasia went on eagerly. 'And the other years are delaying their plays too – they'll all be judged together. Just think, Edie, everything's being held over, just for you.'

Edie turned her head. It was not Anastasia's voice she heard now, but that of Lyle, calling after her in the woods: '*If you hate us, go. Go on, run away . . .*' Edie had run, but now her job was over. She wasn't needed at Knight's Haddon any more.

'But next term . . .' she began.

'Next term what?' came a quiet voice, and Edie looked up to see the tall angular form of Miss Fotheringay advancing towards the foot of the bed.

'The headmistress has been waiting to speak to you for days now,' Matron said. 'Do you feel well enough for it, duck, or shall I tell her to go?'

'I can talk now if – if you like,' Edie said to Miss Fotheringay, smiling uncertainly at Matron's cheek.

'I hope that doesn't mean *I* have to go away too,' Anastasia moaned, seeming quite unabashed by the headmistress's presence.

'I am afraid it does,' Matron said firmly. 'One person at a time. Doctor's orders. Now hurry along or you'll be late for supper. Or is Daddy taking us somewhere fancy again?'

'Don't be horrid,' Anastasia retorted playfully. 'Papa

can't help it that he spoils me.'

'I think that may be true,' Miss Fotheringay murmured, as she took Anastasia's place by the bed. 'Now what can I get you, my dear,' she asked Edie. 'Some tea?'

Edie shook her head, both pleased and embarrassed at this unaccustomed endearment. Miss Fotheringay looked at her kindly, but even when the others had gone she did not speak.

'It's not very easy to talk,' Edie said faintly, wondering if she were supposed to account for what had happened.

'I know that,' Miss Fotheringay replied. 'It's my turn to talk, and there are things I should have told you long before now. But I might begin by saying that you are the bravest child I've ever met. Or perhaps,' she added thoughtfully, 'there is one other person who was your match.'

'It was much worse for Anastasia,' Edie began earnestly. 'She—'

'I'm not talking about Anastasia. She had no choice but to be involved in the drama. You chose to help her. I'm just so sorry that you couldn't trust me.'

'I – I did,' Edie protested. 'I mean, I could . . . but then—' She faltered, as Babka's hateful words came flooding back: '*With friends like those, who needs enemies? She said she was a dangerous woman, Editha. Her urge to control was out of control. A dangerous woman.*'

'You discovered that I had not been straight with you?' Miss Fotheringay suggested.

'I know that you knew my mother,' Edie said, hearing the accusation in her voice. 'I found out that weekend, when your parents came. I didn't mean to eavesdrop but your mother talked so loudly I couldn't help it. I was excited, but I wondered why you hadn't told me, especially after all the things we'd talked about. Then the next day I asked Babka and she said—' She stopped, at the end of voice and strength. 'It doesn't matter, anyway,' she said, in a quite different tone.

'Of course it matters,' Miss Fotheringay said fiercely. 'And now, Edith, you must listen to what I have to say.'

Edie looked at her headmistress, and noted the flushed cheeks and the imperious light in her eyes, and she felt a strength come to her from she knew not where. 'Why must I?' she cried. 'I don't want to hear about my mother from you! I thought I did but I don't, not any more. I've built up a picture of her, you see, and it's all I've got and I don't want to let it go.'

'And I don't want to take anything away from you, Edith, except—'

'Then don't!' Edie said, with sudden violence. 'Don't talk to me about my mother! I don't want to listen and you can't make me.'

For a moment Miss Fotheringay looked angry. Then she got up and walked to the window. 'You win,' she said, lowering her eyes. 'For now.'

Edie sank back on her pillows. 'D-did Miss Winifred light the fire in Helen's tower?' She wanted suddenly to bring Miss Fotheringay back.

'Yes,' the headmistress replied, without turning round. 'It was part of her plan to make Anastasia look as though she needed help. Ah,' she added, pressing her face against the glass. 'The police have just found another journalist lurking in the bushes.'

'A journalist?' Edie asked in surprise.

'The place has been swarming with them. *Russian Princess in Boarding School Kidnap Plot.* Pretty good headline, wouldn't you say?'

'I suppose so, although . . .'

'What?'

'Is that the whole story? I mean, if Miss Winifred and the doctor wanted to kidnap Anastasia, why didn't they just snatch her? Why did they first have to make her appear mad?'

'Time, Edith. Time explains everything. If they'd snatched her in the village we'd have alerted the police within minutes. They needed the alibi of the doctor's appointment to give them time to get to the coast. But maybe something else will emerge at the trial. You are quite right to look behind the headlines.' Miss Fotheringay turned to face her. 'It is what your mother always did,' she said, in a voice that was almost harsh.

'I – I know . . .'

'Edith, if you would only—'

'No!' Edie cried, stumbling into the speech she had rehearsed in her head. 'I know that you and my mother hated each other, and I don't want to hear about it. It doesn't mean that I have to hate you. I . . . I don't hate you . . . I . . .'

Edie saw an expression of puzzled horror on Miss Fotheringay's face, but she went on, fitfully: 'J-just because you hated my mother it doesn't mean that I have to stop loving her—'

'Hated her?' Miss Fotheringay cried. 'I didn't hate your mother! I loved her! She was the best friend I ever had!'

Edie looked at her headmistress in astonishment. She wondered if it was some sort of cruel jest, but Miss Fotheringay returned her stare with one of cool perturbation. Her eyes were bright and her cheeks even redder than before, but when she spoke her voice was steady.

'It's true that we quarrelled. And the fact we didn't – *I* didn't – put things right before your mother was killed is my greatest regret.'

'What – what did you quarrel about?'

'Risk,' Miss Fotheringay answered gravely. 'We quarrelled about risk. Now, will you let me tell you the story?'

Miss Fotheringay paced the length of the room, as if winding herself up to speak. Edie did not hear the deep intake of breath, or see the tightening of her eyes. By the time the headmistress returned to her seat by the bed her face was composed again. But she talked as if to herself, her eyes fixed in the distance.

'I met Anna at school, when we were both the age that you are now, and even then she stood out from all the rest,' Miss Fotheringay began. 'She had a restlessness about her, an energy that lit her like a flare. She wasn't happy at home. She didn't get on with her sister – your Aunt Sophia – and she felt that my parents understood her better than her own. We were day girls, and she liked to come back to my house after school, and often she would stay the night. We all looked upon the spare bedroom as hers.

'After school we went up to university together, to the same college at Cambridge, and after university we shared a flat in London. Anna was often away in those days – she was making her name as a journalist, reporting on the break-up of the old Soviet empire.'

Edie listened, spellbound. No one had ever before spoken openly to her about her mother's life.

'Everything changed the year we both turned thirty,' Miss Fotheringay went on. 'Anna was in Moscow, covering a story, and we were in touch often. But then her emails stopped. I had no idea what she was doing, and feared it was something dangerous. A month later, she called to say she was coming home. I went to the airport to meet her and that was when I met Michael for the first time.'

Edie detected a stiffening in Miss Fotheringay's manner at the mention of her father's name.

'I guessed at once that he and Anna were together, though she didn't say so. I felt hostile to him – I could see he was a risk-taker, and I knew he would lead Anna into danger. They spoke to each other in Russian – or maybe it was Polish – and then he melted away. She said that he was a journalist, based in Moscow, but that he had come over to see his Polish mother, who lived in London. I wasn't interested in any of that – I was just relieved to see that she was safe. And I'd missed my friend, of course.

'Anna discovered she was pregnant about a week after

coming home. I was happy for her – she had always wanted children. But I was worried too. I knew Michael wouldn't be able to look after her and a baby. She was annoyed by my questions, said she didn't need looking after, but I think she was more anxious than she let on. She couldn't get hold of Michael – he was off on some job – so she turned to me. I sat in on doctors' appointments with her, bought a cot for the spare room, even started knitting—'

Miss Fotheringay paused, and shook her head as though in disbelief at the story she was telling. 'She was nearly six months pregnant when Michael suddenly turned up and took over,' she continued in a harsher tone. 'Suddenly I wasn't needed any more. Michael and Anna spent hours talking about the Moscow story and I was horrified to learn that they planned to go out there together, after the baby was born. I told Michael he should let Anna and the child stay behind, but he said it was nothing to do with me. There was a violent row. I said that it was mad to think of taking a child somewhere so dangerous, and Michael started shouting, telling me I was an interfering fool. The next day they moved to his mother's flat in Queensway.

'They both turned on me. Anna wrote to me and said that I had to accept that it was her life, not mine. She accused me of being controlling, of wanting too much of what wasn't on offer. I could see that I had to step back, so I did. I let out my flat and took a teaching job at the English school in Rome, and did not even tell Anna my address. I next heard of her six months later, when her death was reported in the press. A baby daughter, I read, had been left in the care of a grandmother.'

Miss Fotheringay's eyes closed a moment, wincing as if against a physical pain. Then she turned and looked at Edie very clearly.

'Not a single day has gone by, Edith, when I have not thought of my friend Anna and her child. When you swam, unsought, into my ken, I felt that the gods had forgiven me, at last, for falling out with my dearest friend. And now I hope you will forgive me too.'

'For what?' Edie whispered.

'For not finding you sooner.' Miss Fotheringay looked at her, as if for confirmation, and Edie smiled.

She did not know how long Miss Fotheringay sat by her bed. She felt very tired, and though she summoned all her strength to stay awake, she could see the pale glow of the nightlight blurring before her half-closed eyes. She was aware of a bell ringing, and of Miss Fotheringay's low voice talking about Anastasia, and next term, and Christmas, as if pronouncing from a dream.

'What did you like most about her?' Edie asked suddenly, hearing her mother's name.

Miss Fotheringay looked thoughtful, her eyes distant and half smiling, as if watching a scene from long ago.

'Her courage,' she said.

Shades of Gold

Edie felt like the Queen as she sat propped against the pillows in the back of Prince Stolonov's brown Bentley, her blanket tucked regally about her knees. *But the Queen*, she thought ruefully, *would not be twiddling her thumbs waiting for her best friend to say her goodbyes.*

It was the last day of term at Knight's Haddon, and the courtyard was full of parents trying to get away, delayed by daughters passionately hugging each other goodbye for the umpteenth time and arranging to meet in the holidays. Trunks and tuck boxes were being lifted into boots while toddlers tripped over their sisters' lacrosse sticks and dogs were told to 'Get down boy, down!'

Edie thought back to her lonely vigil at the dormitory window when she had watched the school empty for the *exeat*, knowing she would be the only one left behind.

This time she was going away too – with Anastasia.

'Ansti tells me you've never been to the South of France,' the prince said from the front of the car, slipping the mobile phone on which he had been talking into his pocket. 'You should feel quite at home in Menton. It's full of invalids.'

'I hope I won't be an invalid much longer,' Edie said quietly, but she was glad all the same that she had been ordered out of the December cold and into the warmth of the waiting car. She knew she would get better, but she wasn't yet. She had had to promise to obey doctors' orders to the letter before Miss Fotheringay had agreed to let her go on holiday with her friend.

Aunt Sophia had been much easier to get around. '*Of course you should go to the South of France with Anastasia, darling,*' she had written. '*Wish I was coming too – I've heard the prince is an absolute dish! But can you really bear to be picked up by Miss Fotheringay on Christmas Eve? She says you've agreed to spend Christmas and the rest of the holidays with her and her ancient parents. If you're happy, that's fine, but don't let her bully you into it. I can't believe it's what you want.*'

Edie smiled. Aunt Sophia had no idea. Miss Fotheringay had offered her something she had wanted all her life.

Lyle had also written:

Dear coz, prince's villa in the South of France???!!! Bum in the butter or what???!!! Don't forget Folly.

And now here was Anastasia, climbing into the back of the car in a welter of possessions and half-finished sentences.

'Oh, Papa, I'm so sorry . . . I didn't realise you were in the car already . . . I was trying to find Fothy . . . completely disappeared . . . Helen says it always happens on the last day of term.'

As Anastasia spoke the prince turned the first corner in the drive, and from her window Edie noticed a tall, familiar figure on the far side of the park. She pressed her face to the glass, and watched as Miss Fotheringay walked alone up the low hill towards the beech wood. Then the drive twisted again, and she was gone.

'Oh, Edie, just think how silly we were,' Anastasia's voice sang on. 'I can't believe we *ever* thought she'd be capable of doing anything wrong – can you?'

Edie was reminded suddenly of Babka, who believed that there were only good people and bad people, '*Good people and bad people, Editha, and no people in the middle.*'

She had a shrewd idea of what Babka would have to say about her present adventure, sitting in the back of Prince Stolonov's car, on her way to his villa in the South of France: '*All that glisters is not gold, Editha. You would do well to remember that.*'

'Edie, what are you thinking about?' Anastasia asked.

Edie smiled, enjoying the caressing touch of heat as the car turned towards the sun. 'Shades of gold,' she murmured, and closed her eyes against the glare.

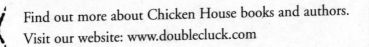